Praise for

Captain Lacey Regency Mysteries series

The Hanover Square Affair

(Top Pick!) With her vivid depiction of the era, Gardner brings her novel to life, from the streets inhabited by the destitute to the mansions of the wealthy.

— *RT BookReviews*

The Sudbury School Murders

Winner, RT BookReviews Reviewers Choice award for Best Historical Mystery

The fourth Gabriel Lacey mystery is another compelling entry in this outstanding series.

— *Fresh Fiction*

A Body in Berkeley Square

[Captain Lacey] is an irresistible character in another engaging tale, so it's no wonder this is an ongoing series. *A Body in Berkeley Square* is an excellent historical mystery that I highly recommend.

— *Romance Reviews Today*

A Covent Garden Mystery

Realistically set in the sometimes unseemly environs of 19th-century London, the suspense is at an all-time high in this swiftly paced installment.

— *RT BookReviews*

Books in the
Captain Lacey Regency Mysteries Series
by Ashley Gardner

A Death In Norfolk

Ashley Gardner

Captain Lacey
Regency Mysteries
Book Seven

Chapter One

England, 1817

In September, amidst a driving rain that swept across the northern Norfolk coast, my hired coach rolled up the drive to my ancestral home and deposited me at the house's front door.

My valet-in-training, Bartholomew, a lad used to working for the very rich, gazed at the edifice in doubt. "You lived here, sir?"

The house stood silently under lowering skies, the roof over one wing completely collapsed. The windows were dark—those that weren't broken. Bricks and rubble decorated what was left of the lawn, and the drive was pitted and covered with weeds.

"Indeed I did," I said.

My father had closed off rooms rather than spend money on repairs. Instead, he'd wagered away all he had or used it on gifts for his mistresses.

The house had at one time been a fine Palladian affair, with fanlights, columns, and a pleasing symmetry. Now the gray-white stone was chipped and fallen away, the Corinthian columns at the door dark with grime. Bits of brick and fallen slates littered the ground.

"And you intend to invite her ladyship here?" Bartholomew's doubt rose several notches.

My wife-to-be, the Dowager Viscountess Breckenridge, daughter of an earl, had grown up on an elegant estate in Oxfordshire and now dwelled in a modern, costly townhouse in South Audley Street in London. I had spent a month at the Oxfordshire estate this summer, and the comparison between the two houses was dire indeed.

"Her ladyship insists," I said.

"Well, you've got your work cut out, sir, I must say."

"That is why I'm pleased you've come along to help, Bartholomew."

Bartholomew's mouth popped open, his face taking on a look of dismay. "Yes, sir."

Bartholomew, former footman to the great and wealthy Lucius Grenville, held himself high above common laborers. I could not resist teasing him.

"I was not suggesting you try a bit of carpentry," I said. "But you can help me coordinate and supervise the repairs."

That was more to Bartholomew's liking, and he looked relieved.

I had another errand to run while I was here in Norfolk, a letter to deliver which had weighed in my pocket all the way from London. I was reluctant to carry out the errand, though it was a simple one, but doing so would be symbolic.

Deliver the enclosed to one Brigadier Easton at Easton House south of Cley. Completion of delivery deducts twenty guineas from your debt. Denis.

James Denis was a criminal but a very subtle one. Very few deeds were traced back to him, and he had magistrates in his pocket. He also owned MPs outright and had aristocrats dancing his bidding. He and I had played a thrust-and-parry game for more than a year now, he constantly trying to coerce me to work for him, and recently he'd assisted me enough to put me firmly in his debt.

A letter written by Denis would not be innocuous. If Grenville had asked me to deliver a message, I'd think nothing of it, but anything involving James Denis could never be that simple.

The enclosed message hadn't been sealed. Denis had known I'd insist on reading what I delivered, and he'd not tried to hide it. But when I opened the message, I found a note that made no sense to me.

I decided I'd make the delivery in case it proved important to Brigadier Easton, but I would not let Denis or the brigadier draw me into any intrigue. Nor would I become a permanent go-between. I'd deliver the letter, and that would be that.

The front door to my house was locked but I had a key, kept among my possessions for twenty years. I hadn't been back to this house since I'd left it to follow my mentor to the army and India, to fight the Tippu Sultan long before the Peninsular Wars began.

The lock proved to be frozen, the key useless, but a firm shove broke the bolt right out of the wall.

I walked into a dim, dust-coated interior. A carpet lay on the floor but so thick with grime that its original color was indiscernible.

I left footprints in the dust as I moved through the wide entrance hall and looked into rooms on either side of the corridor. I expected memories—good and bad—to come flooding at me, but this ruined house looked so different from what I'd left that it spoke to me not at all.

I vaguely remembered the fireplace in the dining room, where my father had leaned while he regaled my mother and me with his pompous lectures. The fireplace had been painted wood, but now the mantelpiece had fallen, exposing the brick behind it.

Bartholomew coughed and pulled out a handkerchief. I moved on to the next room, the library with windows looking over the back garden. The garden was nonexistent now, a stretch of weeds that ran down to join sapling trees at the bottom of the field.

In here, at least, I did feel the touch of my past. My father had beaten me bent over the desk so often, my face pressed into its wooden surface, that I remembered every swirl of the grain.

He'd beaten me for every sin, real and imagined. He'd been trying to make me obedient, and instead had made me rebellious. As I'd grown older, I'd started deliberately inviting the thrashings, because I'd realized that if Father were beating me, he wouldn't be beating my mother.

Memories were hell. As I stood in this room, I remembered why I'd been so keen to follow Aloysius

Brandon and his young wife into the army, why I'd hurried to procure a wife of my own. My mother had died long before, and I'd wanted out of this existence, to get away, to find the world outside these walls, to live.

Well, I'd done that. And now here I was, twenty years older, injured, world-weary, far more cynical, and about to marry again. To a lady who'd have put my father in his place faster than a cat swats a sparrow out of the sky.

"Captain!"

Bartholomew's shout cut through my musings. I hurried out, my walking stick tapping in the dust.

I found Bartholomew at the front door. Coming up what was left of the drive was an elegant carriage with high-stepping horses complete with silver-gray plumes. The coachman had a matching brush in his hat, and the door of the carriage held the crest of the viscounts Breckenridge.

"Bloody hell," I said.

The horses shook their heads at the rain, plumes dancing. Bartholomew hurried forward at the same time a footman jumped from the back of the coach into the mud. The footman unhooked a box from beneath the coach and placed it under the carriage door.

The footman opened the door, and a well-formed ankle came down, foot in a pristine leather shoe. Bartholomew and the footman stretched a canvas between them, holding it high to shield the lady who prepared to descend, and I came forward to hand her down.

Donata Anne Catherine St. John, Dowager Viscountess Breckenridge, was thirty years old and my betrothed. That she'd agreed to marry me still came as a bit of a shock.

Lady Breckenridge ignored me completely, thanked Bartholomew and her footman, and lifted her skirts to walk the few feet into the house. She said nothing as she tilted her head back to take in the entire wreck of it.

"I thought you were to stay with your friend near Blakeney," I said, following her. "With its wonderful view of the sea."

"I am, but I could not resist seeing the house of your birth." Lady Breckenridge turned in a circle in the hall, staring up the wide staircase. "A man's home can tell much about him."

"That is what I fear," I said dryly.

"Nonsense. It is falling apart, obviously, but there are good bones here. Well designed. Late seventeenth century, with later additions."

As I stood, rather uncomfortably, on the bones of my ancestral home, Donata turned her dark blue gaze on me. "Now, Gabriel, I know it's bad of me to pounce on you without warning, but I did so want to see the place. Do show me everything."

I complied.

A marvelous thing happened as I took Lady Breckenridge from room to room, explaining what was what. The past became just that, the past. My father was no longer the ogre who ruled my life. He'd become a distant ghost, gone for eight years now, releasing his stranglehold on me.

"Good bones, as I said," Donata remarked as she stood in the largest bedroom, empty of all furnishings. "Well anchored. The wing that has fallen in was an eighteenth-century addition, was it not? A good architect can restore it and fix the flaws that kept it from standing."

"The Lacey fortune hardly runs to architects," I said.

"But the Breckenridge one does." She watched me, waiting for me to object.

"I know you berate me for being too proud, Donata, but the last thing I want is to run through your money to repair my life. Every member of the *ton* supposes that's what I'm doing, but I want *you* to believe that I am not."

She shrugged. "I like you being proud, and to the devil with what my friends believe. But I am not being charitable, Gabriel. I am being practical. I will have to live here too, and so will my son, and I hardly want to worry about bricks falling on us as we walk about the passages. Besides, I will be inviting Lady Southwick—the friend with whom I am staying—and this house is ever so much better than hers. The Southwick house is gigantic, but modern, gaudy trash. I do so want to best her."

I was torn between amusement and alarm. "You say you care nothing for what your friends think."

"And I do not, but Lady Southwick and I have always been rivals. She even had it off with my husband—briefly—a long time ago. I believe she was as appalled by him as I was, so that did not quite work out as she liked."

As always, whenever Donata mentioned her brute of a husband, whose face I'd once had the pleasure of bruising, I felt both irritated and protective. "Why do you stay with her, then?"

"We rather enjoy the game, I think. You'll understand when you arrive. And she will try to lure you from me. It is her way, I must warn you."

Her words were flat, but her eyes flickered.

"I have no wish to be lured, I assure you," I said.

I had little wish to stay at the house of Lady Southwick, but I did not have much choice. The nearby inns were hardly fit for a viscountess used to the very best of everything, and I'd been pleased that she had a friend of equal rank and wealth nearby. I'd been included in the invitation to stay at Southwick Hall, and it would have been churlish of me to refuse. Lady Breckenridge would be the one to bear the brunt of disapproval at my rudeness, so I had capitulated.

I did finally persuade Donata that she should leave the cold dankness of my home and return to her rival's house, which would at least be comfortable. Donata kissed me lightly on the lips and let me lead her back to the carriage.

Once she was gone, vanishing into rain and mist, I went back through the house. I knew I was simply delaying my errand for Denis, but the rain was pouring down, and Denis's mission could wait.

I ended up in my mother's sitting room—her sanctuary—once a room of whites and golds and pinks, light and airy. The windows looked past the garden to a rise of ground and a little copse. Beyond it was the gray green that marked the marshes that lined the sea. In the distance, a windmill, with a tall, cylindrical body and a four-bladed fan, turned slowly in the storm.

The windmill had been there, beside a stream, for as long as I could remember, built in the last century.

The pumps drew water out of the marshy ground, lifting it to spill into the rivers and streams that carried it out to sea. The drained earth left behind was rich and fertile, allowing men to farm where once had been only grass and water.

I'd sneaked into in the windmill more than once as a child, only to be hauled out by the keeper before I ruined the pumps. The great creaking machinery had always fascinated me.

I turned back, the interior of the room dark after the rain-soaked glare. As I stood waiting for my eyes to adjust, I realized that something incongruous lay across the mice-chewed chaise.

I went to the chaise and leaned down to look. In the dim light I saw a dress—a long, high-waisted pale muslin that a young debutante might wear. The garment was thick with dust, the hem tattered. When I lightly touched the sleeve, the netting that covered the sleeve crumpled to nothing.

I straightened up, puzzled indeed. I had no sisters. My mother had died when I'd been a lad, and she'd not brought out any young women as favors to friends or even had them to visit. My father, as far as I knew, had chosen his mistresses from the glittering demimonde, ladies with much experience who'd never wear a gown so innocent as this.

Why the dress was there and who it had belonged to was a complete mystery. If a couple had broken into the house for a tryst—they'd have found it quite easy to gain entrance—why leave the gown behind?

I did not touch the dress again, fearing it would dissolve further if I handled it. The fabric was so very fine.

I needed to complete my errand before the paper burned my pocket to ash. I left the intriguing puzzle of the dress and closed the door of the room, locking it with the key I'd found in the lock. I put the key into my pocket.

My hired coach had returned to Norwich, and I prepared to walk the two miles to the brigadier's house. Riding and walking much this year had given me back strength, though my left leg still tired easily, and I'd never rid myself of this limp. However, I could face a two-mile walk without much dismay.

I told Bartholomew to meet me at the public house in Cley and indulge himself in a well-earned ale, and I went to the brigadier's alone.

The rain had lightened a little. I could see across the farmland to the marshes that ran along the coast. Grasses bent in the wind, and all was as wet as could be.

I remembered the brigadier, though through the perspective of a boy. Brigadier Easton had been a martinet, like my father, but with a streak of fairness that my father had lacked. He lived in a brick house that was as tall and deep as it was wide, windows in even rows covering all three floors.

The butler who opened the door took my card, gave my damp clothes and muddy boots a disdainful look, but at least he let me wait inside, out of the rain. The brigadier must have recognized the Lacey name, because the butler quickly returned and bade me follow him upstairs.

I was shown into a long, narrow study whose windows looked north to another windmill. This windmill had been shut down and abandoned, its work done, its spindly arms still.

The brigadier was in his sixties, as my father would have been had he been alive. While my father had been a big man—the same six-foot, broad-shouldered build as myself—the brigadier was small and slight. He made up for his stature with a powerful voice, which had, before his retirement, bellowed orders to troops in India.

He came to me, hand extended. "Gabriel Lacey. The young hothead who eloped and raced away in the middle of the night?" He chuckled as I shook his hand. "I had wondered when you'd make your move and become a man. Captain now, eh? Commended for bravery at Talavera; you and all the Thirty-Fifth Light. Damned bloody battle, that."

It had been. I'd begun the morning a lieutenant and had been given captain that evening, both for my actions and because too many other captains had died. My father had died here in Norfolk that night, though I had not known until I'd received the letter weeks later.

Easton released my hand but peered up at me nearsightedly. "Back home now, are you? What are you going to do with the place?"

"I have some idea of repairing the house and living in it," I said.

Easton's look told me he doubted my sanity but wouldn't argue. "And, you are getting married. Do not look so surprised. We read the London newspapers even here. My felicitations."

I bowed politely in thanks. I put my hand into my pocket and withdrew the message from Denis.

"I did not come here only to call on a neighbor," I said. "I was charged with delivering this to you. From London."

Easton frowned. He took the folded paper—thick, cream-colored, and expensive—walked to his desk, sat down, and opened a drawer. He removed a pair of spectacles, put them on, and opened the paper. He read the one word on it and went utterly still.

I approached the desk. Easton stared down at the page, his face drained of color.

The one word on it was *Corn*. Obviously a code, but what Denis meant by it I could not say.

The expression on Easton's face was telling me, however. The brigadier stood slowly, his skin wan, the man looking ten years older than when I'd walked in.

"You brought this from Mr. Denis," he said.

"I did. Denis . . . asked me to."

Now what was in his eyes was abject fear. Easton studied me anew, taking in my large build, my big hands, the walking stick I held, inside of which rattled a sword.

"I suppose I ought to have known. What else did he ask you to do? Tell me quickly; I've faced it before."

I looked at him, puzzled. "Nothing. To deliver the message was my only charge. What does it mean?"

The brigadier let out a breath and sank to his chair. He put both hands on the desk and looked up at me, shoulders slumped in defeat.

"You've brought me my death sentence, my boy. That's what it means. This is my last day on earth."

Chapter Two

A death sentence. Denis's first commission to me had been to warn a man that his life was in danger.

I might have suspected Denis of playing a jest on me, but one look at the terror in the brigadier's eyes made me know that he, for one, took it seriously.

"Why should James Denis want to kill you?" I asked.

Easton's face was damp with sweat. "You do not know?"

"I told you, I was directed to hand you the message, that is all. I know nothing about it."

Easton got to his feet again, fists on the desk. "I must ask you to leave, Captain."

"Tell me what this is about, and I might be able to help you."

"I will make it an order."

I set my feet, my hand firm on my walking stick. I was twice the brigadier's size and the creaking butler who'd answered the door would be no match for me.

"Neither of us are in the army any longer," I said. "I advise you to get away from here. Denis was polite enough to give you a warning, perhaps even a sporting chance. I would take it."

"Yes." The brigadier nodded, swallowing. "I must . . . prepare my carriage."

"And have Denis or one of his pugilists accost you on a lonely road? You have an ocean at your disposal. A boat to France or the Netherlands is what I'd advise."

"A boat." Easton's eyes focused a bit, and he looked around his study. "If I leave, I can never return. My wife . . ."

"Where is your wife?"

"Visiting my daughter and grandchildren. In Kent."

"Let her stay there. You go, and I will talk to Denis. Send no word to your wife or daughter, in case he intercepts it. Send a message when you're safe—not to your wife or to me, but to Lucius Grenville in London. I will see that your family receives it."

"Grenville?" Easton looked puzzled. "That self-important dandy? Why should I involve him?"

"He is a friend and trustworthy. Now, you need to be off. The tide is out, but if we go to the point you might be able to hire someone willing to take you at once."

"I have a boat of my own. Down in the Broads."

"Which Denis will no doubt be watching. Hire someone, chosen at random, and go. Denis is not a man to hesitate. Gather what you need—quickly—and be off."

*** *** ***

In the end, I had to go with him to the boat. The brigadier and I rode out on a pair of his horses, he with a small pack strapped to his saddle.

I took a direct route to the coast, deciding that if Denis's men were watching and following, they would be less likely to attack us in the middle of a village high street than on a deserted back lane.

In any case, I saw nothing of the hired pugilists Denis employed to do everything from serve brandy to dispose of men who disobeyed him. What Easton had done to draw Denis's displeasure I couldn't imagine, and Easton wasn't about to tell me.

At the point, I refused a fisherman far too eager to sail Easton across the North Sea, and chose one I more or less had to threaten to do it. I could too well imagine the eager fisherman taking Easton's money and dropping him overboard halfway to Amsterdam.

The rain continued without abatement, and I was soaked through by the time I helped the fisherman and his son push the boat off the sands and into the waves. Easton had already disappeared into the tiny cabin, clutching his bundle of belongings, several guineas poorer. The fisherman had driven a hard bargain.

I had no doubt the fisherman would make it to Amsterdam or wherever he was bound. No matter how un-seaworthy a man's craft looked, I knew these fishermen could sail a goodly distance and back in safety.

I was left with the horses. I mounted one and led the other back to Easton's, where I relinquished both to his groomsman. I told Easton's butler to shut up the house and send the servants on holiday. The butler eyed me in trepidation, but I did not give him time to argue before I departed again.

*** *** ***

I seethed that Denis had sent me on such an errand and seethed at the brigadier for making it necessary. I was also angry at Easton for not having the sense to run before Denis caught on that he'd been crossed.

Therefore, I was in a perfectly foul mood when I reached the public house in Cley. I was not happy with Bartholomew's round-eyed stare at my ruined clothes or his, "Oh, sir."

"My baggage has already been sent to Lady Southwick's," I said waspishly, "so they will have to take me as I am. Hire a horse for me, will you? I do not relish the idea of tramping over miles of muddy roads."

"Yes, sir."

Bartholomew had learned to simply vanish when I spoke that sharply.

He could not find a horse to hire, but he did find a cart. It was slow and smelled of rotting vegetables, and the wheels squeaked, but at least I could sit and stretch out my bad leg.

We bumped our way south and east, while a fresh breeze blew in from the coast, bringing with it more rain. Bartholomew hunkered into his greatcoat, but I didn't mind the rain in my face. Though I'd adjusted to living in London, I was country grown, used to sharp ocean winds, not stagnant fog that smelled of

London's many cesspits. London, especially in the summer, could be noisome and appalling. Perhaps I missed my native land more than I knew.

Southwick Hall stretched wide arms across a green lawn, situated so that approaching guests would have a view of magnificent fountains placed in tiers leading to the front door.

"Gaudy trash," Lady Breckenridge had called the place, and I saw why when the cart drew closer.

The long, four-story house had a pleasing symmetry when viewed from afar, but the architect had decided to lavish this pleasant outline with pilasters, columns, hexagonal windows, plaster curlicues, pediments, and half-clothed marble women who held up giant urns or pulled back stone draperies. Much of the decoration was in imitation of the ancients, but in such a mishmash of cultures and eras that it confused the eye and upset the stomach.

The inside of the house was not much better, I saw when I entered. The lofty entrance hall was painted with multicolored gods, goddesses, nymphs, satyrs, maidens, shepherds, mermen, and other creatures of the sea, all surrounded by an abundance of gold-leafed moldings certain to give the onlooker a headache.

Bartholomew had already given the carter his coin and legged it around to the back of the house. I envied him. The servants' quarters would be full of bustle, warmth, and normal-looking decor.

The majordomo, after looking askance at my sorry state, told me that the other guests had begun dinner, but I would be taken to them after I refreshed myself. His look told me he'd allow me nowhere near the other guests until I made myself presentable.

The bedchamber to which he led me resembled the entrance hall in decoration, but I consoled myself that I would be sleeping in the dark. The bed at least looked comfortable.

Bartholomew entered as I stripped off my wet clothes. He looked inordinately cheerful for someone who'd ridden through pouring rain on the back of a cart. He unpacked my things, whistling, while I washed up, then he helped me into my regimentals.

"Something amusing you, Bartholomew?" I asked as I fastened the silver braid.

"You'll see, sir."

His good mood after my race to send Easton out of harm's way then our muddy ride irritated me a bit, but I kept my temper in check. I asked no more questions and went downstairs to the dinner in progress.

The dining room's theme was that of hunting. The mural on the longest wall depicted gods and satyrs chasing helpless oxen and boar through a featureless wood. Most of the animals looked like pincushions full of spears, and those already dead lay broken in pools of blood.

At least ten people gathered around the table—I'd not thought this would be a large house party, but perhaps my ideas of large and Lady Southwick's differed.

The head of the table was empty, but Lady Southwick sat at its foot. Lord Southwick was far away in Greece at the moment. I'd been told that he was often far away in Greece.

Lady Southwick looked to be of an age with Donata Breckenridge, her hair fair with a touch of red. Lady Southwick's gown was a near match to

Donata's, dark green and black to my lady's cream and silver. The two women also had similar bearing and mannerisms, as though the same set of governesses had trained and finished both.

The difference ended there, however. Lady Breckenridge had developed a sharp intelligence, while Lady Southwick wore a sly, predatory look of a person who thought herself more clever than she was.

The guests did not look up or cease conversation when the butler led me to the only empty chair, which was on Lady Southwick's left. This put me nowhere near Lady Breckenridge, who sat at the other end of the table next to a dandy called Rafe Godwin. She and Godwin carried on a merry conversation, neither glancing my way.

When I could pull my gaze from Lady Breckenridge, I looked across the table and saw a man I knew very well indeed. He was the most popular gentleman in England, and his name was Lucius Grenville.

The source of Bartholomew's good humor became clear. While in the servants' hall, Bartholomew must have come across his brother, Matthias, who was footman to Grenville. Bartholomew would think it a good joke to surprise me with Grenville's presence.

It did surprise me, because Grenville was very choosy about whom he graced with country visits. The dark-haired, dark-eyed dandy shot me a look across the table as Lady Southwick signaled to her footman to serve me the sole.

After Donata's warnings, I expected Lady Southwick to pay me embarrassing attention, but, alas for Grenville, he eclipsed me. Lady Southwick spent the meal leaning to him, her bosom resting nearly in her plate, so that Grenville could look straight down her décolletage if he chose. Grenville kept his gaze firmly on his food.

The fish was tender and fresh, served with a hot, buttery sauce, welcome after my afternoon in the rain. The game birds that followed were equally good, and the meal ended with a tart heaped with late berries made piquant with lemon. In spite of her taste in decor, Lady Southwick apparently employed a fine chef.

Once the last plates had been taken away, Lady Southwick rose, and the ladies flowed out of the room, leaving the gentlemen alone.

I disliked the modern practice of ladies and gentlemen parting after supper. I'd always found more enjoyment in the company of the fairer sex. Even well-bred gentlemen were apt to grow boorish in their cups, make bodily noises, and emit odors.

One of the Mayfair men at the table already resembled an indolent satyr in the mural. By the rapidity with which he imbibed port, I predicted he'd soon be splayed like the dead boar in the foreground.

Rafe Godwin lit a cheroot, blew out smoke, and directed a his words at me. "You're from these parts, are you not, Lacey?"

The manner in which he said "these parts" told me he thought little of them. "I am, yes," I said. "My father's house is about five miles distant."

"How's your yield?" Godwin asked. "I hear that farming has been dreadful these last few years."

True, a few years ago, a spate of bad weather had meant a dearth of crops, which had resulted in a sharp rise in the price of grain and of bread. People had starved, both here and in the cities, which had led to violence and riots.

Godwin, who spent his nights at White's and the gaming hells and his days asleep, likely knew little about farms and their yields.

"I have not been to Norfolk in two decades," I said. "I have no idea what my fields yield."

"Oh, dear," Rafe said, as though this were the most amusing thing he'd heard in a twelvemonth.

A thirtyish gentleman I did not know narrowed his eyes at me. "Lacey? Not related to Roderick Lacey, are you?"

"He was my father," I said.

The gentleman studied me for a time then seemed to remember to be polite and held out a hand. "Reaves. Preston Reaves. I have the living at Parson's Point."

Mr. Reaves, with his fine suit and manicured hands, looked nothing like a vicar. I assumed he was one of those clerics who'd gone into the church not for the calling, but because there was nothing else he could do. Younger sons who had no hope of inheritance took clerical orders or joined the army, and Reaves looked a bit soft for army life.

In the church, an ambitious man could progress until he was made a bishop, with a seat in the House of Lords. Money could be had in the higher positions, although a vicar could have a good living if the local lords and gentry were generous enough.

My father had held the living for Parson's Point, which meant that I now did. However, because my family had grown notoriously poor, Lord Southwick had begun paying the vicar's living many years ago, as well as the living for the vicar of his own parish. It was one of those things everyone knew and no one mentioned.

"In my youth, the vicar here was one Dr. Quinn," I said.

"He passed on about seven years ago," Reaves said. "They had a curate for a short while, then Lord Southwick proposed me for the living."

"Did you know my father?" I asked.

"Not at all, actually. He, too, passed on, not long after I arrived." Reaves stared at me a moment, as though reconciling himself to the fact that he now, in theory at least, worked for me.

Grenville rose, helped himself to port, and removed a snuffbox from his pocket. He opened it, one-handed, and held it out to me. I declined, not much caring for snuff.

"No doubt the captain would prefer a pipe," Rafe Godwin said, grinning. "Shall we ask our hostess if she can locate a corncob?"

Baiting the yokel was to be Godwin's entertainment for the evening, I saw. After all, I wore old regimentals and had arrived in a cart, late and covered with mud. Perhaps I ought to be chewing on a straw.

I got up and made my way to the humidor on the sideboard. "I do like a pipe, it is true," I said. "But I will make do with what our hostess has provided." I chose a cheroot, rolled it between my fingers, and lit it from a candle on the table.

Grenville took a pinch snuff from his fingertips, wiped his nose with a silk handkerchief, and ignored Godwin. I seated myself in the chair Lady Southwick had vacated.

Godwin began a raucous conversation with the other gentlemen, and Grenville leaned to me. "I can only say, thank God you are here, Lacey. The company, apart from Lady Breckenridge, is appalling."

"You did not need to accept the invitation," I said. "I am amazed you did."

"It was Lady Breckenridge's invitation. I imagine she was as appalled as I and needed reinforcements. While Lord Southwick is away, Lady Southwick is free to have as many house parties as she pleases. Notice the high proportion of gentlemen to ladies."

I had noticed. Three ladies to seven gentlemen, including myself.

"Lady Southwick does not like to share," Grenville said. "But it would not look well for her if she had no ladies in the party at all."

I had puzzled over the reason Donata wanted me to stay in the house of a predatory woman, but I thought I understood. Lady Breckenridge's first husband had practiced infidelity without shame, even bringing his mistresses into the Breckenridge household. Had Lord Breckenridge been here, he'd already have let Lady Southwick net him and then moved on to the other ladies of the party. I'd once witnessed Lord Breckenridge fondle another woman while his wife stood not a yard away.

Donata had professed not to care, but I'd seen the hurt in her eyes, the anger that had turned into acerbic humor and a cynical view of the world.

Lady Breckenridge wished to determine, before she married me, whether I'd do as Lord Breckenridge had done. I could not grow offended at her worry — Breckenridge had put Donata through a terrible time of it. If she needed to be certain that I would not do the same, then so be it.

"At least the food is not bad," I said. I pulled on the cheroot, following it with a deep drink of port. The port was rich and smooth, complimenting the dusky taste of the cheroot.

"Lady Southwick has a fine chef, yes, but he's temperamental. As long as he does not grow angry, we eat well. The moment he goes on a tear, we dine on hardtack and water."

"Continental, is he?"

"As English as the pair of us. Local born, son of a fisherman, happened to stow away on a boat to France and get an education in food." Trust Grenville to know the pedigree of every chef in England. "Luckily for us."

"What of Marianne?" I asked. Marianne Simmons, former actress at Drury Lane Theatre and once my upstairs neighbor, was now more or less openly Grenville's mistress.

I did not ask why Grenville hadn't brought her with him — Lady Southwick, for all her reputation for chasing gentlemen, was a lady of the aristocracy, who would hardly invite a stage actress turned courtesan to her gathering. If Marianne had been famous — another Sarah Siddons, say — leeway might be given, but Marianne had never risen higher than the chorus.

"She is in Berkshire," Grenville said. "I told her I'd take her to Paris when this visit was done, and she agreed. She has the full run of the Clarges Street house now, as well as use of my carriage. There are those who wonder when she'll get at the family plate. I have become a laughingstock."

He spoke lightly, and I knew that Grenville, in truth, did not care what people said about him in regard to Marianne. The challenge of Marianne, for him, was too interesting to abandon because the dandies at White's sneered.

"You will make it highly fashionable to take lesser actresses as paramours. I believe Mr. Godwin already is pursuing a lady of the chorus."

Grenville glanced down the table at Rafe Godwin, and took another, and somewhat derisive, pinch of snuff.

The conversation of the Mayfair gentlemen grew louder, as though they were determined not to care that the great Grenville ignored them to speak to a rube like me. Reaves was the only one who remained decorous, listening while he sipped his brandy.

Grenville suggested a game of billiards to me, and I gladly followed him across the hall to the wide billiards room. The decor here was of naked gods and goddesses cavorting, enough to put a man off his game.

I fetched balls while Grenville chose a cue. "Now that I've cornered you, Lacey, I must pick a bone. Matthias tells me that Bartholomew told him that you'd disappeared into the mists on your way over here and returned looking as though you'd swum the channel. *After* you'd wallowed in mud a bit."

I rolled white and red balls onto the table, lifted my port and cheroot from where I'd set them on a side table, and enjoyed another mouthful of both. "Our footmen need to find other things to discuss."

"Nothing interests them more than what you get up to. What about it?"

"A complicated story," I said.

"For God's sake, Lacey, put me out of my misery and tell me."

I decided to lay off tormenting him. As Grenville took his first shot, I briefly related what had happened with Easton.

Grenville stood up as the balls rolled gently across the table. "Good Lord. And you got him off safely?"

"I hope so. Unless Denis has all fishermen on the Norfolk coast in his pay, I believe the brigadier will reach Amsterdam without too much mishap."

"What about you, Lacey? What happens when Denis discovers his bird has flown?"

"I will cross that bridge when I come to it. I know I owe Denis a debt, but I refuse to repay it by helping him with dark deeds."

"But he did not ask you to kill Easton for him. He asked you only to deliver the note."

I took another drink of port, emptying the glass. "To make me aware of what he intended for Easton and to ensure that I was part of it, no matter how remotely. Captain Lacey visits Brigadier Easton, Easton is agitated, and then Easton is dead. What will a magistrate make of that?"

"And now Easton has disappeared. What will a magistrate make of *that*?"

"Another bridge I will cross."

Grenville retrieved a ball that had rolled to a stop. "You walk a knife's edge, Lacey."

"As ever." I lifted my cheroot, waiting for him to shoot again. "Better entertainment than watching Lady Southwick stalking her prey."

"As I believe that prey is me, your comment is less than amusing."

I had a smile at his expense, then we bent to the game.

*** *** ***

Later that night, when Bartholomew had left me and I'd gone to bed, I heard my bedroom door open. I did not worry that Lady Southwick had come to pounce, because I knew the sound of Donata's movements and her scent.

I had slept without my nightshirt in hopes she'd come, and when Lady Breckenridge slid her warm, bare body over mine, I forgot about Denis and Easton, the sneers of the gentlemen in the dining room, and the wreck of my father's house. For a brief and wonderful while, all was right with my world.

*** *** ***

Donata did not stay, and I woke early and alone. While I knew that most people in her circle were aware that Lady Breckenridge and I sometimes shared a bed, it would never do to be seen practicing our sins. *Appearance is all, in my set,* she'd say. *A ridiculous thing, but there it is.*

Before she went, I asked her to accompany me to my father's house, and she agreed we would go there in the afternoon. Donata habitually stayed in bed until after one, so with Bartholomew's assistance, I rose, dressed, and breakfasted, then borrowed a horse and rode off on my own.

I went back to Easton's house. I'd helped the man escape Denis's rather brutal form of justice, and I wanted to know why.

When I reached the house, I found the butler outside, arguing with and gesticulating to a beefy man. The large man was familiar to me—one of the pugilists who worked for James Denis, and who usually stood guard in Denis's study, watching visitors with a cautious eye.

The man saw me and gestured for me to follow him inside. I dismounted and handed the reins to the butler, who was quivering in terror.

I walked inside the house and stopped in astonishment. At least half a dozen of Denis's men swarmed the hall and the downstairs rooms, pulling up carpets, tearing off paneling, and breaking holes in Brigadier Easton's walls.

Chapter Three

"What the devil?" My voice rose above the noise of the demolition. Two of the men looked up, saw me, and went back to work. The others paid no attention.

The pugilist who'd led me inside was large, a little taller than my six or so feet, and I put him at least eighteen stone. He'd once held me back when I'd made to lunge across Denis's desk, so I knew he was incredibly strong.

"Sir," the man said, giving me his hard stare. "What did the brigadier take away with him?"

Not the question I'd expected. "Take away with him?"

"You helped Brigadier Easton get away to the Continent. What did he take with him when he went?"

No anger, no outrage that I'd thwarted his master. A simple question in an even tone. "Very little," I said. "A change of shirt and a few necessities."

"How large a bundle did it make?" the man asked. "These necessities?"

I measured off about a foot by a foot with my hands. "That large."

"You're sure he had nothing else?"

"Quite sure. He got into a boat with barely enough room for the fisherman and his nets. The brigadier did not have time to pack a trunk nor the room to take it with him. You can be certain that by now, Mr. Denis knows exactly what boat Easton boarded and where he disembarked."

The lackey shook his head. "Mr. Denis don't know he's gone, not yet."

I stopped in surprise. "Why are you here, then, if he doesn't know?"

The man looked uneasy. I'd seen him look so once before, during the affair at the Sudbury School, when he'd offered up information he'd kept to himself, not realizing it was important. Under Denis's stare, this big, mean-looking man had wilted.

"We came last night, as instructed. I was to visit Brigadier Easton and bring back what he took from Mr. Denis. But when we got here, the brigadier had gone off, and there's no sign of the stuff. If you took it, sir, best give it back. Mr. Denis, he likes you, and he might go easier on you if you 'fess up right away."

Took what? "I am afraid you have me at a loss, Mr. . . . I don't believe I've ever learned your name."

"Cooper, sir. Martin Cooper. I know you didn't take the things for yourself, sir. You're not that kind.

But you might have done to help the brigadier. It's misguided, sir. The man is a thieving bastard."

Now, I was completely in a fog. "I assure you, Cooper, I have no idea to what things you refer. I sent Easton away, I admit. I had no wish to see the man receive what Denis sent you to do to him. I took him to a boat and got him away. That is all. I did not help Easton pack or take anything from this house. He never told me his business with Denis — there was not time."

Cooper regarded me with skepticism. "That so, sir? You did not make him tell you? You're an inquiring sort of man, I've noticed. "

"True, but this time, I did not have a chance." It had been more important to get Easton away, and quickly. "You look worried, Cooper. What do you think Denis will do when he discovers that I spirited Easton out of the way? You are not to blame for the actions of the impetuous Captain Lacey."

He rubbed his forehead. "It's not so much Easton flying the coop, sir. It's the things. Mr. Denis will want them back, and I can't put my hands on them."

"Now you have stirred my curiosity. What sorts of things?"

"Paintings, sir. From the Netherlands, mostly. A few from the Italian states and from Russia, even."

I began to understand. "The brigadier kept these painting for Mr. Denis?"

"Brought them back to England for him, with no one the wiser. The brigadier likes to travel."

"Ah." So, Brigadier Easton had smuggled stolen artwork into the country for James Denis. The brigadier, well respected and with many connections, might not be questioned about the bits and pieces he brought back from the Continent.

I recalled the picture I'd often seen in Denis's house, that of a young girl standing by a window in a pool of sunlight, the painting small, quiet, and serene. I wondered if Easton had obtained that for him as well.

"And the brigadier decided it might be lucrative if he held on to one or two of these?" I asked.

"More than one or two. A bucketful, more like. Claimed he had to leave the last load behind in Amsterdam, as they were too difficult to move, but Mr. Denis figured Easton had them here."

Mr. Denis was rarely wrong. No wonder the brigadier had looked so terrified. Denis had a long reach—only a fool would try to steal from him.

Not that I hadn't gone against Denis's orders myself in this instance. I'd been sent to frighten the brigadier so that he'd give up the paintings to Denis. Instead, I'd gotten him away, leaving Cooper unable to put his hands on either Easton or the artwork.

"I am sorry," I said. I truly was. Denis would vent his wrath not only on me, but on Cooper. "I had no idea about the paintings, or I would have made Easton tell me about them before he went." Whether I would have passed such knowledge to Denis was another matter.

"As you can see, I'm in an awkward patch," Cooper said.

"I do understand. The least I can do is help you look."

I did not need to ask him to describe the paintings Easton had stolen. I'd know them when I saw them. The artwork on Easton's walls were original watercolors of the house and grounds, likely done by Easton's wife, daughter, or a local fledgling artist. Any painting Denis acquired would be old, famous, and painted by a master.

I went upstairs, past two men taking out the paneling on the staircase, and to Easton's study. The room looked much the same as when I'd left it last night, Cooper's men not having reached it with their sledgehammers.

The room was long and narrow, with Easton's desk in the exact center of the carpet. The windows did not let in much light—though the rain of yesterday had abated, the sun was hidden by a thick bank of clouds.

I found spills in a jar on the mantelpiece and lit candles about the room. The painting above the fireplace was a rather dull one of the house surrounded by the flat green of Norfolk. Again, if not painted by Easton's wife or daughter, probably done by a local lad wanting to sell his services.

A good place to hide a painting was behind another painting. I took down the picture of the house, found a paperknife in the drawer, and cut the painting out of the frame.

I found nothing behind it but wood to hold the canvas in place. I searched every inch of wood, frame, and canvas, but concluded there was nothing else there. I laid the picture aside and started on the next one.

The room had five paintings, but each frame held only the picture that had originally graced it. The tops of all the frames were thick with dust, which told me they hadn't been disturbed in a long while and that Easton's maids were less than diligent. I doubted that a mote of dust would be allowed to linger in one of Lady Breckenridge's houses.

I set the paintings aside and started looking behind furniture. The furniture was better dusted, but even so, I found nothing.

After a thorough search of every visible place, I resorted to what Denis's men were doing. I started pulling up the carpets. Easton's study had three carpets—a large woolen one with an oriental design on it, on which the desk sat, and two smaller, much finer ones on either end of the long room. The smaller ones had come from the Near East, woven in a tent among hot desert sands.

None of the rugs concealed paintings or loose floorboards under which paintings could be hidden.

I finished in the study and returned to the hall. I took down a painting there, laid it facedown on a table, and carefully cut it out of the frame. One of the men tearing up the paneling dropped his tools and yanked down another painting—a shaky watercolor of the sea at Blakeney Point. Denis's man plunged a knife straight through the painting and ripped it from its frame.

"Have some respect," I snapped.

Cooper came up the stairs. "No time, Captain. Have you found anything?"

I shook my head. "The study looks empty of fine artwork, but I did not rip out the paneling."

Cooper snapped his fingers at the second man on the stairs and pointed to the study door. The second man shouldered his sledgehammer and trudged up the stairs and into the study. A few seconds later came a *thud* and the splintering of wood.

"They could be anywhere," I said. "Rolled up and sewn under a chair or sofa, flattened between boards in the ceiling, inside a window seat, folded behind books—although I hope he did not fold any priceless masterpieces."

"If the paintings are in this house, sir, we'll find them," Cooper said.

I had no doubt he would. "They may not be in the house at all," I said. "Easton might not have risked bringing them here."

"That is true." Cooper's eyes glinted. "I thought of that, sir. That's why I sent a couple of men to look over your house."

I stared at him. "*My* house? What the devil for?"

"It's reasonable, sir. The house is empty, no one to bother it. You haven't been there in a donkey's age—it's been shut up since your dad's death. No one goes there, now."

Lady Breckenridge would be going there this afternoon. Not for several hours yet, but what if she grew impatient, or annoyed at Lady Southwick, and decided to make the journey early?

I put down the paperknife and headed down the stairs without a word to Cooper.

The man followed me. "I'll just go with you, sir."

He would whether I liked it or not. I gave him a grim nod. "Fine, but hurry."

An excited shout stopped me from charging out of the house. Cooper brushed past me on the way to the dining room, and found one of the pugilists pulling a rolled canvas from behind a few ripped-out boards of paneling.

"Give that to me." Cooper snatched the canvas from the man's hands and unrolled the large thing across the dining room table. He went carefully, I was happy to see, understanding the consequences of damaging Denis's loot.

All the men had stopped working and came crowding in to see. An incredible painting spread itself before us. Colors glowed against a background that brightened from sable on the left to a golden light on the right that surrounded two rather muscular angels. A group of round-cheeked women faced the angels with expressions of astonishment, their gowns vibrant red, lavender, and blue.

I'd seen, in my travels, copies of paintings of the great Rubens, enough of them to realize that he'd painted this one himself.

"Good God," I said. "*This* was thrust behind the paneling?"

"Keep hunting," Cooper said to the other men. "We need the rest."

I touched the paint that a Flemish genius had stroked on two hundred years before. "Amazing." This should be hanging in the drawing room of a king—and maybe once had been. "How did Brigadier Easton get hold of something like this? And why would Denis trust him with it?"

"Couldn't say," Cooper said. "Are you staying or going? Sir."

"Going," I said.

It hurt to look upon that beautiful painting and leave it here with Denis's men. They'd roll it up and cart it off to him so that he could sell it to a rich banker who didn't mind buying stolen goods. War-wrecked Europe was an open market to James Denis and others like him, who stole from the weak and sold the booty to the very rich. Rubens was dead and gone, and all the people who'd owned this painting were probably dead and gone as well.

Cooper still insisted on accompanying me. The other men must be quite trustworthy if they could be left in a house with one and possibly more priceless pieces of art.

I rode the horse I'd borrowed from Lady Southwick's stables. Cooper didn't like horses and didn't ride. He walked along beside me and insisted I pace him. I did, because I wanted to keep an eye on him as much as he wanted to keep one on me.

The rain had finished, and wind had sprung up to send away the mist and open the sky. As a lad, I'd loved the enormous skies arching over the farmland that rolled to miles of marshes and gray sea. This was the land of my childhood, where I'd played among the tall marsh grass and hidden in fishing boats so I could go out to sea with the men. The fishermen had taught me to fish, and I'd brought the spoils home to our cook, who was careful not to tell my father where she'd obtained them.

I'd roamed fearlessly, brought home when I strayed too far by farmers, villagers, fishermen, or the publican at Parson's Point. I'd found many ways to elude the nannies, tutors, horse masters, or whatever teacher of the moment my father saw fit to employ. None stayed long, and he'd always try to cheat them out of their fee.

It was in this land that I'd learned the lure of the fairer sex, the first in the form of a barmaid in Blakeney the summer I'd been fifteen. She'd been older than me — sixteen — and I'd thought her the most beautiful creature I'd ever seen.

I'd reveled in the conquest until I returned to school at Michaelmas, to later learn that said young woman was quite loose with her favors. Ours would hardly be the love of legend. She'd married at eighteen and gone to Suffolk with her husband, and was there now for all I knew.

Cooper said nothing on the road, a man with a habit of silence. I who never liked talking for the sake of it started to find him restful.

We went through the gate to the weed-choked drive. Cooper glanced about askance as he climbed over bracken on the way to the house. A cart stood in front of it, the horse let loose to graze as he liked. I dismounted, removed my horse's saddle and bridle, and let it join the carthorse.

I heard the sound of pounding before I entered the front door. No one was in the main hall, but the banging went on below us. I opened a door at the back of the house and descended to the kitchens and servants' quarters, where I found two men tearing out the walls.

They looked up when I came clattering down, saw that it was only the captain, and returned to smashing. Cooper came down behind me.

"Anything?" he shouted.

"Not yet," one of the men said.

"This paneling is fifty years old, and intact," I said over the hammering. "It's doubtful anything will be behind it."

Cooper shrugged. "No stone unturned, sir."

I ought to have been far more upset to see them bashing away at my ancestral home. However, the memories I had of this house were far from pleasant, and it was a wreck in any case. The best memories were of this kitchen, in fact. The cook would secretly feed the ravenous appetite of a growing youth when my father had thought a little starving would make me more obedient.

I surveyed the wreckage for a time then said, "Pull out all the paneling, every bit of it. We'll take it up to the stable yard and build a bonfire. Then you can start on the upstairs."

The men looked at me in surprise. Cooper nodded at them, and they turned back to the task with more gusto.

I picked up an axe one of the men had laid aside. Cooper kept a keen eye on me as I approached a wall they hadn't yet touched. I raised my arms over my head and let the axe slam into the wall.

The white-painted wood splintered. I hacked at the paneling until it began to come away from the solid stone that had sat on this spot for more than two hundred years.

I drew a breath, wiped my brow, shucked my coat, and raised the axe again. I moved to the next patch of paneling and struck another heavy blow.

There was release in the destruction, a sort of joy. I pounded at the walls again and again, until sweat ran down my face, and I was laughing.

*** *** ***

Lady Breckenridge did not arrive until late afternoon. She reached the house twenty minutes before the appointed time, which was the only indication of her curiosity. She arrived in a luxurious carriage — Grenville's — and Grenville came with her.

One of the men had moved up to the entrance hall, and he shouted to me that I had visitors. I came upstairs and went outside in my shirtsleeves, too hot to resume my coat. I left the axe behind.

"Good heavens," Lady Breckenridge said, looking at me.

Grenville, out of habit, raised his quizzing glass and ran his gaze over me, but he looked slightly envious. Someone like Grenville could not roll up his sleeves, open his collar, and do a bit of honest toil without the entire world commenting on it.

Lady Breckenridge lifted her skirts and strolled past me and inside, as unafraid as I thought she'd be. My first wife had been dreadfully timid—though I came to learn that she always managed to have her own way despite that. My second wife, it appeared, would not be bothered by timidity.

"You there," she demanded of Cooper's man. "What are you doing?"

I was inside a second later with Grenville behind me. Cooper's man lowered his sledgehammer and regarded Lady Breckenridge uncertainly.

I answered for him. "They're tearing everything out. The wood is worm eaten anyway."

"I can see that, but if you go at it like a madman, you'll ruin the wall behind it." Lady Breckenridge pointed upward, and spoke to the man with the sledgehammer. "Break the panels at the joints and keep the beams intact. If they prove faulty we'll replace them, one at a time. That's good stone behind it." Lady Breckenridge slapped her palm against the wall, as though she patted horseflesh. "If you destroy all the beams at the same time, my good man, you'll bring the entire house down on top of us."

She turned away without waiting for his response. Denis's man stared at her a moment, then returned to his task, breaking away the paneling as she'd instructed.

"Mr. Grenville, it might be time for those chairs," she said. "Gabriel, since you have absolutely nowhere to sit in this house, I had Grenville bring some camp furniture. It's dreadfully damp in here, but I assume we'll conclude our business shortly. Now, what did you wish to show me?"

Grenville departed out the door to whistle at Matthias and Bartholomew, who were waiting at the coach. As they started unloading, I beckoned to Donata.

"This way," I said, and led her up the stairs to my mother's sitting room. Cooper's men had not worked their way this far yet, and I did not intend to let them in there.

"I wanted to show you this," I said. I pointed at the pale dress lying across the chaise where I'd found it. "And ask you what you made of it."

Chapter Four

Lady Breckenridge reached a gloved finger to the gown's fine netting, but I stilled her hand.

"When I touched it, it crumbled to dust," I said. "I hoped you could tell me a bit about the style, when it might have been made, what sort of woman would have worn it . . ."

The two of us stood in a bubble of quietude as she leaned to study the gown. I heard Grenville giving orders to his footmen outside and the men continuing to break the paneling downstairs, but in the hushed peace of my mother's sitting room, even those noises were muted.

"I haven't seen a gown like this in years," Donata said after a time. "See how very simple it is. No adornments, just the little bow on the bodice. Silk netting on the sleeves, yes, but only there, and the sleeves are so very short. I had a dress like this, but the whole thing was covered with silver netting. It shimmered when I moved." She smiled in memory. "That was nearly ten years ago. I loved that gown."

She'd been a young bride ten years ago, alone in London while Lord Breckenridge was far away on the Peninsula.

The simplicity she described was a far cry from what Donata wore now—a dress of black-and-white striped broadcloth under a military-looking black spencer. Her skirt's hem was decorated with wide black braid embroidered with silver flowers, and her white straw bonnet had a turned-up brim with a black lining. She wore gloves of black leather that fitted her hands like a second skin. I, in my shirtsleeves and dusty breeches and boots, was a sharp contrast to this painfully fashionable lady.

"Am I correct that this was a debutante's gown?" I asked. Ten years ago, I'd been up to my neck in mud in Portugal and rarely saw a debutante. The colonels or generals in my regiment who had daughters to bring out took them back to London.

"At the time, white was in fashion for everyone," Donata said. "Pure Greek, you know. But this gown is certainly virginal. Made for a debutante, yes; say a girl between the ages of fifteen and twenty. After twenty, a woman gives up trying to be the youthful belle of the ball looks to take her place on the shelf. Or else, she is married."

Donata had married at eighteen. Her young innocence had come up against the brutality of Breckenridge straightaway.

"Ten years is a long time," I said. "Could the dress have been made at a later date? Or perhaps the girl wore it for several years? You change your entire wardrobe every season, but a girl from a poor gentleman's family would not have that luxury."

"That is true," Lady Breckenridge said without taking offense. "She *could* have been wearing this seven or eight years ago. But after the year 1810, it would have been difficult to convince a seamstress to make it. Once gauze-thin muslin went out and satin and velvets came in again, we never looked back. Dresses had more ornamentation, though they were certainly not as decorated as they are now. And this gown was not cheap, Gabriel, despite there being so little of it. The young woman for whom this dress was made came from a reasonably well-off family, or at least had a wealthy benefactor. It would have been the first stare of fashion in about 1807—or, in the country, 1808. 1809 at the very latest."

"My father was still alive then," I said.

Lady Breckenridge gave me a sharp look. "Are you contemplating the idea that your father enticed a debutante here, got her out of the gown, and persuaded her to leave it behind when she left?"

"I am not certain what to think. There are many possibilities."

"Do be logical, Gabriel. If such a thing had happened, the event would become known. Even if this debutante said nothing, *someone* would have noticed—a servant, someone from the village. You know what country gossip is like."

I did know. Her words made me feel better, but I remained a bit uneasy.

Lady Breckenridge went on, "Gowns are passed on as well—given to lady's maids, sold secondhand. This one looks in fine condition, except for its stint lying here gathering dust, of course, but it could have had a second or third owner. Perhaps a maid and her young man came here for a tryst, or perhaps the maid hid here, changed her clothes, eloped with said young man, and didn't bother to pack the gown. She had limited space and would not need it."

"That is possible," I conceded. Farfetched, but possible. "Though a maid and her young man might take it with them to sell it. I would think that the gown would fold up to nothing."

"Perhaps she feared someone would trace her through its sale. I have no idea, Gabriel. I am speculating."

"I understand. Thank you for your insight."

"May I take it?" Lady Breckenridge asked. "If it does not fall apart. Perhaps one of Lady Southwick's maids will recognize it."

I saw no reason not to let her. Bartholomew entered at the moment, bearing camp chairs. I heard Grenville below, talking in his easy way with Denis's men.

"Bartholomew," Lady Breckenridge said. "Bring me a blanket from the carriage, will you please? And open the windows before you go. The rain's gone, and it's a bit close in here."

Bartholomew said, "Yes, m'lady," set two camp chairs in the most solid part of the rug, wrestled with the two windows until they opened, and departed.

Lady Breckenridge went to a window and looked out, careful not to touch the filthy sill, then turned away and sat in one of the camp chairs. Because the chairs were Grenville's, they had cushions and rugs to ensure comfort.

"A lovely room," Donata said. "I can see why your mother liked it. The view is splendid. Tell me about her."

Lady Breckenridge, sitting with legs crossed, black-gloved hands relaxed on the arms of the camp chair, looked thoroughly at home in my mother's room. Her elegance befitted the feminine sanctuary this had once been.

"She passed away when I was nine," I said. "My memories are those of a child."

"You were not much older than Peter is now," she said.

"I had my father," I said. "Not that this was compensation. I was at school already, called in to see the headmaster when she died. The headmaster was sympathetic—I see that now—but at the time he told me to bear up and be a man about it. I was a man, all right. I was convinced that my father had killed her."

"A bit gruesome for a child. Why did you think so?"

"Because he used to beat her." I did not like to think about her cries, stifled because they'd make my father angrier. "Not until I came home between terms did I learn that she died of a fever. Even so, I'm certain my father sped her into the grave. He had no patience with her, thought she was too weak, thought she was overly fond of me."

Donata looked surprised. "You were her son. Why shouldn't she be fond of you?"

"*Overly* fond. The poor woman wanted to speak to me at least once a day, and my father was certain this would make me weak. He tried to forbid it, so my mother and I began to meet in secret. My father's greatest fear was that his son would not grow up to be strong."

Lady Breckenridge roved her gaze up and down my six-foot and more height. "He had no need to worry in that regard." I could not tell whether she meant it as a compliment. "My husband never forbade me to see Peter, but then, Breckenridge could rarely be bothered to remember he had a son."

Another strike against Lord Breckenridge in my book.

"The result is that I do not know much about my mother," I said. "I know she loved this room, that she found sanctuary here from my father. He had no patience with feminine frippery, and so he never came here. I used to creep up the back stairs and slip inside when he was busy. At least I have those memories."

Whether Lady Breckenridge would have expressed sympathy for this I was not to know, because at the moment, Bartholomew entered the room with a thin blanket over his arm. A well-trained servant, he simply came in without knocking, not drawing attention to himself. Lady Breckenridge rose. "Thank you, Bartholomew."

She took the blanket from him, laid it on the chaise, and very carefully slid the gown onto blanket. More of the gauze fell in on itself, but Lady Breckenridge folded the blanket over the rest of the dress and lifted the bundle.

"Carry this back down to the carriage, please," she said, holding it out to Bartholomew. "Over your arms, exactly like that."

Bartholomew looked bursting with curiosity, but he managed to keep it to himself as he took the blanket-wrapped garment. When he opened the door again, the man who'd been tearing up the bottom staircase came in with his hammer.

"We're to start on the upstairs, guv," he said. "You and her ladyship might want to go somewhere less dusty."

I was in front of him before he could take a step into the room. "Not in here."

The man was a bit shorter than me but wide of shoulder, and he carried a large sledgehammer, but I did not care.

"Mr. Cooper's orders, sir," he said.

"Mr. Cooper does not own the house. I do. This room is not to be touched. Tear up the rest of the house, but not this room."

The man did not look intimidated. "Mr. Cooper says the whole house must be searched, sir, before Mr. Denis arrives."

"I will deal with Mr. Cooper. And Mr. Denis. The chance that Easton hid anything here is remote."

He remained stubbornly fixed. I'd seen these lackeys obey Denis's slightest whim without question. Their devotion was admirable, but at the moment, their devotion was irritating me.

"What is that, then?" The man jerked his chin at the blanket Bartholomew held in his arms.

"Not a priceless painting," I said.

"I'll just have a look, shall I, guv?"

I got in front of him again. "You will not have a look, and you will leave this room. I give you my word that Bartholomew is not spiriting away anything you are looking for. It is another matter entirely."

The bloody man didn't move. "I need to ask Mr. Cooper, sir."

"You need to leave this room before I thrash you."

"Really, guv, you should stand aside."

The man kept his voice cool, an emotionless automaton used to carrying out James Denis's orders.

I on the other hand, lost my temper with a vengeance. "This is *my* house," I shouted at him. "In it, you do not work for Denis or Cooper or anyone else. You obey my orders and mine alone. *Do you understand?*"

The most hardened soldiers had slammed to attention when I'd roared at them thus, and I saw this man's spine straighten in spite of himself. He looked me up and down, his eyes as blank as ever, but they flickered when they met mine.

"Yes, sir," he said.

"Tell Cooper to come and talk to me," I said. "Now, if you please."

"Yes, guv." The man backed his way out the door. I hadn't cowed him, I could see, but he'd decided he did not get paid enough to deal with me.

Bartholomew chuckled as the man clattered down the stairs. "That was a fine thing."

"Bartholomew," I said, still out of temper.

"Right, sir." Bartholomew hastened out room with the dress, and I returned to the window.

I was still tight with anger. Ever since I'd seen my daughter back to France this summer, I'd experienced something like peace, no more rages or melancholia. But seeing one of Denis's brutes ready to tear up my mother's sitting room with his heavy hammer made my simmering anger boil up with nightmare force.

Lady Breckenridge had said nothing during the entire exchange, listening with her cool air of observation.

"You will have to replace the carpet," she said after a time.

I turned around. "What?"

"You will have to replace the carpet if this room is to be used again. The vermin have been at it. The wallpaper too, I am afraid. I understand why you do not wish Mr. Denis's pugilist to wreck it, but do not seek to make the room a shrine, Gabriel. That is always a bad idea."

She looked in no way dismayed at my outburst. Instead, she stood before me, quietly logical, giving me sound advice.

"Not a shrine," I said. "My father forbade anyone in here after she died. Not the same thing, but also a bad idea."

"Quite right," Lady Breckenridge said, looking around. "This will make a pleasant little sitting room. Keep the pictures and things she liked, but redo the rest. She would have wanted it to be used, I think."

Lady Breckenridge had compassion without sentimentality. I liked that very much about her.

I went to her. "I apologize for my temper."

"No, indeed. You were quite right. They should not run tame in your house." Her eyes sparkled with curiosity. "But what on earth did you mean about a priceless painting?"

Grenville chose that moment to come in. "An excellent question. What about it, Lacey? Why are

James Denis's pugilists sinking hammer and claw into your house?"

"Where is Cooper?" I asked.

"I believe the other two are looking for him," Grenville said. "Tell us, Lacey. Your brief tale about Easton has whetted my appetite for more."

Without further hesitation, I related all to them. The smuggled artwork was Denis's business, but he'd involved me in it. His own fault if I spread the knowledge.

I knew, even as I spoke, that Denis did not fear what I would say. He was expert at winding his nets around those he wanted to control, and he would not have chosen me for this errand had he wanted to keep its true nature secret. That mean he was not in the least worried about me or who I'd tell.

"Good heavens," Lady Breckenridge when I'd finished. "As I have observed before, Gabriel, your acquaintance is interesting."

"And as I have observed, you need to have a care with James Denis," Grenville said. "He is a dangerous man, with dangerous men in his employ."

"I know that," I said, "Though, truth be told, I could become grateful to him for some of the things he's done. He found my wife and daughter. When my daughter was in danger, he made every effort on her behalf. I cannot hate him for that, no matter what his motives."

"He did once save me from a fiery death," Lady Breckenridge put in.

Grenville gave us both a severe look. "That is all very well. However, it does not negate the fact that Denis is a thief, a smuggler, an extortionist, a sometime murderer, and deep in corruption of all sorts. Such a man does things only for his own gain, and he cannot be trusted not to turn on you at any moment. Remember that."

He stopped talking when Lady Breckenridge looked past him and raised her brows. The pugilist I'd chased away had opened the door quietly.

Grenville scowled at him, looking in no way embarrassed. "Yes, what is it?"

The pugilist addressed his words to me. "I can't find Cooper, guv."

"No?" I asked. "Did he go back to Easton's?"

"Couldn't say. Want us to carry on?"

"In all other rooms, yes. Keep dragging out the debris for the fire."

The lackey touched his forehead in an approximate salute. "Right, guv."

He disappeared and the banging recommenced. I drew a breath. "Donata, this is a precarious place for now. I'd rather see you lounging in luxury at Lady Southwick's."

"Where the decor hurts my eyes," Donata said, but she came to me and kissed my dusty cheek. "I will start making lists about what to do in these rooms. Your mother seems to have liked pink and yellow, so we'll keep those colors. Do give a thought to letting those men take out the paneling, as long as they do not damage the beams as I instructed. The wood is rotting, and they seem keen. Why not make them do the work?"

As always, her clearheaded practicality bandaged my rather messy emotions. She'd have made an excellent officer's wife—one who followed the drum, that is. Breckenridge had been an officer but had left his lady well at home.

"Make use of my carriage and my lackeys, my lady," Grenville said. "I'm for a walk. The rain has cleared, the air is deuced fine, and my English heart is lifted. How about it, Lacey?"

I declined. "I want to stay here and keep an eye on things."

"I do not blame you. In that case, I will tramp alone and wend my way back to Lady Southwick's. I'll observe the birds soaring over the trees and rejoice in the countryside as I go."

We agreed on our separate courses, and I walked with Donata out to the carriage. Part of Grenville's motivation for his walk was that he grew ill in carriages swaying through the countryside. He did not have as much trouble in the city, where the distances were short, and his coach moved slowly through traffic. He also did not succumb when he drove his own conveyance. But put him in a chaise and four on the open road, and he became a slave to nausea and dizziness.

I kissed Donata on the cheek before I helped her into the waiting coach. She clung to my hand a moment and whispered, "You are a good man, Gabriel. Never forget that."

Then, with her usual aplomb, she settled into the landau and directed Grenville's coachman, Jackson, to drive on.

Matthias asked leave to join Grenville on his tramp, and the two of them walked off across what had been the park. I was glad Matthias accompanied him, because though the country seemed open, there were hidden corners and marshy hollows to traverse. Grenville was so obviously a wealthy man, and who knew what strangers lurked in the shadows, waiting for a mark. In these times, people grew desperate. Matthias, a sturdy lad, could protect him.

Once my friends had gone, I returned to helping Denis's men tear down my house. We carried timber and rotted floorboards into a clear space in the old garden and piled it for a bonfire. I fetched an old spade and broke the grasses away from the pile so the fire wouldn't spread.

In this flat country with its huge sky, the sun stayed well in sight through the evening. When we lit the bonfire at seven o'clock, the sunset still outshone it.

Cooper had not returned. Denis's men and I warmed ourselves around the welcome bonfire, and were still there when, around half past seven, Matthias came running, running up the path from the park.

"Sir," he panted. He had to bend double, hands on knees to catch his breath. "You need to come, Captain. Now!"

Chapter Five

"Grenville," I said, my heart in my throat.

Matthias shook his head, sweat dripping from the blond giant's hair. "No, sir. Not Mr. Grenville. You need to come."

I wasted no time. Grenville had, once before, investigated by himself on my behalf and come to grief. Despite Matthias's assurances, I wanted to find him quickly.

The horse I'd borrowed from Lady Southwick had wandered off who knew where. Searching for him would take too long, so I hobbled after Matthias the best I could.

Denis's men followed us, and Matthias led us south and east, a couple of miles across farmland to a silent windmill. It stood dark and tall above us, and I recognized it as the one I had seen through the windows at Easton House.

The fan blades hung still, one coming to rest just above the windmill's door, which had been broken open. Grenville stood in the doorway. Four of Denis's men were there as well, one with a lantern, and Grenville was arguing with them.

He was trying to keep them out. Matthias pushed fearlessly through the lot, opening the way for me.

Grenville did not bother with a greeting. He beckoned to me then stepped through the door into the windmill. I confiscated the lantern and ducked under the low lintel.

The interior of the windmill was dark and silent, with a wide board floor covered with broken pieces of a stair that had once led to the rooms above. Water trickled somewhere below us. In this dank place, my lantern shone as a warm star.

The light fell on the outstretched body of a man lying on his back, his face black with blood. It was a gruesome sight, a bloody pulp where his face had been, his hair soaked red, his arms outstretched, hands open.

"Dead." Grenville sounded stiff. "He's cool, and I couldn't detect breath."

The man was tall, his limbs large, hands and feet huge. He wore a workman's shirt, serge coat, cotton knee breeches, and heavy shoes, a costume no different from those of the men who waited outside.

"Is it Cooper?" I asked.

"I have no idea. I never met Cooper."

"Do they know?" I gestured to the men peering through the doorway.

"They were all for dragging him out, putting him in a cart, and dumping him into the sea. But this was a murder. We need a magistrate."

I looked down again at the man sprawled on the damp stone floor. James Denis was a law unto himself, the men who worked for him, his deputies. I did not know whether they wanted to keep the death quiet so they could exact vengeance on their own, or to keep up Denis's façade of invulnerability. Much of Denis's power lay in the myth that he and his could never be touched.

The men at the door turned way abruptly, and worried conversation arose. I handed Grenville the lantern and went back outside.

Another large man was coming down from the house, also carrying a lantern. Next to him walked the unmistakable form of James Denis.

Denis was striding down the path toward the windmill, his tall, slim form emphasized by his high hat and the cloak that flowed from his shoulders. He walked briskly, and his lackeys fell silent as he approached.

Denis swept his gaze over the scene. He was a youngish man, thirty at most, with an unlined, square face, a long nose, and dark blue eyes that looked black in this light. Those eyes were cold, as always, and now the look in them was glacial. I noted that his men tried very hard not to be caught in the path of that icy stare.

He ignored them to rest his gaze on me. "Who is in there, Captain?"

"It might be Cooper," I said. "He's not been seen all afternoon. But the man's been beaten, and I cannot tell who it is."

"Cooper." Denis's gaze flickered. Had he been any other man, I would have sworn he showed uneasiness, even concern. "Let me see."

I stepped aside to let him through the door. Denis removed his hat and handed it to a startled Matthias, then he swept his cloak behind his shoulders, entered the windmill, and got down on one knee. Grenville obligingly brought the lantern low.

Denis touched the dead man's chin, the only thing not battered. He stayed there in his half-kneel, staring at the wreck of the victim's face.

"It is not Cooper," he said.

Did I detect a faint loosening of the shoulders . . . in relief? I'd never seen Denis show an emotion other than irritation or anger, and even those had been muted.

"Who, then?" I asked.

"His name is Ferguson. William Ferguson."

"Bill Ferguson?" Grenville asked in surprise. "Good God."

The name meant nothing to me. Grenville noticed my blank look and continued, "One hell of a fighter. Unbeatable. Retired a few years ago, to the dismay of the Fancy."

The "Fancy" consisted of mostly upper-class gentlemen who were avid admirers of the sport of boxing. Prize fighting was illegal, but having two men fight for show was not, and boxers and their sponsors found many ways around the laws. The private betting that went on among the Fancy moved fortunes.

"Ferguson came to work for me a year ago," Denis said. "He'd tired of every youth wanting to prove themselves on him, and he sought obscurity. He also needed money." He spoke in a flat voice, whatever emotion I thought I had seen gone. "Who did this?"

Again, he directed his words at me. "We do not know," I said. "Grenville chanced upon him here not thirty minutes ago. I've been at my house all afternoon, trying to keep a few walls standing at least."

The increase in Denis's frown as he got to his feet told me he hadn't been informed of events here. I leaned down and lifted a heavy piece of wood, which had once been part of the stair leading to the next floor. It was covered with dried blood.

I showed it to Denis. "Someone fought him and fought him hard."

"This Cooper fellow, perhaps?" Grenville asked.

Denis swung to Grenville so quickly that Grenville, who had as much sangfroid as Denis ever did, took a step back.

"No," Denis said, his voice going colder still. "Cooper would not have done this."

"Is he here?" I asked. "He left my house early this afternoon, without saying good-bye. I assumed he'd returned here."

"He is not at the house," Denis said. He obviously was not at the crowd around the windmill either. "What the devil was Ferguson doing out here?" This he asked of the men at the doorway. Not one of them answered.

"Looking for your artwork, I imagine," I said.

"Looking for it," Denis repeated. "And Cooper? Why was he with you, Captain?"

"The same reason. He was worried about what you would do when you arrived and found Easton gone, the artwork nowhere in sight. I sent Easton away—Cooper and your men had nothing to do with that."

I sensed every witness within earshot tensing. These men had been in a frenzy all day to find the paintings before Denis arrived so that his anger at their failure to kill Easton might be assuaged. The fact that Easton had run away, leaving the artwork hidden, had not yet been conveyed to Denis.

Denis's expression did not change. "I fully expected that you'd help Easton flee," he said. "Cooper should have understood that."

His dark blue eyes held no ire, but I grew suddenly angry.

Of course. If Denis had wanted Easton dead, a silent assassin in the night could have done the deed quite easily, and Denis would not have bothered to warn Easton at all. But he'd sent me, because he'd wanted Easton to run, not die—for whatever reason, only Denis knew. He'd used me and my ever-present sense of honor.

I broke away from him. "Matthias, find something with which to cover the body. We'll need the magistrate and coroner out here."

"No." Denis's word was flat and final. "He was one of mine. I will take care of it."

"Someone fought and killed a very strong man," I said. "The killer might still be wandering the countryside, a danger to others. He should be found."

"And I will find him. A coroner will tell us only what we already know—that Ferguson died from blows to his head, delivered by a person or persons unknown. That will be the end. Or the coroner and magistrate will accuse and arrest someone at random, probably one of my men, guilty or innocent. Tell me what good that would do, Captain."

As we spoke, Grenville removed his greatcoat and handed it to Matthias, who spread it over Ferguson, lying battered and silent. The man who'd accompanied Denis from the house directed others to fetch a board on which to carry Ferguson's body.

I could only let them. Denis was correct about the conclusions the local magistrate and coroner would draw. Many of Denis's men had criminal pasts, and it would be simple for a magistrate to pick one at random to arrest, not caring much which he chose to be the culprit. Denis would at least try to ferret out the truth.

Denis went outside again, followed by Grenville. The others got Ferguson onto a makeshift litter and carried him back toward the house. I was struck by the care they all took of him, if not showing grief then at least reverence and respect.

Denis remained behind as the train of men moved slowly up the path. Once they were out of earshot, he turned to Grenville. "I wish to speak to Captain Lacey by himself. Please take your footman and go home."

Grenville did not much like taking orders. He sent me a swift glance, but I nodded at him.

"Tell Lady Southwick not to wait supper for me," I said. "And bid Lady Breckenridge good night for me if I do not return before she retires."

Grenville kept his cool demeanor in place, gave me back the lantern, and tipped his hat. "Good night then, Lacey. I'll have brandy waiting for you on your return. Matthias."

Matthias gave me a nod as well and fell into step with his master. They began their walk eastward, in the direction of Southwick's grand home, leaving me alone in the night with James Denis.

Chapter Six

Denis and I stood in silence. The wind was rising, that steady Norfolk wind that blew from the North Sea and straight through everything in its path. Clouds tore across the moon, giving the land an eerie glow.

"Easton had become a problem," Denis said. He gazed across the flat farmland around the quiet windmill, its job of pumping water from the earth finished. "You were the best person to take care of that problem."

"Meaning you did not want him dead. Of course not; you can always use him again, or at least his contacts. So, send a cavalryman, a local son Easton would trust, to warn him off, to help him escape, and you are rid of your problem for now. He stole from you. Now that he's running far and fast, you can recover your property."

Denis nodded without looking at me. "My surprise is not that you have discerned this, but that it took you a day to do so."

I realized something else. In this place, in the darkness, was the first time since I'd met Denis that he'd let himself be alone with me, no one to guard him. I had my sword in my cane, and I was strong. He knew what I was capable of, and yet . . . here we were.

"The men who work for me understand that it is dangerous work," Denis said. "But I pledge to take care of them. I do not like it when I fail."

His voice was flat, uninflected. But I could see from the rigidity of his back that he was angry. Exceedingly so.

"Whenever your men have been harmed, it has happened only when they've been out of your reach," I pointed out. "Ferguson came here with Cooper in a frantic rush to find the artwork before you arrived. Cooper was terrified that you'd punish him for letting Easton get away and wished to soothe your temper with the paintings presented to you, fait accompli."

"And yet, Cooper is nowhere to be found."

I glanced at the dark windmill. "Perhaps he and Ferguson quarreled, Cooper agitated because he wanted the task finished before you arrived. The quarrel grew violent, and when Cooper saw that he'd killed Ferguson, he fled."

Denis finally turned to me, eyes icier than ever in the light of my lantern. "Ferguson was one of the best fighters in England. He was younger than Cooper, and he had a fiery temper. Why is it not Cooper lying dead?"

"A man may be a magnificent fighter and still lose against a stout beam of wood. Cooper might have landed a fatal blow out of great luck. I still wish that you would let a coroner look at Ferguson."

"And I said, a coroner can tell me nothing I do not know already."

"Not necessarily true. He could tell whether the man met his death because of the blows, or whether his face was disfigured after death."

"Why should he be beaten afterward?"

"I have no idea. But I'd rather be certain."

Denis returned his gaze to the gray horizon, none of the anger I sensed showing on his face. "I know a surgeon I can summon."

One who would obey Denis to the letter. "The local people will wonder why you've taken over Easton's house. It might not be a good idea to stay here."

"On the contrary," Denis said. "I own the house. I have for several years now. Easton was leasing it back from me."

I should not have been surprised. Denis was very good at arranging things. "Even so, the world here is small and closely knit. Strangers are not tolerated."

"The world is changing, Captain, even here. The war changed it, and now peace is changing it still more." He looked at me again. "But I take your point. How fortunate for me that I have a native son to vouch for me."

My irritation rose, but I said nothing. Let him make what he would of my silence.

"I want you to find out what happened, Captain. Discover who killed Ferguson and why, and bring the man to me, not to the magistrates."

Of course I'd find out what happened. I wanted to know as much as he did. "You are not the law."

"He faces me first," Denis said, ignoring me. "And, do, find Cooper."

Now I heard worry. Quite a range of emotions this night for a man who rarely let any show.

"If Cooper killed Ferguson, he might be far from here," I said. "On the sea already."

Denis settled his hat against the wind. "Cooper did not kill him. This, I know. But find him. He might be a witness to whoever did."

Another tweak to his hat, and Denis set off up the path to the house, leaving me alone with the windmill in the darkness of the night.

*** *** ***

I went back inside the windmill. I had one tiny lantern and no idea what I looked for, but I searched the dusty wooden floor for anything I might have missed.

Ferguson's blood had spattered across the room. The walls, once whitewashed, were gray with grime and now splashed red. Already, insects had come to inspect and feed.

I wanted to wash the place clean, but at the moment I had nothing with which to do so. I brought in handfuls of damp earth to spread across the floor where most of the blood had pooled, but that was all I could do.

I left the windmill and closed the door. I wanted to lock it, but the hasp of the lock had broken. I noticed that while the windmill, one of the older ones, was crumbling, the lock was new. Now it was broken. Had Ferguson done that, or his killer?

I looked up the hill to Easton's house, Easton's no longer. Most of the windows were lit, Denis wealthy enough to afford to illuminate any room he wished.

I wondered what the domestics had done—the butler who'd admitted me and Easton's cook and other household staff. Had they taken the holiday I'd commanded them to, or had Denis recruited them to wait upon him?

I turned from the house's warmth and made my slow way back across the fields toward my own home. The going was slow, the wind coming across the land, chill. I went carefully, my eye out for Cooper or any murderous wretch still in the area.

The Lacey house sat on a rise of ground among low hills, a bulk in the darkness. Unlike Easton's place, all my windows were dark.

Behind the house, the bonfire still flickered, but no one had remained to man it. Most of the wood, brittle and old, had burned quickly. I smothered the fire the best I could, bringing in sand from the bottom of the garden to scatter over it. I waited until the fire had died to a tiny smolder before I left again.

The horse I'd borrowed from Lady Southwick's stables was nowhere in sight. Horses had an uncanny knack for finding their way back to their own barns, so he might have gone home, or else someone had come across him wandering and taken him. I'd have to hunt for him in the morning or be prepared to give Lady Southwick the cost of the beast.

I made my way on foot a mile and half north to the village called Parson's Point, a tiny place south of Stifkey marsh on the coast. Local history said that in medieval times, the village had been a port, with an inlet cutting to the center of the village. Drainage and time now put it half a mile inland. The village had begun life as a Roman camp, renamed Parson's Point a few hundred years ago.

I needed to hire a horse or put up for the night. I'd never walk to Lady Southwick's, five or so miles away, on my stiff leg in the cold.

The public house in Parson's Point beckoned me with warm light. I was tired, my leg hurt, and the wind howled. I entered the brightness of the taproom with relief.

This was the first time since my arrival that I'd sought familiar haunts. I stood in the doorway, struck with a strange feeling of time whirling backward. Since I'd left Norfolk at age twenty, I'd experienced war, hardship, and loss, yet also intense friendships and a wild joy at being alive. But it seemed that the world of Parson's Point had stayed in an untouched bubble while I'd been gone.

The faces I'd left twenty years ago were still here. The publican, Mr. Buckley, had been thirty-five, just taking over from his elderly father. He was fifty-five now, but still had the fat cheeks and ruddy complexion of his youth. Fishermen I recognized sat in the corners, nursing pints and smoking pipes. The shopkeepers and boat makers took up benches in the middle of the room. In a corner, a man scraped a bow over a fiddle, playing softly.

But, I realized as I stood there getting my bearings, that there had been changes. Some of the older faces had been replaced with younger ones, sons who were near replicas of their fathers but not quite. One of the shopkeepers I did not recognize at all, and in the shadows, I saw men I'd known, now broken and battered, soldiers home from war.

Buckley the publican saw me. "Now then, young master. Best bitter for you?"

The few gazes that hadn't yet turned to me did so now. About half the room nodded in a quiet way, unsurprised that I'd walked into the public house twenty years after I'd walked out of it. Others sang out greetings, lifting tankards in my direction, and still others regarded me sullenly. My father hadn't been well liked, and the saying, *The apple doesn't fall far from the tree,* was a popular one.

I put down my coin and lifted the ale, taking a pull. I swallowed, refraining from making a face. The ale was different, not nearly as good as I remembered it. Either they'd changed brewers or experience had made my palate more particular.

I sat down at the middle table, uncomfortable but not wanting to be standoffish. I leaned my cane against the table and saw gazes go to it. One soldier in the corner was missing an arm, another's face had been burned.

"Come back to the land of your fathers, have you?" a boat maker asked. "Hope you'll open the old house again. It's been a blight on the land these eight years gone."

Buckley said from the bar, "Saw you'd brought some fellows from London to help you go at the place. You didn't need to. Plenty here that will do it for you."

One of the soldiers spoke. "Hard, when work's going begging. What about it, Lacey?"

I recognized him now—Terrance Quinn, nephew of the old vicar at Parson's Point. Terrance had been my friend, eighteen to my twenty when I'd left for the army. He'd followed a few years after that, from what I had heard, an infantryman all the way to Waterloo.

I chose my words carefully. "Those two happened to be at the house today, and I took advantage of them. Certainly, put out the word—anyone wishing to help tear apart the Lacey manor and put it back together should apply to me in the morning. Not too early," I finished, holding up my tankard. Those around me chuckled.

"You've come into money, have you, Lacey?" Terrance asked, his eyes glittering with dislike. Everyone knew the Laceys had pockets to let.

"He's come into a *lady*," Buckley said. "Our felicitations to you, Master Lacey."

The room laughed and drank to me. I was not at all surprised they knew. Someone would have heard through the gossip network common to all villages that I was staying at Lady Southwick's, that I was betrothed to Lady Breckenridge, and how high a standing Lady Breckenridge had.

"Saw the fine carriages on the road," Buckley went on. "Soon you'll have the house opened up and be hosting posh do's."

I gave him a good-natured smile. "If my lady has her way, yes. In that case, I imagine I'll be right here most nights."

That brought a collective laugh, hands thumping on tables.

"Surprised you deign to come here at all, Lacey," Terrance broke in. "Don't want your London friends despising you, do you? I hear tell you are great friends with the man who turned the brigadier out of his house."

Faces turned to me again. Some men looked as belligerent as Terrance, others threw me glances of apology for Terrance's hostility.

"I would not say he is a great friend," I said, keeping my voice steady. "But yes, I know Mr. Denis. Apparently, he purchased the house from Brigadier Easton some years back."

"First I've heard of it," Terrance said.

"That he did," Buckley broke in. "The brigadier's boot boy is the wife's sister's son. This Mr. Denis used to come and shut himself up with Mr. Easton for days. Butler there said to the staff one day that Easton no longer owned the house but would live there same as always. Up 'til yesterday anyway."

More eyes on me, some curious, some accusing. "The brigadier went to the Continent," I said.

"Why'd he want to do that, then?" Terrance asked.

I shrugged. "Business, I suppose."

Another man spoke up. "Men crawling all over his house now, staff gone. Big, muscular gents. Maybe he's turning it into a brothel for unnaturals."

This brought a laugh, one that held an edge of relief. Better to laugh at the ridiculous than stir tempers, as Terrance was determined to.

Before the laughter died away, someone told the listening fiddler to play. He started a lively tune, and men began to sing. I joined in, an old song, and I again felt the strange sense of going backward in time. I'd spent many an evening in this public house in the summers before I'd gone, using it as my sanctuary from the stifling anger of my father.

I stayed much longer than I meant to, singing and drinking with men I'd known long ago. When the publican finally turned us out, I paid him a few shillings for the use of his horse to get me back to Southwick Hall.

Terrance Quinn materialized from the shadows in the yard after Buckley had boosted me onto the horse and handed me my walking stick. Terrance caught the bridle with his good hand as I started to turn the horse away.

"You have a lot of cheek coming here, Lacey," he said.

Terrance spoke in a tone I'd heard many times in soldiers — frustration with something in their lives led to fistfights about anything and everything.

"I live here." My words slurred with too much ale. "The cheek was in staying away too long."

"You know what I mean. Rubbing our faces in your lofty friends and your lady viscountess, while the rest of us came back to nothing. *Nothing.*"

"If you think I've not suffered loss, you are wrong," I said. "Very wrong." I could have begun a litany of the tragedy I'd been through but decided against it. Terrance and I trading a catalog of sorrows would border on the absurd.

"You don't know the meaning of suffering, *Captain,*" Terrance said, then he strode away into darkness.

Buckley had remained in the shadows during this exchange, and he came back to me once Terrance had gone. "Never mind him, young master. He's a changed man. Can't blame him, you know, leaving an arm behind in Belgium, and then returning to find his cousin what he was betrothed to gone. No one knows where."

Chapter Seven

Something stirred the fog beneath the large quantities of ale I'd consumed. A dress of virginal white, Lady Breckenridge touching it and frowning. "His cousin? You mean Miss Helena Quinn?"

"Aye. She eloped with a man, so they say. None have heard of her since. Young Mr. Quinn has taken it hard."

Well he might. The revelation sobered me a bit, and I rode out of the yard into the wind.

I was far gone in my cups, and how I reached Southwick Hall without sliding off that big horse, I never knew. Fortunately, he was a patient beast, a farm horse, and he knew the roads better than I did.

One of Lady Southwick's grooms got me dismounted. Bartholomew, anxiously waiting in the stable yard, took me upstairs to my chamber, but he left me there without helping me undress. I found out why when I let myself fall across the bed, still in my coat and boots.

I landed on something very soft and fine-smelling. She woke, and began to scold me.

In my exhaustion and inebriation, and to erase the picture of Ferguson with black blood clotted on what was left of his face, I gathered Donata to me and held her until I could breathe again.

*** *** ***

I slept much later than I meant to, and when I awoke, Donata had gone. She'd left an indentation in mattress and pillows, but those had already grown cool with her absence. I snuggled into the nest she'd left, still half asleep.

I was pulled out of this pleasurable state by Bartholomew breezing into the room. "Awake then, are you, Captain? Lady Southwick's compliments, and she wishes to see you."

Not what I wanted to hear this early after a night of drinking. "Why?" I mumbled.

"Couldn't say, sir. Message was conveyed to me by the butler who said it was not my place to ask. I'll have you fixed in a trice, sir."

As he spoke, he banged about at the washstand. The scent of water steaming with mint came to me, along with the sound of Bartholomew stropping a razor against a long piece of leather.

I'd learned to succumb to his ministrations. First, because it saved argument; second, because Bartholomew was skilled. He'd learned how to take care of a gentleman from Gautier, Grenville's able manservant. Bartholomew could shave me without cutting me, would wrap a warm towel around my face to ease the razor's sting, and assist in my toilette without being too intrusive.

He had me shaved, bathed, and the ends trimmed from my unruly hair without taking too long and without rushing. Someday, a gentleman of means would catch on to how good a valet he was and snatch him away.

Bartholomew had even brought me a private repast, which I could barely touch, and mixed me the pick-me-up he'd learned from my landlady. My ability to think had returned by the time I reached the sitting room downstairs, and found that Lady Southwick had arranged a tête-à-tête.

She waited for me on a divan near the wide windows that looked out to her garden. The wind had blown away the clouds for now, and the wide Norfolk sky soared blue above the riotous flowers of the late summer garden.

I bowed to her. "My lady, I apologize. I have been a most cavalier guest. I faced several unexpected turns of events yesterday, which kept me from your hospitality."

Lady Southwick looked pleased. "A pretty speech. Lady Breckenridge has much praised your politeness."

As she smiled up at me, I was struck again by how similar she was to Donata. The two ladies had different coloring, but her high-waisted, dark green gown with cream stripes must have been created by the same dressmaker; her cream silk cap with three feathers could have been made by Donata's milliner.

Lady Southwick, however, looked at the world as though she expected and believed that it would behave exactly as she wanted it to. Lady

Breckenridge looked at the same world and knew that it never would.

"Forgive me if I upset you," I said.

"Oh, you have not upset me. Lady Breckenridge is a bit put out with you, but you must expect that. Wives are always put out with husbands. I know I am constantly put out with mine."

I did not point out that I was not yet married to Donata, because for some reason, I did not wish to remind this lady of my unmarried state.

"The other guests are a bit chatty about you as well," she said. "The subject of your very country manners has come up time and again. Mr. Grenville speaks highly of you, however, so your manners will be overlooked. You can make things up to me if you like in our little game this afternoon. Partner me, and all will be forgiven."

"Game," I repeated.

Lady Southwick rose and twined her fingers around my arm. "Croquet. On the lawn. Now." She gave me a smile.

"I have many errands this afternoon," I said, not moving. Pressing ones. I needed to find people and finds things out, not tap a blasted ball around a green.

Her fingers sank deeper into my arm. "Now, Captain, you must show these Mayfair gentlemen that you've risen above your country upbringing. A polite game, with the ladies, will do this."

I knew that the gentlemen here didn't give a damn about me rising above my upbringing—which had been similar to theirs, in any case. But Lady Southwick was dragging me out the French windows to a little terrace that led to a lawn.

As we stepped outside, I saw Donata already walking on the grass. She had her hand on Grenville's arm and looked sublimely uninterested that I'd emerged from Lady Southwick's private sitting room with Lady Southwick, alone. Bless her.

"Ah, Lacey," Grenville said. "Good afternoon."

He wore his man-about-town look, the one that said he was weary with ennui but would endeavor to be polite.

Rafe Godwin wandered by on his way to the croquet green. Rafe lifted his quizzing glass and studied me through it, turned away, and made loud, piggy noises to his companion, who tittered.

Grenville glanced at Rafe's retreating back. "I might have to cut him," he said.

Lady Southwick's butler handed me a mallet. "If you cut every gentleman on my account, you'd have no one left to speak to," I said.

Because Lady Southwick had turned away to give instructions to her butler, Grenville dropped his persona for the barest instant. "What a relief that would be."

Lady Breckenridge patted his arm. "Nonsense. If you cut everyone, that would only make you the more popular. Human beings strive more to catch the attention of those who hate everyone than of those who like everyone. A strange thing, but I've observed it to be so."

I smiled at her, then leaned to Grenville and spoke in a low voice. "Can you get word to Bartholomew and Matthias? I'd like one of them at my house to keep Denis's men from tearing it up too much, and I'd like the other to have a look inside that windmill again. We might find something in the light of day that we missed last night."

"And this afternoon is so very bright," Donata said. "Do not worry, Gabriel. Placate Lady Southwick with this tedious game, and then make your escape."

I exchanged a look with Grenville, who had the impudence to grin at me. Lady Southwick returned at that moment, and we could speak no further.

"We are the blue team," Lady Southwick said. "Excellent. I hope that you are a good player, Captain. It's a guinea a wicket."

A guinea . . . I had forgotten that ladies and gentlemen of the *ton* could not do anything so simple as play a friendly lawn game without gambling like mad. Knocking balls about the grass could become deadly expensive.

Grenville looked unconcerned, and I knew he was prepared to spot me the cash, though he knew how such things grated on my pride. Very well, then, I decided as I shouldered my mallet and led Lady Southwick away. I would have to play to win.

*** *** ***

The game commenced, the house party alternating between standing about gossiping and giving intense attention to play. Grenville played politely — that is, he showed he did not intend to best everybody in sight, while giving the impression that he could if he wished.

Donata had no such compunction. She ruthlessly knocked her ball into her opponents' at every opportunity, and reveled in driving their balls off the pitch. She did not spare me. When her red-striped ball clacked into my blue-striped one, she put her well-shod foot over her ball and plenty of muscle behind the stroke that smacked mine away. My ball galloped across the green and dropped into the marsh grasses that pushed against Lady Southwick's cultivated lawn.

"What say you, Gabriel?" Lady Breckenridge said, a sparkle in her dark blue eyes. "Five guineas on the game?"

"Of course," I said. "I always pay up my wagers."

Her smile grew satisfied. She referred to the wager we'd made the first day we'd met, when I'd played billiards with her in a sunny room, and she'd challenged me.

I had to search through the grass for my ball, while Donata went on to score double points behind me. I took the opportunity to coerce Reaves, the young vicar, into helping me look for the ball, and so into conversation.

"What became of the Quinns?" I asked him, "when you took the living? Dr. Quinn, you said, passed on. What about the rest of his family?"

Reaves blinked. "Devil if I know. No, a moment. I believe the wife lives in Blakeney with her sister-in-law. I know her nephew is still about."

"Terrance, yes. I spoke to him last night. What about the Quinns' daughter? Helena?"

"Couldn't say. She was gone before I arrived. Some scandal, I think, but I know little about it. You know what villagers are. Rattle on amongst themselves but close ranks against outsiders."

Reaves was certainly an outsider. He was a city man, probably had lived his entire life in the circle of Cambridge and London.

"I remember Helena," I said. "When I was a boy, she'd follow me about, wanting me to teach her to climb trees and so forth. I thought her a nuisance."

"Yes, well, apparently about—oh, ten years ago?—she up and ran off. Probably with someone her family did not approve of. Provincials can be quite close-minded. She's likely living in some cottage not far from here, teaching her own daughters not to run off with scoundrels."

Reaves bent to tap his ball, finished with gossip.

Ten years ago. Had Helena Quinn gained entrance to my father's house, changed her debutante's gown for traveling clothes, and then gone off with her unsuitable man? My father had still been alive then. I could not see him helping illicit young lovers, nor could I see him allowing anyone outside the family into my mother's sitting room.

Perhaps one of the Lacey maidservants had found the dress discarded by Helena after her flight and had put it into the sitting room for safekeeping, knowing no one would disturb it there. Said maidservant could always bundle it away later to sell.

But if so, why hadn't she, why had the gown been spread so neatly, almost reverently, across the chaise, and why had my father allowed it to remain there?

I renewed my intent to find Helena Quinn, or whoever had left the gown, and ask for the story. In spite of Donata trying to persuade me out of my fears of the discarded gown meaning something sinister, I could not shake the feeling.

I gained some respect from the house party by winning half the wickets, but Lady Breckenridge and Grenville won the game.

"That is five guineas you owe me, Gabriel," Lady Breckenridge said as we returned to the shade of the terrace. The butler passed among us with a tray of lemonade.

"And I will pay the debt," I said. "At the moment, I need to return a horse and make some inquiries."

"Lady Southwick has planned an outing for us, it seems," Grenville said, sipping lemonade. "She's going to cart us all down to Binham to stroll about the ruins of the priory. And have a picnic."

"I will have to join the house party there," I said. "Or perhaps I should excuse myself to Lady Southwick altogether and take rooms over the tavern at Parson's Point."

"Do not, Gabriel," Lady Breckenridge said severely. "I do not tell you this only because I'd never forgive you if you left me to deal with Lady Southwick alone, I tell it to you for your own good. *I* know that other matters are pulling at your attention, but *they* will accuse you of not being able to hold your own at a society house party. The story will be told and retold through the shooting season and on into spring. They'd make a laughingstock of you."

I hardly cared, but I knew Donata did. She had to live among these people, and she was drawing me into her world. She had once told me that she liked me because I did not behave as expected, but she took a large risk, socially, attaching herself to me.

"Then I will stay," I said. "But I must see about the horse, and I must make certain that the Lacey house remains in one piece."

"I will placate Lady Southwick for you," Donata said. "And continue my discreet inquiries about the gown."

"Ask Lady Southwick about Helena Quinn, and whatever scandal surrounds her."

Lady Breckenridge looked surprised. "You have a woman in mind already for the owner of the dress?"

"I might. She disappeared about the same time that the gown was made. Helena was the vicar's daughter; I imagine Lady Southwick knows the story, or at least the gist of it."

"Hmm." Lady Breckenridge took a sip of lemonade, made a face, and dumped the rest of the glass's contents into the rhododendrons. "I shall endeavor."

"What shall I do, Lacey?" Grenville asked.

"Look after Donata, for now," I said. "Especially on this jaunt to the priory, and stay on guard for yourself. Ferguson was killed in a brutal fashion by someone very strong. That someone is still at large. I'd rather not have him decide that you saw him and can identify him."

Grenville's exuberance dimmed. "Do you know, Lacey, when I found the man, I felt a very sharp pain in my chest—exactly where that knife went into me. I thought, for a split second, that the killer was there and had stabbed me to keep me silent. I swore I felt myself falling to the ground. But no, Matthias was next to me, holding me up, taking me outside. When I looked down, there was no knife in me, no blood. I even opened my waistcoat and stuck my hand inside my shirt to make sure I was whole. Is that not odd?"

Not at all. I woke in the night sometimes, thinking I hung upside down from a tree, my left leg a torn and shattered mess, while French soldiers laughed up at me. They'd enjoyed themselves swinging me like a pendulum.

"It is to be expected," I said.

"I make too much of it," Grenville said. He drew out his handkerchief and dabbed his face. "I've styled myself as a man not afraid to face danger, but I realize that before someone stabbed me in the dark, I'd never truly faced it. Stepping into that place last night, finding Ferguson there . . . Please tell no one how suddenly terrified I was."

Donata touched his arm. "You are among friends."

I said, "I am not astonished at your fear. What astonishes me is that you went into the place at all."

"Curiosity and arrogance. I had stout Matthias with me and no idea that violence lurked in the corner. I will take more care at the priory."

"Please do." I said. I kissed Donata's smooth cheek and left to make my excuses to Lady Southwick.

*** *** ***

When I reached the stables, I discovered that the horse Buckley in Parson's Point had lent me had been returned to him by one of the under grooms. The head groom told me this, and also told me, looking very put out, that the horse I'd borrowed from Lady Southwick yesterday had not turned up.

I told the man I'd hunt for the horse and asked if anyone nearby would allow me to hire a horse for the day. Before he could answer, Grenville's coachman, Jackson, stepped up and said that Grenville had told him to keep the carriage ready for my use whenever I wanted it.

Because I did not much want to drag myself to the next village to try to find a horse for hire, I took up Jackson on the offer. Grenville had brought his landau, open for the warm weather, and I rolled off in this luxury.

I was anxious to reach my own home, but I was equally anxious to talk to Bartholomew, who'd gone to search the windmill. I directed Jackson to Easton's house, and we reached it in a short while.

Easton's household had definitely gone. One of Denis's pugilists came out of the house to open the carriage door for me. This particular man had helped me search for missing girls from Covent Garden earlier this year, and knew Jackson, who'd also helped with the search. He gave me a salute and stayed behind to speak to Jackson while I started to walk down the footpath toward the windmill.

Another man came out of the house before I could get far and told me Denis wished to speak to me. I did not want to see Denis; I'd come to the house to look at the windmill and to inquire whether Cooper had returned.

The man stood solidly in front of me, however, until I agreed to follow him back to the house and inside. He led me upstairs and ushered me into Brigadier Easton's study.

Denis had commandeered the desk. Easton's personal papers and trinkets had gone, replaced by Denis's usual thin stack of paper, one inkwell, and a pen tray. Denis had been writing but when I entered, he laid the pen in the pen tray and moved the paper aside.

"Captain," he greeted me. "What have you discovered?"

"Nothing," I said with some impatience. "I came to find out whether Cooper has returned."

"No." The word was succinct but conveyed Denis's unhappiness. "And I want you to make every effort you can to find him."

"I thought you wanted me to discover who killed Ferguson," I said. "Or do you think the tasks are one and the same?"

"No." Again the short sound, charged with meaning. "I have sent Ferguson's body back to his family. I did not like that I had to send him home dead. The surgeon I employ confirmed what I told you a coroner would, that Ferguson had been beaten, and that one of the blows certainly killed him." Denis twined his long fingers together. "My fear, Lacey, is that Cooper has been murdered as well. And I do not like to contemplate this idea."

"You are well and truly worried about him."

A long pause followed. Denis looked at me, but not at me, then he turned to the man who stood guard inside the room. "Leave us," he said.

I stilled, surprised. James Denis never let himself be alone in a room with anyone, especially not with me. The pugilist looked surprised as well, but he stifled any question and left the room without a word.

Denis stood up. He walked to the window, his back to me, and looked out to the sunny day. The tall windmill stood silently, arms still.

"I *am* worried," Denis said, his back still to me. "You need to find him, Lacey. If something happened to Cooper, I am not certain I could bear it."

Chapter Eight

I had never in the year or so I'd known James Denis heard him speak with concern about another human being. He did not, even now — his voice held the stiffness of a man confessing something he did not want to, nor thought he'd ever have to, confess.

I did not reply. If Denis wished to tell me more, he would. If he did not, he would not, even under torture.

After another silent moment, Denis turned around, his face as impassive as ever. "I had an unusual childhood, Captain. I will not give you the details, but suffice it to say, urchins who pick pockets on the streets have more usual childhoods than I. I met Cooper when I was ten years old. He had just retired from exhibition fighting — not of his own will. The man who'd trained and kept him commanded him to lose a fight to a younger man the trainer was trying to bring out as his next sensation. Cooper refused, and so he was turned out without a shilling.

"I tried to rob Cooper on the street. When picking his pocket did not work, I pulled out my knife and tried to fight him." He shook his head. "Me, a stripling of ten, and Cooper as large and tough as he is now, but twenty years younger. He bested me easily, but instead of turning me over to the Watch, he took me home. He told me that he'd teach me to fight if I stole for him so we could eat. I tried to tell him to go to the devil, but he landed me on the floor and left me there to think about it.

"I did think about it, long and hard, and decided his scheme might be a good one. If this man taught me to fight, I reasoned, in time, I'd be able to fight him, and get free of him. Meanwhile, if he protected me and kept me away from the magistrates, we might be able to make a good living together. I called to him and told him I agreed, but that I would choose the targets and do nothing I thought too dangerous for me. The only way this would work, I said, was if neither of us got caught. We made a pact then and there, a contract, if you will, about what I would do and what he would do, and that we would protect each other."

Denis let out a breath. "So it began. Cooper taught me how to fight—with fists, with knives, with pistols. He taught me how to take down a larger opponent with a minimum of moves, and how to render them unconscious before they realized what was happening.

"I scoured the city looking for targets, reported to Cooper, and planned our moves. Simple robberies at first, of things that were easy to take and easy to sell.

We made a good team, me slipping in while Cooper provided a distraction, Cooper getting in the way of any who might have caught me. But as I grew, so did my ambition. Our targets became more complicated, more lucrative, and I started to hire more men to help us. Cooper remained in thick with the world of pugilists, and he knew who could be trusted, who would be loyal, and who would welcome employment."

He opened his hands. "So you see, Captain, Cooper has been with me every step of the way. He protected me, fought for me, taught me how to fight for myself when no help was coming. It did not take long before I abandoned the idea of besting and killing him and so ending the association. We got on, and nothing could stop us. And now, he is missing, and one of the men he handpicked is dead."

Cooper had always been deferential to Denis, calling him "sir" and doing his slightest bidding. I imagined that Cooper had recognized, even in the ten-year-old Denis, a being of intelligence and great ambition. Cooper must have realized that his impulse to use the little boy had been a stroke of luck so pure he could bathe in it.

Relationships were never simple, I well knew. What was between Denis and Cooper, changing and developing as the two men grew older, would be enmeshed and complex.

"Cooper would never have killed Ferguson without telling me or explaining why," Denis said. "I know this."

I understood what he feared. The killer could have struck Ferguson and then gone after Cooper. Or the other way around. Perhaps we simply hadn't found Cooper's body.

"I will look as thoroughly as I can," I said.

Denis looked straight at me again, as cold and hard as ever. "See that you do. Report to me or send messages through your lackey."

I did not bother arguing that I did not work for him. "If a fine-blooded horse wanders into the stable yard, please tether it for me. I mislaid it, and it belongs to Lady Southwick."

"I will have my men keep an eye out. I will also send my regrets to Lady Southwick that you will not be attend her outing to Binham Priory. I prefer that you keep searching for Cooper."

How the devil he knew about the Binham ramble I did not know, but I had learned long ago not to be surprised at the information Denis had at his fingertips.

"I confess that riding about the heath and marshes will be preferabie to another game of bloody croquet," I said.

"Have a care, Captain. I am certain that wedded bliss with the upper classes will land you in many more games of bloody croquet."

I turned back. "Is that why you've never married? An objection to croquet?"

Denis gave me the barest hint of a smile. "You will get no more stories out of me today, Captain. Good afternoon."

He sat down at the desk, pulled the half-finished letter back to the center of the desktop, and lifted his pen. I'd been dismissed.

*** *** ***

I went downstairs and told the man talking to Jackson to fetch me a horse. I'd search much better on horseback through back country than from the landau on the roads. If Denis expected me to scour the land, he could provide the means.

I traversed the footpath to the windmill, but Bartholomew was not there. I found nothing more than I had the night before—blood I'd not been able to soak up with the dirt was now dried on floor and walls. Someone from Denis's household had brought at ladder reach the upper floors. I climbed this to a much cleaner room above, wide windows on two sides letting in daylight.

This floor had been part of the keeper's rooms, but every stick of furniture had been removed. A thick layer of dust coated the floor, undisturbed. No one had been up here, including Bartholomew or Denis's men. They must have looked at the dusty floor, and concluded, as I did, that no one had been there and it was not worth the bother to ascend.

I left the windmill, took the horse led out for me, and rode north and west toward Blakeney, crossing a river and cutting over fields.

Farmland rippled around me, the centuries-old practice of draining the marshes rendering the land dry and fertile. Late crops were still growing, this year a little thicker than had been in the past few years, when a cold summer had meant small yield. I saw the blight the bad years had left—farms abandoned, cottages standing empty. Farmers and farm laborers had gone to the cities to find work, to be buried in the dirt and smoke of the factories.

As I rode, I saw farmers bending to labors, and as I neared the sea, fishermen walking back to the villages from their day out, nets over their shoulders, ready for mending. Nowhere did I see the large form of Cooper, nor did I see Lady Southwick's blasted horse.

As I rode into Blakeney, I took a chance, dismounted in front of the public house, and asked inside where I could find Mrs. Quinn, widow of the Parson's Point vicar. I knew fewer men in this taproom than I had in the Parson's Point pub, but still a good many greeted me with quiet acknowledgment.

The publican told me that Mrs. Quinn lived in the high street near the pump, next door to him, in fact. He pointed the way, I thanked him, left the horse with the hostler, and walked to the house.

The cottages in Blakeney, as they were in Parson's Point, were made of, or partly of, flint, which was found in abundance in this part of the country. The walls of the Blakeney cottages were pebbled with the gray stone.

I knocked on the green-painted door of the house, to have the door wrenched open from within by Terrance Quinn.

"What do you want, Lacey?" was his greeting.

I removed my hat and bowed. "I came to pay my respects to your aunt and mother."

"Did you?" Terrance filled the doorframe, preventing me from looking past him. "I do not see you hobbling around to pay your respects to other men's mothers."

"I was fond of your uncle. I heard about his demise and wanted to give my best to his family."

Terrance scowled. "You're a lying bastard, Lacey. You came to pry. Do you think we don't know what you've been getting up to in London since you came back from the war? In thick with magistrates and the Runners. Chasing murderers. You've turned thief taker."

"Not quite."

"I think *quite* describes it. You scent a whiff of scandal about my family, and here you come to pay your 'respects.'"

I could not say he was wrong. The dress I'd found had intrigued and worried me, and yes, learning of Helena's flight had made me uneasy.

"Perhaps we should not argue about it on the high street," I said.

"Why not? Our neighbors know all our business. Ask them."

Terrance started to close the door. I put my shoulder against it. "Listen to me," I said, my voice low. "Your cousin was my friend, and at one time, you were too. I want to help you find her."

Terrance opened the door, grabbed me, and hauled me inside, his one-handed grip amazingly strong. He slammed the door, and I righted myself before I could unbalance on my bad leg. We made a sorry pair.

"My mother and aunt have gone to Norwich," Terrance said. "The cook and maid are taking their day out, so no one is here to stop me beating the devil out of you."

"You'd find it a tough fight," I said. "I am not as feeble as I appear."

"Neither am I." Terrance's face was red.

I gestured with my walking stick to his empty right sleeve. "How did that happen?"

"How do you think? Fighting the Frenchies at Waterloo. A ball went right through it. The surgeon said I'd have to lose it or die of gangrene, so I let him take it. I should have told him to shoot me in the head."

I tapped my bad knee with the stick. "This was French deserters amusing themselves with a lone prisoner. The only reason I lived was because of the kindness of a Spanish woman and her small children. I, the brave soldier, was reduced to begging for water from a six-year-old boy."

Terrance looked at my injured leg with a little less belligerence. "I suppose we both have harrowing tales. I thought my family would welcome me back with joy, but they've let it be known that I would have brought them more honor if I'd stayed and died. What good is half a man to a poor family?"

"Which is why I make myself useful by prying into other people's affairs."

"And now you've come to pry into ours. To hell with this, Lacey. Helena ran off with a man. She went to Cambridge. That is all."

I debated whether to tell him about the gown, but I decided not to. Terrance was unhappy and volatile, and I was by no means certain the gown had been Helena's.

"Arguing is thirsty work," I said. "Step with me to the pub, and I'll stand you a tankard."

I thought for a moment he might accept, for old time's sake, but Terrance shook his head. "I have things to do before my aunt and mother return. I'll tell them you called."

"Fair enough." I made for the door. "Send for me anytime you wish to jaw, or drink, or argue. A message to the old Lacey house will reach me."

"Do not wait for it," Terrance said.

I gave him another half bow and stepped out of the house. He slammed the door before I could turn and walk away.

*** *** ***

I made my way down the southwestern road to the Lacey house. When I reached it, I found that Denis's two men had returned to continue the search for the stolen artwork, but no Cooper.

Bartholomew was there, as well as Matthias, the two brothers helping one of the men break up the debris from the bonfire. Bartholomew had found nothing in the windmill, he said, as I stopped to speak to them.

A sudden shouting from the house startled us all. It was Denis's man, who had gone below stairs to continue demolishing the servants' passages and the kitchen.

Matthias and Bartholomew raced to the house, and I followed as quickly as I could. We found the second man in the kitchen, he having torn half the mantelpiece from the fireplace. I do not now what I expected him to show us—the skeletal remains of Miss Quinn?—but I was fully prepared for horror.

What he held, pulled from the fireplace, was a piece of canvas folded around things that clanked.

As we all hurried in, he spread the canvas open across the massive kitchen worktable, the one piece of furniture still whole.

"There, guv," he said. "What do you think of that?"

I stared down at four silver candlesticks, a wide and deep silver chalice, and a small silver plate, tarnished now, but the metal shimmered here and there in the sunlight from the high windows.

These dishes had never graced the Lacey household. The plate and chalice had been made to hold a host and wine, and I'd stared at the silver candlesticks on the altar of the chapel at Parson's Point all my young life.

Someone had robbed the Parson's Point church and stuffed the booty up the chimney of the Lacey kitchen.

Chapter Nine

The man who'd found the stash hefted one of the candlesticks. "Nice silver there. Fetch a good price."

"Put it down," I said. "I know where these things belong, and I will return them."

The man looked astonished but stood the candlestick upright on the table. "Why, guv? We know they're nicked, but none but us know they're here, eh? I have just the chap to sell them to, and we split the take. Stands to reason. I found them, but it's your house."

A fair-minded thief. "They came from a parish church that is by no means well off," I said. "I am taking them back."

The man still had his hand on the candlestick. He eyed me in confusion then sighed and stepped away. Denis must have ordered him to obey me no matter how daft my commands.

Bartholomew stared at the silver. "But what is all that doing *here*?"

A very good question. I laid the candlesticks and communion dishes in the middle of the canvas and folded the cloth over them again. "Someone robbed the chapel, stashed the things in an empty house, and did not have a chance to return for them."

I could see that Denis's lackeys thought I'd lost my mind. Perfectly good nick, me with no money, and I wanted to return it?

"I'll ride up to the village now," I said. "But I agree about keeping it quiet."

I picked up the clanking bundle, balanced it over my shoulder, and leveraged myself up the stairs with my walking stick. Bartholomew came out with me and brought my horse to me.

"Keep an eye out," I said as he helped me into the saddle then handed up the bundle. "I'll return directly."

"Aye, sir," Bartholomew said, and I rode away.

I clattered into Parson's Point not long later, which had filled with cooking smells for evening meals. I went through the village, past the flint houses that looked very much like those in Blakeney, and out the other side of the village to the church, half a mile beyond.

The Parson's Point church had been built at least seven centuries ago, and repaired yearly by its congregation ever since. It had very little in the way of ornamentation, having been constructed before the wild gothic fantasies of pointed arches, flying buttresses, and gargoyles.

The church's only decoration was frescoes painted high on the walls above the altar. They were pretty pictures, faded with time, depicting the holy family on their flight to Egypt and the young Jesus teaching in the temple. I'd always envied the boy Jesus as I'd studied the paintings during the learned but dull sermons of Dr. Quinn. He'd done what he pleased while his parents looked on in astonishment. Christ's story might have ended differently had Joseph been anything like my father.

The rest of the church was whitewashed, and the rows of polished pews for the masses were a fairly recent addition. Until twenty-five years ago, the villagers had stood for their worship. My family and other prominent members of the community had always had enclosed pews in the front.

Preston Reaves was not at the vicarage. Of course not—he was picnicking with Lady Southwick and her guests at Binham Priory. Likely he was looking at the ruined splendor of the priory and regretting he hadn't been born before the advent of Protestant frugality.

The vicarage housekeeper, Mrs. Landon, a bit more faded than I remembered her, answered the door and peered up at me without surprise.

"I heard you'd returned, young master Lacey. And about time too. Come in and shut the door. Mr. Reaves is not here, if that's who you've come to see. He isn't much for tending his flock, is Mr. Reaves. Not like dear Dr. Quinn. But come to the kitchen, and I'll fix you a bite."

Mrs. Landon's son, still working here too, took my horse away to the tiny stable behind the house. I hefted the bundle of silver and followed Mrs. Landon down the hall to the large kitchen.

She fetched a cup from the kitchen dresser and poured steaming coffee into it. "They say you're opening the house again," she said. "And getting married. Happy times, happy times. Now, what are you carrying there all secretive?"

I cleared a space on her kitchen table, extracted the items one by one, and set them on the table. Mrs. Landon's eyes widened, and she sat down hard on a kitchen chair.

"Good Lord." She stared at each piece in turn. "I never thought to see these again."

"Then I am correct that they're from the chapel?"

"That you are. Wherever did you find them? At a pawnbroker's somewhere? Is that why you came back to Norfolk, to return them?"

I touched a candlestick. "I found them stuffed up the kitchen chimney in my house a mile away. I imagine the thief thought an empty house a good hiding place."

Mrs. Landon gave me an odd look. "But the house wasn't empty when these went missing."

My brows rose. "No?"

"No, indeed, dear. They went missing about the same time Miss Quinn ran off. Everyone was convinced that Miss Quinn and her young man took them away with them."

I sat down at the table, my hand tight around my coffee cup. Helena Quinn had run away nine or ten years ago. What might or might not be her gown had been left in my mother's sitting room. At the same time, someone had robbed the chapel and hidden the stash up the chimney. My father had been still living in the house, growing poorer, sicker, and more alone as the years went by.

"They could not have been put in the kitchen chimney then," I said. "It would still have been in use. Someone would have found it."

Mrs. Landon gave me a pitying look. "You weren't here for your father's last years. Not your fault—you were off with the fighting. My nephew was there, you know, in the war, and we didn't hear from him for years and years. He came back right as rain, cheerful as ever, but a bit deaf from all the canons. Not like young Mr. Quinn, poor soul. And for Mr. Quinn to find his cousin had eloped out from under his nose. They were to have been a match, you know." Mrs. Landon paused to pour out more coffee. "Mr. Quinn thought Miss Helena would wait for him. They grew up so close, and everyone thought they'd marry and settle down right here."

"My father," I prompted when she stopped to drink.

"Oh, yes, I was telling you about him. Old Mr. Lacey, he started letting the staff go a few years before he died. He knew he was ill, poor lamb, and understood he wasn't long for the world. Not much money left, either. When I was a girl, the Lacey estate was a big, fine house with a big, fine farm. All gone now. The world changes. Anyway, he let go the cook and took his meals at the public house. When he got weaker, he had a local lad come and do for him, bring him food and so forth. No hot meals anymore, though I sometimes went and brought him a bit of dinner. And he'd be so angry, not liking to take charity. A proud man, was your father. So you see, someone *could* have hidden the silver there with no one being the wiser."

"Who was the local lad that brought him the food? Perhaps he saw something."

"Robert Buckley, the publican's boy. Robert's grown up now, got a farm of his own down by Letheringsett. He didn't much like your father, but he'd deliver the food, make sure Mr. Lacey wasn't too ill or hurt, and leg it again. He wouldn't have nicked the silver, though. He's a good lad."

I believed that Robert probably hadn't stolen it. If he had, he'd have had plenty of opportunity to go back and fetch it from the kitchen chimney. "How does young Mr. Buckley have his own farm? Did he inherit it? Come into some money?" I did not think the business at the public house ran to buying land.

Mrs. Landon chuckled, her faded blue eyes showing amusement. "He married it. She's the daughter of a farmer who didn't have a son to leave anything to. Farmer fixed it up so his daughter and her husband could get the lot. Robert was lucky. The wife is a sweet thing too, and now they have a little boy of their own. I always say that marrying money is much easier than grubbing for it yourself. But you know that. I hear your lady is quite plump in the pocket."

I took another sip of the good coffee. I should be offended, but I'd always liked Mrs. Landon. She spoke her mind but had no resentment in her.

"Does everyone in Parson's Point suppose I'm marrying for money?"

"Of course, dear. Your father left you nothing, and your lady has plenty to go around. One of the aristocracy too. You played your cards well."

I gave her a severe look. "Please put it about that I am very fond of Lady Breckenridge."

"Fondness never hurts. Mr. Landon and I were very fond of one another, rest his soul. I'm sure you and your lady will get on well. Not like that frivolous chit who was your first wife. I'm sorry she passed on, of course, but it was not a good choice. You were only a lad yourself at the time. You weren't to know."

My first wife, Carlotta, was not, in fact, deceased, but living in France with the French lover for whom she'd deserted me. My marriage to her had been legally ended, thanks to James Denis, but to save reputations all around, we'd agreed that Carlotta Lacey would be deceased, and Madame Colette Auberge would return to France with her husband.

"The follies of youth," I said. "Miss Helena made a bad choice too, do you think?"

Mrs. Landon gave me a dark look, then she rose and moved about the kitchen, bringing out a loaf of bread, slicing it, and putting pieces on a toasting fork. "Miss Helena Quinn needed a swat on her behind, in my opinion. Twenty-two she was, old enough to know better." Mrs. Landon showed her disapprobation by thrusting the toasting fork hard into the fire. "Young Mr. Quinn was off to war, and she was acting virtuous about waiting for him. Then in comes a bloke from Cambridge. Well dressed, swanning about, turning Miss Quinn's head. After that, Terrance Quinn was as nothing to her."

When the bread had toasted to her satisfaction, she plopped the pieces onto a plate and scooped a hunk of creamy yellow butter onto the toast. The hot bread melted it, spreading rivulets of yellow across the blackened surfaces. Mrs. Landon shoved the pile at me and sat down again.

"Who was he?" I asked. I wiped my hands on my handkerchief and dug into the buttered toast, feeling ten years old again. The bread was chewy and nutty, the butter creamy light.

"A man called Braxton. Let me see. His Christian name is Edward, I think. That was it. Edward Braxton. A solicitor by trade. He'd come to settle the estate of a Cambridge gent who owned a farm near Binham Priory. Braxton adored the sea, and he liked to come up and walk along it when business didn't press him. He met Helena on one of these walks. We knew nothing about it, or about him, until someone saw her with him. And they weren't simply walking, if you take my meaning. Well, her father was a bit put out, as you can imagine. Scolded her something horrible. Next thing you know, Mr. Braxton has returned to Cambridge, and Miss Helena has disappeared. Up and gone with him."

"You are certain of that? Did she leave a note, tell anyone?"

Mrs. Landon shrugged. "Not that I hear. But she was gone, with a change of clothing, and Mr. Braxton was gone too. And we all suspected she'd crept into the church and stolen the plate—to set herself up in housekeeping maybe. But now you say it was in the chimney at your house all this time? Why would she have put it there?"

"Miss Quinn might not have stolen the plate at all," I said.

"Well, that's true, dear. You finding this lot puts a different view on it. Mr. Reaves will be happy to see it again. Though the villagers never liked the fancy chalice and platen. Communion is not something we have truck with here. Mr. Reaves needs to remember that."

Parson's Point had always been very low church, I remembered. The chalice had been locked away — lovely to look at but rarely used.

"Did no one go to Cambridge to find Helena?" I took another bite of the heavenly toast while Mrs. Landon refilled my cup.

"To be sure. Mrs. Quinn and her sister-in-law had word of Helena — I am not certain from where — but they learned she was right as rain, but not exactly where she was. Mrs. Quinn was content to let the matter go. She was ashamed of her own daughter, never wanted to speak of her. Young Mr. Terrance went out to Cambridge when he came back, but too much time had passed. Mr. Braxton was no longer at the house Terrance found. Neighbors said he'd gone north somewhere, with his lady wife. And that was that."

"If everyone here thought Helena or Mr. Braxton had stolen the silver, why did the magistrates not try to find her?"

"We kept it quiet. The Quinns were so heartbroken. They didn't want anyone chasing after Miss Helena and silver plate no one wanted. They begged us all to keep it quiet. Oh, everyone *knew* what happened, but we pretended not to, do you see?"

I did see. The plate belonged to the church, not the Quinns, and if Helena had been arrested for stealing it, she would have been tried and possibly hanged or transported, and her solicitor husband along with her. Better to be silent about a chalice and candlesticks no one used than watch a beloved daughter be carted to Newgate. My discovery showed she hadn't taken the things away with her, in any case.

"No one has tried to find her since?" I asked.

Mrs. Landon shrugged. "Let bygones be bygones. Miss Helena broke her parents' heart, and Mr. Terrance's. Best not to bring it up." Mrs. Landon creaked to her feet. "I'll put this lot in Mr. Reaves's study. He'll be surprised to see it, that is if he ever comes back from wooing the gentry."

I rose, realizing my visit was over. "Does he woo the gentry much of the time?"

"To be sure. He's not at all right for a country parish, though he tries his best on Sundays. You'll be there Sunday morning, will you? Sitting in the Lacey pew. It's been empty too long."

I knew a command when I heard one. "Certainly, Mrs. Landon. And thank you for the repast. It was excellent."

"You were always were too thin, young master Lacey. I hope that lady you marry has a fine cook who will fatten you up."

Lady Breckenridge's town chef enjoyed experimenting with odd Continental cuisine, so I wasn't certain about that. The man would never serve something as wholesomely good as toasted bread with butter.

I departed the vicarage, knowing that the silver plate would be as safe with Mrs. Landon as in the Bank of England, and resumed my search for Cooper.

*** *** ***

Cooper had disappeared from my house yesterday afternoon about the time Grenville had arrived. I went back to the Lacey house and hunted in a pattern that began there and radiated in an ever-expanding circle.

I found no sign of him anywhere—not stuck in a marsh, buried in a dune, hiding in an outbuilding at a farm, nothing. I began to be annoyed with the man. No farmer had taken a man fitting his description anywhere in a cart, though they were happy to tell me about Brigadier Easton hightailing it to Amsterdam in a fishing boat.

I hoped Easton had landed safely. I'd told him to write to Grenville, so I'd have to wait until a letter arrived at Grenville's London house to be certain he was all right.

In spite of the closeness that Denis claimed with Cooper, I wondered if Cooper hadn't simply returned to London or found something new to do. Perhaps Ferguson had found the artwork in the windmill, and Cooper had knocked him on the head and absconded with it. On the other hand, if Cooper and Denis had such a bond, I could not see the man walking away without word. *Something* had happened to him, and I hoped it was not something sinister.

I saw no sign of Lady Southwick's horse either. I started assuming both disappearances were not coincidental.

I returned to my house again to find that Buckley had indeed put out the word that I wanted help with the repairs. Several village men had come. It was too late for them to start today, but I told them I would be working on the walls and roof very soon. I sent them and Denis's men away for the night, and

Bartholomew and I closed up the place as best we could.

I told Bartholomew to make his way back to Lady Southwick's. The evening was still light and warm, so I turned my horse down the road to Binham.

My route took me past a flint quarry and ruins from Roman times as well as several modern windmills, all pumping, pumping, pumping to drain the perpetually wet land. Some of the windmills were a hundred years old, others built within the last twenty years.

Binham Priory, once the home of Benedictine monks, was now picturesque ruins. Indeed, when I arrived, it was to see that several of the ladies had sketch pads on their laps, drawing the empty stone arches.

I left the horse with one of the Southwick servants and made my way to the waiting group. Before I could reach them, Rafe Godwin stepped in front of me.

"You've been damned insulting, Lacey," he said. "I have half a mind to call you out."

Chapter Ten

I was tired, unhappy with my progress, and at the end of my patience. "Done. I will meet you in the morning."

Rafe took a step back, face going white. "I do not *truly* mean we need to draw pistols. But I take umbrage at your behavior. You've slighted our hostess—coming and going as you please, sending messages that you refuse to grace us with your presence. Lady Southwick has shown you the kindest condescension allowing you to stay in her house, and you have taken the worst advantage of her."

I continued walking, planting my stick firmly. "I spoke to Lady Southwick about my wanderings, and she knows that much business keeps me from entertainment."

"It is insulting to Lady Breckenridge as well," Godwin went on. "She should toss you out and have done with you."

"I rather believe that is her choice, Godwin."

Godwin gave me a look of intense dislike. He was a London dandy who'd attained dandyhood alongside the great George Brummell. Brummell, unhappily, had fled to France, ruined by debt, and Godwin had decided he was Brummell's heir. The rest of the world, unfortunately for Godwin, considered Grenville to be Brummell's natural successor.

Godwin, however, did not adhere to Brummell's Spartan dress sense, as Grenville did. Godwin liked bright colors and strange trends in fashion, such as puffed pantaloons and brightly striped waistcoats. Today he wore a waistcoat of loud pink and green and had so many things dangling from his watch fob that he rattled.

"If you find me insulting, then choose your seconds and have them call on mine," I said. "But tomorrow. This evening, I have pressing business."

I knew that Rafe Godwin was, at heart, bone lazy. He often talked about meeting people at dawn or boxing them at Gentleman Jackson's, but in truth, he avoided any activity that made him so much as perspire.

Godwin scowled. "See that it doesn't come to that."

Lady Southwick, coming toward me, heard our last exchange. "I have a better idea, one far less violent," she said. "A shooting match. In the garden, tomorrow morning. I will have my majordomo set it up. You will shoot, won't you, Captain? I hear that you are a crack shot."

I was not certain where she'd heard that. She seized me by the arm and dragged me to where Grenville politely held a pencil box for one of the sketching ladies. Lady Breckenridge was deep in conversation with Reaves and another of the gentlemen a little way away.

"Captain Lacey is going to show us how well he shoots," Lady Southwick announced to the company, then she drifted determinedly toward Reaves to take him from Lady Breckenridge.

"Ah, Lacey, there you are," Grenville said in his ennui-filled dandy's voice. "I'm afraid you've missed the repast, old son. We made short work of it."

"I found sustenance," I said. "Toasted bread and butter."

"Toasted bread and butter," Grenville said, with a half-wistful look. "Takes one back to nursery days."

"I was visiting the housekeeper at the vicarage," I said. "She used to give me bread and butter when I was a lad. Perhaps she hadn't noticed I'd grown."

"Shortsighted, is she? Well, so good that you could come. Have a look at the ruins. So frightfully medieval." Grenville nodded at the priory then directed his gaze at the lady's sketch as though it absorbed his entire attention. The lady, the wife of a minor aristocrat, ignored me completely.

I walked to the ruins as Grenville had directed me. I'd found them a wonderful playground as a boy—the soaring pointed arches, especially in moonlight, had fulfilled the chilling fantasies of a nine-year-old lad.

Lady Breckenridge deserted her admirers to meet me for a stroll around the tallest of the standing walls. "This is too ghastly, Gabriel," she said, rubbing my arm as though she thought me cold.

"Picturesque, the guidebooks say."

"I am hardly in the mood for flippancy. I do not mean the ruins; I mean this house party. Poor Grenville is put out at you, and Lady Southwick is full of innuendo. I will endure one more day, and then I am returning to Oxfordshire. Yes, I do know that staying with Lady Southwick was my idea. Do not cast it up to me."

"I said not a word."

"I will make a brief hiatus in London to speak to an architect about your house. Then I will be off to Oxfordshire. I miss my boy." I heard the sadness in her tone. She loved her son, though she rarely spoke of him. It was a private thing, I'd understood when I'd at last seen them together.

I laid my hand over hers. "Next summer, we three will come here together. My house might be livable by then."

"An excellent plan. Do you know, Gabriel, why I am annoyed with myself?"

I smiled down at her. "Because you wanted to observe how I would respond to Lady Southwick, who so blatantly makes herself available to any."

"So you guessed that. I profess to be ashamed."

"A natural worry, after what your husband put you through."

Her fingers closed more tightly on my arm. "He hurt me, Gabriel. I will admit that to you. And so I became a callous, rather reckless woman in response.

I pursued you with a ruthlessness that makes Lady Southwick tame in comparison."

"There is a difference," I said, stopping. "I never minded you pursuing me."

We stood for a quiet moment, while the peace of the ages flowed around us. It must have been a terrible day here, when King Henry's men came to tear down the walls.

Lady Breckenridge cleared her throat then went on in a brisk voice. "You flatter me, Gabriel. I found out about your Miss Quinn, by the bye. She eloped with a banker's clerk from Cambridge."

"I heard he was a solicitor."

She looked annoyed. "I do wish that if you meant to find out these things yourself, you wouldn't set me to ask questions of ladies I do not like."

"I found out by chance, and I think more than one version of a story is beneficial. Tell yours, please."

We'd walked far from the others and stood beneath the archways of the long-fallen priory. I wanted to know what Donata had discovered, but I was distracted momentarily by sunlight on her dark curls that flowed from under her tilt-brimmed hat. I wanted to lean down and take a curl in my mouth.

"It seems that Miss Quinn pretended to be devoted to her cousin," Donata said, "until he'd been gone to war for about five years. Then she must have realized that she'd be left on the shelf if her cousin did not return, and so she set her cap elsewhere. She had ambition, Lady Southwick said. Wanted to leave dreary village life and have a house of her own in a city. London for preference.

"Then came the banker's clerk. Handsome, citified, sophisticated. He began walking out with

Miss Quinn very quickly. However, the vicar, her father, put his foot down. Helena was to send this man away and wait for her cousin Terrance, like a good girl."

"Hmm," I said. "I can imagine how well that went over."

"Precisely. Next thing anyone knew, Miss Quinn was off and gone in the middle of the night with the banker's clerk and the silver candlesticks from the church. Never to be seen again. Her father wanted to declare her dead, but her mother cried and begged him not to take such a dreadful step. Her cousin Terrance returned, rushed to Cambridge, and could not find her. He gave up, came home, and is now sunk in melancholia. So ends the saga."

"Except for the candlesticks," I said. "I found them."

To her wide-eyed stare, I told her the story and about my visit to the vicarage.

"Good heavens," she said when I'd finished. "It seems you have had a much more interesting day than I've had. Why would they leave the goods behind? I assume they wanted to use them to fund their elopement to Gretna Green. Come to think of it, why would this banker's clerk or solicitor or whatever he was, need to rob the church, if he were so prosperous? Presumably he had the money to take Helena away, hence the reason she wanted to go with him at all."

"The theft of the silver might have nothing to do with Helena and her Cambridge gentleman."

"Humph. The vicar's daughter and the church silver going missing on the same night is too much of a coincidence. And there is the fact of the gown lying in your mother's chamber. What of that? The two maids I asked about it did not recognize it. Rather useless of them."

"I'd like to show the gown to Mrs. Landon," I said. "She would know if the dress had belonged to Helena, since Mrs. Landon has lived at the vicarage as long as I can remember. I would have thought of asking her immediately, but I had no idea she was still there."

"Take them to her tomorrow—after this bizarre shooting match Lady Southwick has decided to hold. I will be going then anyway."

I stopped. The late summer air wafted around us, cool with the hint of fall.

"I'll not be able to leave with you," I said. "Too many things to do here."

Her blue eyes were calm. "I know."

"I am growing used to not sleeping alone," I said. "I find I rather like it." After years of bitter loneliness, having the scent and warmth of a woman next to me all night had grown intoxicating.

"I rather like it myself." Lady Breckenridge touched the lapel of my coat. "No matter. You finish here and come to Oxfordshire. I will instruct our housekeeper to once again put our bedchambers side by side."

I lifted her hand to mine and kissed it. "I believe I would like that," I said.

*** *** ***

Because of the picnic, there was no formal supper at Lady Southwick's that night, for which I was grateful. Bartholomew coaxed a bit of cold meat for me from the kitchens, and I ate it with pleasure. I had no complaints about Lady Southwick's chef.

The only benefit of Lady Breckenridge departing tomorrow afternoon would be that I could leave Lady Southwick's as well and take a room above a pub, which I'd wanted to do in the first place. The other bachelors could stay at Southwick Hall as they liked, but I would show devotion to my lady by moving out.

Lady Breckenridge brought me the white gown, which she'd rewrapped in paper, much later that night. I was already asleep, and the crackling of the paper when she laid it down woke me.

I did not leave the bed, and a few moments later, her sweet-smelling warmth was beside me. "I've come to say good-bye," she whispered, and kissed me.

*** *** ***

Bartholomew woke me the next morning by throwing open the drapes surrounding my bed. He'd already pulled back the heavy curtains over the window, and sunshine poured in on me. Donata had gone in the night, and I was alone in the bed.

"Mr. Denis sent word," Bartholomew said as he turned away to prepare my razor and shaving water. "He would like a moment of your time."

I propped open my tired eyes. "Does he wish it on the moment?"

"Afraid so, sir."

I grunted. "Tell him Lady Southwick has engaged me to shoot at things. I will speak to him this afternoon."

Bartholomew did not look up. "His carriage is downstairs, sir, with two of his lackeys. They are waiting for you."

Nothing for it. I threw back the covers and heaved myself out of bed. Bartholomew, like a good servant, turned away from my nakedness as I pulled on my threadbare but comfortable dressing gown.

"It has come to this, Bartholomew," I said, collapsing into the chair next to the shaving bowl. "I am obeying a summons to James Denis to avoid the company of Lady Southwick and her guests. Denis has become the lesser of two evils."

"Yes, sir." Bartholomew said, concentrating on the razor.

"Pack my things while I'm gone. We will remove to the public house in Parson's Point this evening. I am afraid that your soft billet here is at an end."

"Suits me, sir. I've been bunking with three other lads, and they snore something dreadful. And the goings-on below stairs, you would not believe." Bartholomew shook his head. "Catch Mr. Grenville allowing his household to carry on like that."

I'd observed before that Bartholomew had become a snob. But I could not blame him. If below stairs was anything like above stairs, I fully understood.

Denis's lackey, who waited by the carriage, said nothing as I exited the house. As he assisted me into the conveyance, I remembered where I'd seen his scarred face before. I'd stared into his eyes one night on the Thames, when he and a colleague had beaten me senseless. To warn me, Denis had said, and to teach me obedience.

From the glint in his eyes, I knew the man remembered as well. He deftly helped me into the carriage, being careful of my bad leg, saying nothing at all.

I'd ridden in this carriage before, several times now. The polished marquetry was becoming familiar.

Not until the carriage pulled away from the house, me alone inside it, did I realize that it was only eight o'clock in the morning. While I'd always been an early riser, living alongside Lady Breckenridge was teaching me the comfort of sleeping as long as I pleased.

The carriage took me to Easton's, where Denis sat in the dining room. The room's paneling had been restored to its polished quietness, and a lackey was removing a plate with crumbs on it from the table. When I sat down, he busily filled another plate for me.

Denis looked exhausted. I'd never seen him anything but impeccably groomed, and he was clean this morning, his suit unwrinkled, but his eyes were red-rimmed in his pale face, and dark patches of fatigue stained his cheekbones.

I sat down at the place laid for me, to Denis's right. The footman set a steaming plate of eggs and sausage in front of me, and I tucked in, being hungry.

Denis watched me. He motioned with his fingers, and the lackeys departed, except for the man who'd helped me into the carriage.

"You've not slept," I said. The eggs and sausages were good, seasoned with herbs and fortified with butter.

Denis did not answer the observation, but when he spoke, his voice held a sharp edge. "I will come quickly to the point, Captain. When I tell you what you must do in order to work off a debt to me, I expect you to do it."

"If you mean Brigadier Easton, I delivered your message, which had the effect you desired. If you mean Cooper, I have been searching. Diligently."

He did not seem to hear me. "Instead of leaving no stone unturned, you supped at the vicarage and returned to your Lady Southwick's priory picnic. Though I had already sent your regrets."

I laid down my fork and wiped my mouth on a linen napkin. "I searched, I assure you." I explained how I'd hunted in a pattern of ever-widening circles from the place I'd last seen Cooper, describing the farms, villages, and marshes in which I'd looked for him. "He is nowhere in the area, I am certain of it. He must have returned to London or journeyed elsewhere."

"He is not in London," Denis said. "You may be sure that I have inquired. He would not journey anywhere without sending me word."

"I was not indulging myself picnicking or catching up with the vicar's housekeeper—I was pursuing another matter. I not only have searched for Cooper but have turned many possibilities over in my mind. If the death of Ferguson and the disappearance of Cooper are connected, then there are three possible solutions: Cooper was killed by the man who killed Ferguson, Cooper has gone after the killer, or Cooper killed Ferguson himself." I held up my hand as Denis started to speak. "I know you said Cooper would not have killed him. But perhaps he did it to protect you—heard Ferguson threaten you in some way. Perhaps Ferguson wanted the paintings for himself, and this made Cooper angry. Or perhaps the killing was accidental. The two men had a fight, which got away from them."

Denis broke in, voice crisp and cold. "What other matter?"

"Pardon?"

"Do not pretend to be ingenuous. What is this other matter that has taken your attention from what I told you to do?"

I did not want to tell him. Helena's elopement was a private problem of the Quinns—never mind that every inhabitant of every village in the area knew about it. I did not want Denis bothering them. Terrance would not be careful with Denis, not understanding his danger. Grenville had been correct to remind me what Denis was—*a thief, a smuggler, an extortionist, a sometime murderer, and deep in corruption of all sorts.*

Denis stared me down. His eyes this morning were hard and harsh, and I saw in them the youth who'd decided that throwing in his lot with a brutal pugilist would be better than going it alone.

I decided to skirt around the story. "A young woman disappeared about ten years ago. I have been looking into it."

"A young woman," Denis repeated. "Of course. I notice your interest is caught by anything involving a woman. After ten years, why is it important that you find her today?"

"There might be more to it than people guess." I told him briefly, naming no names, that I worried that no one had actually spoken to or heard from Helena. I also mentioned the strange return of the church silver, which Denis likely had already been informed about by the man who'd found it.

Denis watched me with a heavy stare. "A girl who eloped. The church silver. Yes, I can see where these things have commanded your attention."

"They might sound trivial to you—"

"Whereas one of my men being murdered and the other disappearing must be trivial to you," Denis said, words clipped. "You will drop this other matter. You will be given a room in this house, and you will stay here until we discover what has become of Cooper and what happened to Ferguson. You may bring your manservant if you like, as I know you use him to do things you can't. Your lady, however, will be barred the door. She distracts you."

My temper rose. "I have told you that I will help. But I will not stay here. I will take rooms in the village, which will put me near to the place Cooper was last seen."

"No." The word was loud in the quiet room, the closest I'd ever heard Denis come to shouting. "You will stay here, where I can know when you retire to bed and when you rise from it, where you go and with whom, and how long you stay there. You will remain here until we know what happened to both Cooper and Ferguson, for good or for ill."

"I am willing to help you, damn you, but I must do things in my own fashion. I am not one of the pugilists you employ."

"No, I do not employ you," Denis said, his voice returning to more even tones. "I *own* you. I know where your wife lives in France, and your daughter. I know where lives the mother of your manservant and his brother. I know where your landlady and her sister share a house in London. I know the comings and goings of your Colonel Brandon and his wife. I know everything about your viscountess and her son, all *their* comings and goings. Shall I continue?"

Chapter Eleven

I was out of my seat and lunging over the table at him before the hard hands of the lackey shoved me back down in the chair. I understood now why Denis had asked in particular for a man who'd once beaten me into unconsciousness to bring me in here today.

I held my walking stick in a hard grip. "If you touch any of them," I said. "I will kill you."

Denis sat back, hands flat on the table. "At last, I have raised a spark of interest in you. Have I your attention now, Captain?"

Sitting here, I realized my folly at softening toward Denis even a little. Grenville, usually more generous than me, had been right, and I had grown complacent.

Denis had helped me in a number of situations, it was true, but he'd done it for his own purposes. I'd known that, even as I'd accepted his assistance, but

I'd let myself imagine him interested in my problems. Pride can make a man an idiot. Meanwhile, I'd given him plenty of time to gather information about everyone I knew and cared about.

"I was right when I first met you," I said. "I called you filth."

"Because you believed me to be a procurer."

"Because you use others without regard. I decided you had no honor or decency. I was right."

The chill returned to Denis's demeanor. "Honor and decency are for the highborn. I do what I need to. As do you, so do not become highhanded. My demands have not changed. You will stay here and help me find Cooper, and your friends will be left in peace."

I still clutched my walking stick, but quelled the urge to bash him with it. "If I agree, I do so for *my* own reasons. Not because you threaten me."

"I do not give a damn why you decide what you decide. I simply want you to do it."

I sat in silence, trying to calm my anger. I did not want the anger to go away entirely, but I needed it to lessen so I could think clearly.

"You cannot stop me from searching for Cooper as I see fit," I said. "That means I speak to the local people and consult with Grenville. He is a clearheaded thinker. You chased him away from the scene of the murder, but I would like his opinion."

"Use Mr. Grenville by all means. And your manservant. But do not involve your magistrate friends; or Mr. Pomeroy, your favorite Bow Street Runner; or the local parish constables. I will not have them find Cooper only to arrest him for crimes he committed in the past."

"I agree that this would be unfortunate," I said.

Denis gave me a sharp look, but he let my remark pass. "If you are finished with your repast, I wish you to begin at once. I will make arrangements to have your things brought here."

I gave up. "Happily, my baggage is light."

I wiped my mouth again, pushed back my chair, and made my way from the room, my hand very tight on the walking stick. The lackey stood back and let me go.

*** *** ***

I was still angry when I rode away from Easton's. I knew that one day I'd make it across whatever barrier Denis put between myself and him and punch Denis in the face before anyone could stop me. I looked forward to that day.

A thorough search for Cooper would take more than one man, whatever Denis thought. I could not be his lone bloodhound. I rode to Blakeney and sought Terrance Quinn.

He was not happy to see me. Terrance scowled at me outside the blacksmith's forge where I ran him to ground. He'd come to have a kettle repaired for his mother's cook, and he was displeased that I'd caught him running such a menial errand.

I made certain we were out of earshot of the blacksmith and his apprentice and asked for his help.

"Who is it that's gone missing?" Terrance asked.

"He works for a friend, and my friend is worried that this man might have become lost or hurt."

Terrance's scowl deepened. "Cease lying to me, Lacey. Who is he?"

I conceded. "He works for James Denis—the man who took over Easton's house."

"I knew you had something to do with that."

"Very little, I assure you. Denis bought the house years ago, when I was still in Spain. I'll thank you not to blame me for everything that's gone wrong in Norfolk since we've been away."

"A funny way you have of asking for a chap's help."

"I beg your pardon. I am not in the best of moods. I need to find this man and find him quickly, for my sake as well as his. Will you help or not?"

Terrance gave me a grudging nod. "I'll help. If he's a city man, he could have gotten himself into any number of scrapes. Fools believe they can survive anywhere."

"Can you round up a few trustworthy men to help us? I do not want a hue and cry after him; we need him found, but quietly."

"I do understand, Lacey. I've asked about this Mr. Denis, and the little I could discover is that he is unsavory. He does not like magistrates and constables in his business."

"Exactly."

Terrance looked at me more in curiosity than anger. "Why don't you chuck him?"

"Reporting him to the magistrates would not help, because he has most of them in his pocket. Look what he did to Easton, who was magistrate for this parish."

"I mean, why don't you kill him?" Terrance ducked into the forge, retrieved the cooled pot the blacksmith gave him, and balanced against its weight by tilting his torso to his armless side. "If he's as bad as I think he is, put a gun to his head and pull the trigger."

"I have thought of it," I said. "But I refuse to hang for him."

Terrance gave me a sharp look. "You'd hang if you thought it necessary. I remember you well, Lacey, and I doubt you've changed."

I fell into step with him, but I did not bother offering to help him carry the pot. He'd grow enraged if I did. "You could be right about that," I said.

*** *** ***

Terrance could ride a horse if someone boosted him onto it. He'd learned how to loop the reins together and guide the horse one-handed, a modification of a technique I'd used when I'd had to ride and fight at the same time.

Terrance recruited the blacksmith's apprentice and Robert Buckley, son of the publican from Parson's Point, who'd married the woman with a farm. I'd borrowed a map of the area from Denis, and now I assigned portions for each man to search. We'd meet at the pub in Parson's Point every two hours and discuss what we'd found.

Clouds had blown in from over the North Sea, and they lowered and threatened rain. I pulled my coat closer and rode along the coast road, the blustery weather not assuaging my anger.

Donata and Grenville would be rising now and breakfasting, wondering between them where I'd got to this time. Matthias would tell them, Bartholomew having informed *him* when Denis's man came to fetch him.

Would my friends be angry at me for allowing Denis to ensnare me? Or somehow try to extricate me? I wanted Donata on the road to Oxfordshire, hang the weather. I knew that Denis could reach out for Lady Breckenridge any time he wanted to, but I'd feel better if she resided at her father's house and not here. Her father was a powerful man that even Denis might think twice about harassing.

I passed through Morston, Parson's Point, and Stifkey, and the ruins of a Roman camp. I'd played among the silent, grassy mounds as a boy, pretending I was a soldier fighting the barbaric might of Boadicea and her army. Glorious days, I'd thought. That was before I'd discovered that war was mostly blood, mud, and arguing against the stupid decisions of men who stayed warm and dry in their tents while sending me and my soldiers out to certain slaughter.

After the camp, I turned north to search the marshes.

The edge of the marshes marked where the sea could wash at the highest tides. It was low tide at the moment, and the sands stretched beyond the marshes far into the sea. The land wasn't completely dry — pools glimmered in the gray light, now spattered with rain.

Though my errand was dire, I let myself be entranced with the beauty of the place. I'd met plenty who thought Norfolk flat, wet, and dull, but that was because they didn't take time to have a proper look. The contrast of sea, sky, grasses, dunes, rivers, farmlands, and villages combined to create a pleasing splendor. It was no accident that artists liked to paint here.

I knew that beauty could hide darkness, however. Small farms were full of lonely people who fought amongst themselves and with their neighbors, bad weather meant famine, and the stream of soldiers returning from the war meant more mouths to feed. Many soldiers had nothing to return to, or had been badly injured. In a world where anything less than a whole man was regarded with suspicion, these soldiers, like Terrance, struggled to find their place again.

But out here, where wind and sky met marsh grasses and water, I could clear the cobwebs from my mind, and remember the joy of it. It was cold, and I'd grown to dislike cold, but here it seemed bearable, unlike in my cramped rooms in Grimpen Lane in London.

I crossed a sheep bridge in the middle of the marsh, and there found Lady Southwick's horse. The horse's halter rope looked as though it had been caught in mud and knotted grass, tethering the beast. Dark birds flapped around it, ready to wait for it to starve and die.

The horse jerked its head when it saw me approach, giving me a heartrending neigh. I did not want to dismount, because I always had a hell of a time getting back on a horse by myself, so I rode as close as I could and looked down at the rope.

The rope hadn't tangled. A few stout beams had been driven into the ground here, as though someone had started to build something then given up. The horse had been tied to a thick hook in one of the beams.

I leaned over and untied the rope at the halter, freeing the horse's head. The poor thing took a few running steps to the stream I'd just crossed, lowered its head, and began to drink.

I had rope in my pack, which I could use to lead away the horse without having to dismount. As I twisted around to drag it from the back of my saddle, I saw, on the other side of the beams, a nasty quantity of red.

Nothing for it. I swung my good leg over the horse and slid to the ground. I hobbled back to the posts.

More than the horse had caught the interest of the carrion birds. Blood coated the grasses, and a lone human hand lay upturned to the rain-soaked sky.

Chapter Twelve

The hand was attached to nothing.

In fascinated horror, I drove the birds away and bent to study it. Cooper's? I did not know the man well enough to tell.

I scoured the ground around it, but I did not see the rest of the body. Only the hand, left behind.

In my stints in India, the Netherlands, Portugal, and Spain, I'd seen my share of dismembered corpses. Men missing limbs but still alive had crawled to me for help, leaving bloody bits of themselves behind in the mud. Others had died, their bodies scattered across the hot grass under the Spanish sun.

A lost hand held nowhere near the gruesomeness of those days. And still, it made me shiver.

I did not fancy carrying that hand back and laying it before James Denis, but I supposed I'd better. He'd know whether it was Cooper's.

I hunted in my pack until I found a bit of canvas. Using the end of my walking stick, I tipped the hand onto the canvas and folded the cloth over it, then wiped my walking stick on clean grass. I put the package back into the pack. The horse, scenting blood and dead flesh, moved uneasily.

I searched the area around the bloody patch as far as I could. I found the leavings of a campfire not far away, the ashes still warm. Whether Cooper's killer had built it, or Cooper himself, or a shepherd, or someone passing through, I could not judge.

But I found no more blood, no footprints, or anything to tell me who'd tied up the horse and why. Sheep grazed not far away, uninterested in me. Their wandering likely had trampled whatever evidence might have been left behind.

I returned to my horse and knew I'd never climb onto him out here in the flat. I untied the rope from the hook, caught the other horse, who was grazing by the stream, and led them both out of the marshes on foot.

My leg was aching by the time I reached the road. I had to walk back to Stifkey before I found a mounting block and finally got myself up into the saddle again. I sighed in relief as I eased my weight from my sore leg.

I led Lady Southwick's horse past the curious stares of the villagers and out the other side of Stifkey to make for Parson's Point. At the Parson's Point public house, I gave both horses to the hostler and went inside for a much-needed ale.

"You look all in, young master," Buckley said, drawing a tankard of bitter without me asking, and setting it on the table.

"I'm a bit elderly to be called the young master," I said.

"That's how I think of you. Always did. You and young Mr. Quinn were thick as thieves, laughing together and hiding from your dads in that corner over there. The young master and the vicar's nephew drinking yourselves sick and only fifteen years old."

"And you making sure we got home in our sorry states. You make it sound like happy days."

"They were happy, Captain. Before war and sorrow made you dark."

He had a point. But then, I remembered my youthful misery, my need to be anywhere but in this place.

I tried not to think of the gruesome thing I had in my pack in the stable, but I could not stop picturing how I'd found it—gray skin covered in blood, the birds pecking at it. Dark memories rose in my head, the noise and smell of battle seeming to come back to me. Fighting had been exciting and terrifying at the same time, my body pumping with exhilaration. And then afterward, the exhaustion, the wonder that I was still alive, the days I'd wanted to sleep for hours and not awaken.

"Captain? Are you well?" Buckley leaned on the table and peered at me in concern.

"Tired," I said. "I have much to do."

"Aye, and you're looking for that man what's disappeared. Hope he didn't come to grief."

I nearly laughed, and I covered it by taking a long drink. Though I'd told the others to keep our search quiet, I ought to have known that the news would travel quickly.

Terrance came in at that moment, but he shook his head as he sat down opposite me. "Nothing," he said.

Robert Buckley and the blacksmith's lad entered while Terrance was asking for his pint, with the same to report. I decided, at that moment, not to tell them about the hand. Not here, anyway.

"I hear you have a farm now, Robert," I said as we drank.

Robert brightened. "Aye. Fine bit of land. Better yield this year than last. Come to see it, if you have time. The wife would be honored if you did."

I was not certain what his wife would think, but Robert seemed eager to show off his luck. "I might do that," I said.

Robert nodded and took a pull of his pint.

We finished ales and went back out to search. I told the other three I'd take the western route this time, as I needed to return the horse to Lady Southwick's stables.

The hostler had fixed me with a better rope for Lady Southwick's horse, and he'd rubbed down the beast and given it hay and water. The horse looked better than I did.

The hostler helped me onto my horse, and I led Lady Southwick's along the road that would wind to the south of Blakeney. I decided to take this road, because the Lacey house lay on it as well, and I wanted to stop there.

I rode in through the gates I'd entered three days before, the weeds still in abundance. The house loomed out of the rain, imposing at a distance, even grand. As I drew closer, the ruin of the thing became more apparent.

I was surprised to see Grenville's landau stopped at the front door. The landau was empty, and Jackson was checking the harness. Grenville's groom came forward, unasked, and helped me dismount. I took my canvas-wrapped bundle from the pack, left the horses for the groom to look after, and went inside.

Denis's men were not there. They'd finished stripping my walls to bare stone, and a whiff of smoke from the garden told me they'd burned the rest of the debris.

Lucius Grenville stood on the stairs of the wide hall, with Lady Breckenridge a few steps above him. The two of them did not notice me come in, being too busy arguing.

"You are a pompous prig," Lady Breckenridge said clearly. "I tossed aside being obedient to a man the day after I took my wedding vows."

"It is not a question of obedience—" Grenville broke off his retort when he saw me standing below. "Lacey." He looked embarrassed. "I beg your pardon; we ought not to have barged in without your leave."

"It's raining," I said. I tucked my package more firmly under my arm. "I do not mind my friends running tame in my house, but I must wonder why you wish to."

Lady Breckenridge gripped the wrought-iron railing with a dove-gray leather glove. "I came to pry through your mother's sitting room for any clue to the gown and the takings from the church. Bartholomew told us that you'd been ordered to Denis's hunt and nothing else."

"And I came to encourage her to return to Oxfordshire as planned," Grenville said, his face still red. "Why, Lacey, did we take up with such blasted stubborn women?"

I looked at Lady Breckenridge as I answered. "Because they are more interesting than meek ones. Grenville is right. Please go to Oxfordshire and stay with your son."

"If you are concerned about threats from Mr. Denis, you know I am as safe from him here as I am there," Donata said.

"I know that, but I'd feel better if you were gone."

Something sparkled in her black-lashed eyes. "And the same day I decided to give up obedience, I vowed not to live to make others feel better."

She'd gazed at me as boldly the day I met her, when she'd handed me her cigarillo and then proceeded to trounce me thoroughly at billiards. She'd looked at me without shame then, and she did so now.

"For your own safety then," I said. "Please."

Her eyes were very dark blue in the dim light of the hall. She turned away, lifted her mauve and brown striped skirt, and walked on up the stairs. Neither of us went after her.

Grenville came down to meet me on the ground floor. "What are you doing back here, anyway, Lacey? We thought you'd be busy with Denis's search."

"Because this is the last place I saw Cooper. I wondered if I'd missed something." And, frankly, I was putting off reporting to Denis. "I assume the weather meant an end to Lady Southwick's shooting match?"

Grenville looked pained. "Not a bit of it. Lady Southwick was annoyed that she could not watch you pop at targets, but she made the rest of us capitulate. She regretted it soon, because Godwin almost winged her."

"Good Lord." I thought of Godwin and his bizarre, dandyish clothing. "What happened?"

"I am not certain, to be honest. Godwin lifted his pistol to shoot, we heard a bang, and Lady Southwick gave a yelp and fell. Godwin looked very confused. I could have sworn he fired down the range, but Lady Southwick had stepped off the terrace at just that moment, foolish woman. I thought she'd been hit, but the ball had missed her. Went right past the poor woman's nose. I found the bullet in an ornamental urn down the terrace. Lady Southwick decided we should find our own entertainment for the rest of the afternoon." Grenville dusted off his sleeves. "Lady Breckenridge insisted on coming here."

"There is a second reason I want her gone." I motioned for Grenville to follow me out of the house.

The wind nearly swept us from our feet as we walked onto the old terrace. Another storm was coming, and coming hard.

I pulled the canvas-wrapped bundle from under my arm. "This is thoroughly unpleasant."

Grenville looked curious. "What is it?"

"A man's hand. I do not have to show you."

"Good God." Grenville took a step back. "No, show me. Get it over with."

I gingerly unwrapped the canvas. The hand lay palm down, fingers blackened, fleshy part thoroughly pecked. It was a workingman's hand, blunt-fingered and callused.

Grenville tugged out a handkerchief and pressed it over his nose. "Highly unpleasant, I agree."

I wrapped the thing again and described how I'd found it.

Grenville dabbed his mouth and returned the handkerchief to his pocket. "I suppose, if the appendage belongs to Cooper, we can conclude that Cooper took the horse when you left it, rode out to the marsh, met an enemy, fought, and lost his hand in said fight. But where is the rest of him? Carted away? Or did he drag himself away?"

"If he'd gotten away from his enemy, he could not have gone far in such a state," I said. "Who knows what other injuries he sustained? Yet, no villager or farmer reports having a hurt man wander onto his fields or ask for help. And, if he did survive, why not return to Denis? Or make it to the nearest farm and send a message?"

"The enemy might have taken him away," Grenville said. "Killed him elsewhere. Not a good thought."

I looked across the open land to the copse and the gray curtain of rain coming toward us. "The trouble is, no one in these parts keeps things to themselves. Denis asked me not to let on that we were looking for Cooper, but everyone already knows it. If someone had seen Cooper being dragged or carted away—or even spied an unfamiliar face on the road—everyone for ten villages around would know. And someone would have told me."

"Unless Cooper's enemy was a local person," Grenville pointed out. "Someone so familiar he would not attract notice—if he were seen driving a cart down a road, this would not be unusual. The question is, why should a local man kill Cooper?"

"Many resent Denis taking over Easton's house and are not afraid to say so. I do not believe Denis understands how country people can close ranks. He is very much of the city. But why hurt Cooper and then keep it secret? If villagers wanted to drive Denis away, they would do so much more openly, I'd think."

"Possibly, unless it is a direct resentment neither of us can guess." Grenville looked up at the windows of my house, which were framed with heavy stone pediments. "I understand why you want Lady Breckenridge gone. A dangerous atmosphere. But you will have to persuade her. She will never listen to me."

"I believe you overestimate my influence," I said, smiling a little.

"Not at all. She respects you. She respects very few, not that I blame her. Treasure that."

I did. The fact that Donata Breckenridge was fond of me surprised me every day.

Behind us, Lady Breckenridge emerged from the house. "Are you finished with your secret discussion?" she asked. "I mentioned taking up the carpet in your mother's sitting room, if you remember. If you had done so, you'd have found this in a little niche under the floorboards."

She handed me a notebook. The curtain of rain I'd seen approaching took that moment to strike, and we hastened inside, my bundle again under my arm. Grenville propped the door closed against the wind, and I opened the notebook.

The light in the hall was too dim to show me much, but I saw enough. "This is my mother's," I said.

"I suspected so," Donata said. "I thought I should bring it to you before I pried into your family secrets."

Chapter Thirteen

That had been generous of her. Donata was quite interested in her fellow human beings. I'd caught her one evening in Grenville's private sitting room in his London house, uninvited, looking through his curios. She'd shown no mortification that I'd found her there.

"I once pried through your husband's papers," I reminded her.

"True, but I did not care about that. This is your mother. Quite a difference."

"Thank you," I said.

She pointed to the canvas under my arm. "I suppose you are not going to show me what is in *that*?"

"No," I said abruptly.

"It smells ghastly. I'm not certain I want to see. But tell me, at least."

Grenville broke in before I could think how to put it gently, "A hand that might be Mr. Cooper's. Lacey found it out in the marshes."

Lady Breckenridge's eyes widened. "Good heavens."

"You see why I do not want you here?" I asked.

"Yes, I do understand the dangers, Lacey. I am not a simpleton. I do not like to see *you* here, either, but I have no say in the matter, do I? I believe I shall change my mind and stay on with Lady Southwick. There is a modicum of safety in her house, if one is not blinded by her bad taste."

"And as long as you stay away from the end of Godwin's pistol," Grenville said, snorting.

"Do you know, I do not believe he fired that shot." Lady Breckenridge looked thoughtful. "He seemed absolutely baffled, and there was too much smoke. I think he fired, and someone else fired at the same time, to make it look as though Godwin had accidentally shot at Lady Southwick."

Grenville blinked. "Why on earth would they?"

"Who knows? Perhaps one of the ladies grew tired of her so blatantly chasing the gentlemen of the party. You know that she spent much of the night in the bedchamber of Mr. Reaves."

"With the vicar?" Grenville brought out his quizzing glass and stared through it. "Good God."

"I do not think your vicar prays that much, Lacey," Lady Breckenridge said. "He's a Cambridge man, smooth as butter. Coerced a living out of Lord Southwick, but hopes to work his way back to Cambridge and to a bishopric. A seat in the House of Lords is what he's after."

"A Cambridge man," I repeated. "I wonder if he knew Miss Quinn and her solicitor, or banker, or whatever he is."

"I will ask him," Lady Breckenridge said.

"No, you will not. You will go to Oxfordshire."

She shot me a mulish look. "I am not your wife yet, Gabriel."

"Damn it all, Donata. Do you think I want to ride out to the marshes and find bits of *you* lying about in the grass? Anything to do with James Denis is dangerous, and I want you well out of it."

"What about you?" she returned heatedly. "He is practically holding you hostage. Suppose Mr. Denis decides he likes your services and threatens to make you a permanent part of his household?"

"He will not."

"He might whether you like it or not. I have heard the story of how he had you thrashed, then drugged and trussed up aboard a boat. If you do not return this man he's lost alive, what do you think he'll do to relieve his anger?"

"All the more reason for you to go!" My shout rang through the empty hall. I noticed, distractedly, that Grenville had faded out of sight.

"All the more reason for *you* to," Donata said, undeterred. "Give him what you've turned up and leave him. We will go together."

"I cannot leave until Cooper is found."

"Why the devil not?"

"Because he threatened you!" Again, my voice thundered through the stairwell, an eerie echo of my father's. "He threatened you, Donata. And Peter. He hinted that he'd hurt you, and your son, if I did not help him."

Lady Breckenridge stopped, her lips parting. "Peter."

"Yes." I reined in my anger and took her gloved hands, so small and fragile against my large ones. "Donata, I never meant to draw you into my sordid affairs. If you no longer want. . ."

I could not finish the thought. I was supposed to say, *If you no longer wish to have anything to do with me, I will understand. I will release you. You have no need to stay.*

But I realized I could not open my fingers and let her go. I'd come to care for this lady a little at a time, my affection like a slow-growing flower that at last bursts into exuberant bloom. I had not realized until this moment how much I loved her.

If I let Donata out of my life, she would return to the social whirl of her soirees in South Audley Street, her musicales for the crème de la crème. She'd never again have her life or that of her son threatened, or be tied to a man in the habit of finding severed hands in the marshes. I would return to my small rooms in Grimpen Lane, lonely and alone once more.

I never wanted that life again.

Donata returned the pressure of my hands. "I will go to Oxfordshire and see to Peter," she said. "When this business is done, come to me there."

I lifted her fingers to my lips. "I will finish it swiftly, that I promise."

She gave me a look that was pure Lady Breckenridge. "See that you do," she said.

*** *** ***

Grenville offered to have his groom take the horse back to Lady Southwick, and I relinquished the reins gladly. I had no desire to return to Southwick Hall.

Before the groom assisted Donata into the carriage, I bent and kissed her lips, damn who watched. I savored the brush of her warmth, which would have to last me who knew how long. She touched my lips with her slim fingers, then ascended into the landau. Rain rolled from the landau's canvas top as Jackson started the horses, and the conveyance jerked forward.

I watched the coach recede and vanish into the gray rain, still feeling Donata's fingertips on my lips. I'd thought myself hardened by my disappointments in love, but my heart held a little ache as she went. I was becoming used to her warmth next to me at night.

To keep myself from growing maudlin, I made another search of my house. I lit lanterns that Denis's men had left behind, and I went through the place from top to bottom.

I preferred to do this alone, without Denis's lackeys watching over my shoulder. Again, I went over my home, from the nursery that was now deserted and coated with dust, to the kitchens beneath the house where the candlesticks had been found.

Denis's men had done a through job of removing rotting panels and timber, floorboards that I'd have had to replace anyway, and of ripping open the remaining furniture, which had been cheap and rickety to begin with. Anything of value in the house had been taken by the creditors upon my father's death.

Gutting the house had torn out and discarded the last of my memories. Good riddance to them.

I went to my mother's sitting room last. Donata had been right to search it again, and I put my hand over the notebook in my pocket. I was anxious to look at what my mother had taken such pains to hide from my father, but I needed better light. The ink had faded, and the pages were stained.

I took my time going over the room, looking in drawers and behind the remaining furniture, shining my lantern up the chimney. The chimney was stopped, but with nothing more than years of soot. I'd be hiring a sweep soon.

Planning renovations of the house made me feel better. Donata was right to tell me to strip it to its bones and begin again.

I also knew I was procrastinating returning to Denis. I made myself go back downstairs, where I extinguished the lanterns, led my tied horse to a fallen stone I used as a mounting block, and climbed aboard.

The rain continued to fall in earnest. I pulled my hat down over my eyes and turned the horse down paths that led to Easton's estate. The roads were far too muddy for a good canter, so I took the horse along at a slow trot.

After a time, Easton's square house loomed out of the rain, warm and brick. One of the lackeys came forward to take the horse and help me dismount, and I went inside.

I knew I'd never be given a moment to dry off, fortify myself, or hide my mother's journal, so I thrust my hat and greatcoat at the man who reached for it, retaining the bundle he tried to take from me, and went straight up to the study.

Denis looked up from writing letters. The man was always writing letters, though I never learned what was in them. This one appeared to be long, but he only ever sent me notes of two or three sentences.

When Denis saw my face, he put aside his missive and signaled the two men with him to go. When they hesitated, he actually raised his voice. "Out!"

They went. After they closed the door, I hobbled to the desk and dumped my bundle onto it.

"Is it Cooper's?" I asked.

Denis pulled back the canvas. He stared down at the hand, his expression never changing. His body, however, went very still.

"Yes," he said. "Cooper is dead, then?"

"That, I do not know." I brushed my fingers through my wet hair and explained where I'd found the hand, and how I'd searched for the rest of a body to no avail.

Denis sat back, steepling his fingers. He had not covered the hand again but fixed his gaze on it, as though not letting himself look away.

"I want whoever has done this," he said.

"I'd like to find him myself. I know you do not want magistrates, but he deserves to be caught and arrested."

"No, he deserves *this* to be done to him at the very least."

An eye for an eye. Justice served by James Denis.

After a moment, he asked me, "What do you have to go on?"

"Very little, unfortunately. I went back to the beginning again—my house, the last place he'd been seen. Cooper is not there, nor did I find trace of him in what remains of the outbuildings. I saw no sign of him on the marshes or the sands beyond—no footprints, nothing. No one I have spoken to has reported seeing an injured man, nor have I heard of any gossip of one being so treated."

Denis's fingers tightened the slightest bit. "Leave no stone unturned, Lacey."

"As to that, I would like to speak to your men," I said. "Individually, I mean. I want to know what they know about Cooper, if he mentioned anything about leaving or pursuing a matter somewhere in the countryside—to investigate something he thought might interest you, perhaps. They might have seen or heard something that seemed inconsequential at the time, but might be significant. Also, they might have some clue about Ferguson's death."

Denis was studying me coldly. "You may be certain, Captain, that I have asked them."

"Yes, but they work for you, and I imagine you stood them all in a row and demanded them to tell you what they knew. I want to interview them one at a time, alone, without you listening. That is a different thing."

He fell silent. Though nothing of his thoughts showed on his face, I knew he was weighing every consequence of letting me ask questions, in private, of the men who worked for him. That he was considering it at all told me how much Cooper meant to him.

After a long time, Denis gave me a single nod. "I will have them speak to you in the dining room, after supper. You will use the rest of this day to search. I am not so foolish as to believe you can accomplish this task alone, so I am sending out teams."

I decided not to mention I'd recruited my own team. I had no doubt he already knew. "They need to be careful," I said. "The countryside can be dangerous if you don't know it."

"I agree. That is why you will be directing them."

My mother's notebook would have to wait. I hoped he intended to give me a bedchamber to myself, where I could be alone to read it, rather than expecting me to bunk down with his lackeys. With Denis, one could never be certain.

I looked at the hand. "What will you do with that?"

Denis tossed a corner of the canvas back over it. "Burn it," he said. "It is of no use to Cooper now."

*** *** ***

The afternoon's search proved less fruitful than the morning's. I managed to find Terrance riding toward Blakeney, and I told him I would be conducting the search with Denis's men. If he wanted to continue to help, fine; otherwise, he could go home.

Terrance told me he'd continue. He seemed more animated this afternoon, less morose. I suppose he was happy that he had something useful to do.

I took my handful of men toward Salthouse, with its rise of ground, open heath, and view of the sea. The ocean was gray with rain, the wind strong here. When it grew dark, we returned to Easton's, with nothing to report.

I had been given my own bedchamber, I was happy to see. Bartholomew was there. He'd already unpacked my few belongings, had a fire stoked and the bed warmed and turned down. He asked as he drew off my coat, whether I wanted a bath.

I longed for a hot soak, but I had more to do until I retired. I removed the notebook from my coat's inner pocket and handed it to Bartholomew. "Put that in a safe place. I'll need it later tonight but I want no one coming across it."

"Right you are, sir." Bartholomew's usual cheerfulness was subdued, however. "Will you be all right here, sir?"

"I will," I said, stripping off my damp shirt and reaching for a dry one. "What about you?"

"Below stairs, those what used to be pugilists are mostly leaving me alone. Mr. Denis's chef from London, now, he's ruder than the ruffians, I must say. I have my own billet in the attic—I don't have to share—but I'm to prepare a room for Mr. Grenville, who will arrive tomorrow."

"Mr. Denis arranges everything," I said.

"He does, sir." Bartholomew brushed the creases out of my shirt, tied my cravat, and helped me into a dry coat, then I went back downstairs for supper.

I ate alone in the dining room, with one of the lackeys to serve me. When I asked where his fellows were, he told me they were eating in the servants' hall. Denis did not join me.

The fare was good, the dining room quiet. I contrasted it to the garish dining chamber at Lady Southwick's with its blood-soaked hunting scene and the not-so-thinly veiled insults of her guests. Whatever Brigadier Easton's faults had been, I found his house restful.

After supper, the lackey cleared away the plates, brought me a pile of clean paper, a pen, pen sharpener, ink, and a blotter, and left again. My interviews began.

Chapter Fourteen

James Denis hired men of a type—most of them former fighters, all of them large and strong. Many, but not all, had criminal pasts. Six had accompanied Cooper to Norfolk to search for the lost artwork, which still had not turned up. Denis had brought three more with him. All nine filed in, one after the other, sat opposite me, and answered my questions.

I'd been used to thinking of them collectively—Denis's men—but as each came in and either stood or sat in front of me, they solidified into individuals, men with separate pasts, characters, ambitions.

One man told me he had a son he was raising on his own, his wife having passed six years before. He worked for Denis because Denis paid so much, and if a man kept his head down and got on, he had a place for life. He'd tucked his son away in a school in Scotland, far from Denis's exploits.

Another, younger man, who called himself Tom and gave no surname, had been thought slow in the Yorkshire village where he'd grown up. At age fourteen, his father had more or less turned him out to fend for himself. He'd become an exhibition fighter for trainers who also thought him slow, but had been tossed out when he hurt other, more valuable fighters.

Tom had then worked his way south toward London, doing odd jobs, usually being paid only in a meal and a place to sleep. People feared him and did not like him lingering, so he'd never stayed anywhere more than a day or two. When he'd reached London, street toughs had lit into him, and Cooper had happened by during the fight. Liking how Tom had held his own against four men, Cooper had broken up the fight and brought the young man to Denis. Tom had been working for Denis ever since.

He related all this in short sentences with long pauses between. Not so much slow, I saw, as careful. Tom was happy in his employment now, with no ambition to go anywhere else. He was grateful to Cooper, but he did not know where Cooper was, nor did he know what had happened to Ferguson. He'd been searching Easton's attics for the art when the cry had gone up at the windmill, and he'd run out to see what was the matter.

I believed him. The way he spoke, leaving out no detail but not embellishing, told me that here was a man not comfortable with lying.

The next person to speak to me was the man who'd beaten me on the boat a year ago, the same one who'd stood behind me in the dining room when Denis had explained that he owned me.

He sprawled in a chair, folded his arms, and grinned at me. "What am I supposed to tell you, Captain?"

I shrugged. "Where you think Cooper is, who you think killed Ferguson. Anything unusual you've seen these last few days."

"Besides you poking your nose into our business? Not a damned thing."

I went on asking the same questions I'd put to the others. "Cooper never mentioned wanting to leave, or wanting to follow someone?"

"Not to me. He never talked to me much. And I never talked to him. Never wanted to."

Very helpful. I kept my voice steady. "Is there anything else you would like to mention?"

"Only this." He leaned forward, resting his arms on the table. "Last year, when I did you over, I was going easy on you."

I remembered his ham fists in my face and the way he'd stomped his large boot on my bad knee, not to mention kicked me square in the groin—all of this after I was down.

"I was also half senseless with opium and unable to defend myself," I said. "I agree that a fair fight would produce different results."

The man's grin widened, and he lurched up out of the chair. "When you want to have a go, you just tell me."

"I'll do that," I said, and then he was gone.

*** *** ***

I interviewed the rest, some of whom were quiet and spoke readily, some openly hostile. I was surprised how much they opened up to me, but I supposed Denis would have instructed them in what they could tell me and what they were not allowed to say. But they talked to me more readily than I'd thought.

None, however, had any idea where Cooper might have got to or who had killed Ferguson. None had gone anywhere near the windmill the night of Ferguson's death before Grenville had given the alarm, or so they claimed. Most hadn't had opportunity to know Ferguson well, although the last man I interviewed put forth the theory that Ferguson had it coming.

He was the man I'd yelled at to leave alone my mother's sitting room. He was the smallest of the lot and a bit older as well. He had a wiry build, but I'd seen him breaking my walls with his large sledgehammer without worry. He sat, arms folded, but not in resentment. He was the most evenhanded of the men I'd spoken to, not at all caring about our previous argument.

"Gave himself a lot of airs, did Ferguson," he said. "Stands to reason—he were a champion until he got himself the sack, like a fighting cock who's for the cooking pot. He'd been treated like a princess so long he didn't know how to be a slavey. Fancied himself his nibs' next lieutenant." He chuckled. "Cooper never will leave Mr. Denis's side. He'll die in harness." His smile faded. "Sounds bad now, don't it? Cooper probably got himself offed by the same bloke who did Ferguson."

"You believe Cooper dead, then?"

"Most like. Cooper is that devoted to his nibs. Like father and son, though Mr. Denis is more like the father."

"Is Mr. Denis fatherly to all of you?"

He burst out laughing. "You are funny, Captain. Most amusing. I see why he keeps you around. Mr. Denis ain't fatherly to no one. Me own dad was a drunken layabout, so he wasn't too fatherly either. It is nice to work for someone perpetually sober. As long as Mr. Denis don't expect *me* to be."

"I've never noticed drunken revelry in Mr. Denis's house," I said.

"Course not. He's got rules, and if you break 'em, you're out. Don't no matter what. But that makes sense, don't it? He's got to be so careful, and some drunken fool could muck up the works. His nibs knows how to get the most out of what he has."

He did. I finished with the man and prepared to retire, but the man acting as butler returned and told me that Denis wanted to see me.

I found him in the study as usual, but he was looking out the window into darkness. The storm still raged, rain beating against the windows with the sound of pebbles on glass.

Denis turned when the door closed behind me. "Have you finished?" he asked.

"I have."

"Did any of them confess to murdering Ferguson? Cutting off Cooper's hand and dragging him off into a convenient patch of quicksand?"

"No," I said. He'd known that of course. He'd been indulging me.

Denis did not invite me to sit down. He looked out the window a final time then pulled the drape across it. "I will have to appoint a new lieutenant if Cooper does not turn up. I do not relish the task."

"A change in the pecking order always causes troubles," I said.

He gave me an ironic look. "To be certain."

"One of your men suggested that Ferguson had been hankering for the post."

Denis's brows lifted. "Ferguson did? He never would have been offered it. He is—was—too volatile."

"Perhaps Cooper heard of Ferguson's ambition, did not like the idea, and so decided to give him a drubbing."

Denis sat down behind his desk. Instead of taking his usual upright posture, he leaned back in his chair and contemplated me. "You are fond of the idea that Cooper murdered Ferguson," he said. "You harp on it."

"And you seem to want to ignore the possibility." I stopped waiting for an invitation to sit and sank to the straight-backed chair before the desk. My leg was hurting after the long day. "Think on it—Cooper wants to teach Ferguson his place. Cooper meets him in or near the windmill, they fight, the fight grows violent. Cooper kills Ferguson, whether on purpose or accidentally, who can tell? Cooper comes to himself and realizes he needs to hide Ferguson and get away. He shuts Ferguson into the windmill, and runs off."

"Then what? He steals the horse, rides to the marsh, and cuts off the hand that did the murder in penance?"

"I mean nothing so Shakespearean. Perhaps when the fight grew violent, Cooper's wrist was severed."

"Ferguson had no weapon," Denis pointed out.

"Perhaps Cooper took it with him. Why leave behind a perfectly good blade? When Cooper reached the marshes, he realized that he'd die if he did not lose the hand. It is a difficult decision to make, but I've known men who've made it."

"That still will not wash, Captain." Denis tapped his fingertips together. "Why leave the horse? I understand why Cooper would not seek a local surgeon, lest he be discovered and arrested for Ferguson's murder, but he would have been able to run away faster with the horse."

"The answer could be as simple as Cooper having trouble mounting again. When I was on the marsh, I had to lead my horse back to the nearest village before I could find a way to climb back into the saddle. Add to that, he was injured and in great pain, and likely not thinking straight."

"You seem to have a solution for everything."

"You asked me to find out. This is why you are keeping me on a close tether."

"I asked you to find Cooper," Denis said impatiently. "I am not interested in your theories that he is a terrified murderer. If he killed Ferguson in a private fight, that is their business. He would know that. He would have come to me."

I gave up. I knew that my idea had many holes in it, which Denis was quick to point out, but I could not produce Cooper out of the air.

"I agree he needs to be found," I said. "For better or worse. While I am haring around the country looking for him, will you do something for me?"

Denis pulled his hands apart and slowly rocked upright. "You are working off your debt to me, Captain. Are you certain you wish to pile on more?"

"This will be an easy task for you. I had planned to ask my Bow Street Runner to do it, but you would be more efficient, and Pomeroy always expects a reward for his services."

Denis gazed at me with dark blue eyes that had seen too much. This was a man who had no friends, I'd realized long ago, no one he could call a colleague, no one with whom he could talk at the end of a day. While Grenville and I could spin out an evening over brandy, cheroots, and idle conversation, Denis never allowed himself that luxury. He had to be constantly alert and was constantly alone.

"Tell me what the task is, and I will decide," he said.

"Find a Cambridge man by name of Edward Braxton. He is either a banker's clerk or a solicitor. I gather he no longer lives in Cambridge, but someone there must know where he went. I want to discover his whereabouts, whether he is married to a woman called Helena Quinn, and where she is now."

"Your vicar's daughter, yes. Why does she fascinate you so, Captain?"

"Worries me, rather. It bothers me that no one has heard from her since the night of her disappearance. Her cousin went to Cambridge to find her and could not. I would like to reassure myself — and her family — that she is alive and well."

"A fairly simple inquiry. I will have it done and add it to your debit column."

I ran my fingers along the carved arm of my chair. "I'd enjoy having a glance at this book where you calculate who owes you what, and what sort of thing will pay off the debt."

"You would have difficulty with that, because I keep no such book." Denis touched his temple. "It is here."

I raised my brows. "You remember everything every person in England — or the world — owes you?"

"I remember every favor done me, every one asked of me, every slight, and every assistance." He said it without inflection, without boasting. He stated a fact. "That is why people consider me dangerous."

"Not to mention your small army of former pugilists who carry out dire deeds for you with no questions," I said.

"I suppose that might be part of it. Time for you to retire, Captain. Rise early tomorrow and continue the search."

No brandy, cheroots, and gossip for the pair of us. I stood, said good night, and left him.

*** *** ***

Bartholomew fetched me the bath at last, and I soaked out the day's rain, dirt, and tension. Denis believed in living in luxury, so I had a large tub, plenty of hot water, a big cake of soap, and towels as tall as my body. The bedchamber was lit with a profusion of candles and heated by a well-stoked fire.

The boy growing up on the streets had made certain he never had to feel the pinch of want again. I wondered at Denis's hint that his childhood was unusual, even for a street boy, but I knew he'd tell me only if he thought he'd benefit by my knowing.

He'd told me the story of Cooper to appeal to my compassion so that I'd be more willing to help find the man. I knew that, but I also believed finding him important.

After the bath, I did not succumb to the temptation of the turned-down bed. I told Bartholomew to take his well-earned rest, and I sat in a chair and opened my mother's notebook that Bartholomew had kept safe for me in his coat pocket.

The first part of the book held recipes and remedies, practical things my mother had noted. *For a cold, soak a collection of peppermint leaves in hot water and apply to a towel, to be used as a compress . . . A syllabub of cream whipped with good port layered with fresh berries of the season makes a fine summer pudding.*

Later came more of a journal, and I found, to my surprise, passages about me.

He walks and runs about everywhere now, very sturdy and strong. A fine boy. He has brown eyes like his father and a build that makes me believe he will be as tall. I hear from his nanny that he is very clever too.

A proud mother's words. The page blurred, and I had to wipe my eyes before I could continue.

She wrote of me growing from baby to child to boy, how I confounded my tutors with my constant questions, how I ran about like a wild thing despite frequent punishment, how impetuous I was, how affectionate.

He never minds his mother kissing him, and he returns the kisses, throwing his arms about my neck in true affection. Mr. Lacey does not like this, however, and so I embrace my son only when we are entirely private.

My father had thought any form of sentiment weak and unmanly. Lest his son grow up and seek the company of male paramours, my father forbade any acknowledgment of softer emotions. My mother and I, happily, managed to remain fond of each other. As I grew into boyhood, I became less patient with hugs and kisses, but I always reassured my mother that I loved her.

My mother wrote of missing me when I went off to school, but that she enjoyed knitting and sewing things for me. She'd sent hampers to the school, as well, which she'd done in secret, because my father thought any comforts from home also made boys soft. I'd gained many friends trading the contents of those hampers, keeping the best bits for myself, of course.

My mother hadn't dated her entries, but I followed the passage of the years based on her references to me, my father, my school years, my holidays. About a year before her death, her musings grew strange.

I pen these words to give me courage. To screw my courage to the sticking place, as the Bard says. But what will become of my boy?

I had no idea what on earth she meant. I had been growing fatigued with reading, the clock ticking into the small hours of the morning. The next entry made me come alert.

Miss Quinn is a lovely child. I quite think of her as my own. She is here often when Mr. Lacey is away, and we have tea and play with her dolls. I wish, I so wish, I could have a daughter such as she! But perhaps I will not have to wait so long. My limbs tremble as I think on it.

Think on what? Had my mother been with child? I had never heard word of it. I read rapidly onward.

What a heavenly thing it is to love. It makes one do mad, mad things. I shall have to compose a letter, such a letter as I have never contemplated writing. I want to go. But then I think of my boy, and I falter. I would be kept from him, never to see him again.

My heart beat faster, and I turned another page.

Really, is it so wrong to long for happiness? I am kept from my son, the only person who loved me until now. Mr. Lacey does not even like me to entertain poor Helena, though the vicar and his wife are glad she has such a friend in me.

He is younger than I, yes, but what of it? We love, and we will love. Perhaps a daughter will come of it, to replace the son I must lose.

I turned the page and found it held the last entry. *The time is nigh. I must steel myself. Oh, my boy. My poor, dear Gabriel.*

The rest of the journal was blank. I sat, staring at the last page while the candles around me guttered.

My mother had been preparing to leave my father. Her words never openly stated it, while at the same time, they shouted it.

That she had wanted to leave should not surprise me. My father had made her miserable. What did surprise me, however, was that she'd wound herself into the courage to do it.

Or had she? I wish I knew the exact dates these entries had been written. She'd put the journal under the floorboards and never written in it again.

Because she'd grown sick and died? Or because she *had* run away, and my father had only claimed her dead?

The last thought made no sense. I'd attended her funeral. Someone must have ministered to her in her final illness. Helena Quinn, though she'd been a child at the time, had been close to her. Perhaps Helena would know.

How very convenient that Helena was not here.

And who had been this man with whom my mother had fallen in love, had loved so well that she'd convinced herself to turn her back on her husband and son? She never named him. She'd never even hinted. She'd been faithful to her unknown lover to the last.

I shut the book and clasped it to my chest, closing my eyes. This journal, which I'd bless Donata forever for finding, had brought me closer to my mother, and at the same time, had made her all the more distant.

Chapter Fifteen

I rose the next morning, sandy-eyed, and quite pessimistic about ever finding Cooper. However, I dressed, ate, and rode out again on the search.

I led three of Denis's men west and south toward Holt. We inquired everywhere we went, at farms, in villages, and of shepherds—men who moved back and forth through the valleys and saw everything and everyone. None, however, had seen a man answering to Cooper's description.

I decided to break away and make a brief visit to Lady Southwick, first to apologize for so rudely walking away from her house party, and second to ask her a few things that nagged at me. I had not particularly liked the lady or her guests, but good manners dictated the apology.

Lord Southwick's estate was a large one, and it was easy to send Denis's men to ask questions about

Cooper in the outbuildings and the surrounding farms while I went to the house.

Most of the guests had gone, including Rafe Godwin. Grenville was still there, Matthias and his valet packing him up to remove to Easton's house. The valet would return to London with half of Grenville's baggage, and Matthias would remain to look after him. Grenville doubted he'd need as many evening clothes to reside a few days with Mr. Denis, he said.

Lady Breckenridge, true to her word, had departed yesterday afternoon in her chaise and four, heading back to London before she moved on to Oxfordshire. To this news I breathed a sigh of relief.

Mr. Reaves, the vicar, was still present. I endured his company with Lady Southwick in the drawing room, while I inquired after her health and the accident with the pistol.

"Poor Mr. Godwin," Lady Southwick said. "It quite unnerved him."

Reaves broke in before I could answer. "It quite unnerved *you*, my lady. Godwin should be thrashed."

"Was it certain that he fired the shot?" I asked.

"Of course he did," Reaves said. "His gun went off, and poor Lady Southwick was nearly hit."

"I did wonder," Lady Southwick said. "He looked so very bewildered. I never realized it was he who fired until Mr. Grenville began to shout at him."

"Dear lady, you were most distressed," Reaves said. "Mr. Godwin is uncomfortable with pistols and should not have picked up one at all."

"A gentleman who will not shoot is looked upon askance," I said. "Perhaps he did not want to admit his inability."

"He ought to have left well enough alone," Reaves said, scowling.

I had to agree with Reaves in this instance. I also had a thought I did not like. I had observed that Lady Breckenridge and Lady Southwick were much alike in dress and way of carrying themselves. Had a shooter, seeing Lady Southwick from afar, her fair hair hidden under her large hat, mistaken her for Lady Breckenridge? Had one of Denis's men grown enthusiastic about threatening my friends to make me behave? Or had the shooter fired for another reason?

The speculation made me doubly happy that Lady Breckenridge had gone. "I agree that Godwin should not have tried to shoot," I said. "I see that he was unnerved enough to depart."

"He apologized most beautifully." Lady Southwick sent me a smile. "I do believe his manners are as impeccable as yours."

"And yet, I have been treating your hospitality shamefully."

"Perhaps." Her eyes took on a glint. "But you know how to humble yourself to a lady. Captain, before you go, will you will honor me with a turn in the garden?"

She blatantly left Reaves out of the invitation. He rose politely and bowed to her but flashed me an angry look as I ushered Lady Southwick out the French doors to the rather windy garden. At least it had stopped raining.

We strolled past flowerbeds that held the last of dying summer blossoms and toward silent fountains, empty of water in this weather.

Lady Southwick tucked her hand under my arm and tugged me close. "Lady Breckenridge believed I would try to steal you away from her. She never said so, of course, but I've never seen her jealous before, poor woman. She never gave a fig what her husband got up to. She must think highly of you."

"I would be honored if she did."

Lady Southwick smiled. "As I have observed, you have fine manners, Captain. I am sorry I did not have time to speak with you more, but how fortunate that we are now neighbors."

"I look forward to it," I said politely.

"No, you do not, naughty thing. I know how delighted you were that business took you away from my tedious house party. The gentlemen and ladies I invited do not suit you. You like the unusual, which is why you have become friends with Mr. Grenville and Lady Breckenridge, and that man Mr. Denis. *He* is quite unusual from what I hear. I do believe I am the only person not unhappy that he sent Brigadier Easton packing. He was quite dull, was the brigadier, his wife even worse."

"You have lived in Norfolk some time now?" I asked.

"Casting my age up to me, are you, Captain? But yes, I married Southwick when I was quite a girl and have spent many an autumn in this decidedly quiet corner of England. House parties liven things up, thank God."

"And you were here when Miss Quinn eloped?"

Her plucked brows rose. "You seem extraordinarily intrigued by Miss Quinn, Captain. Lady Breckenridge put me to the question about her as well. What is your interest? Were you in love with the girl?"

"When I left for the army, Miss Quinn was twelve years old—therefore, I would say no. Her cousin Terrance was my friend. I am concerned for the family's sake."

"How very droll you are. I was teasing you. Yes, I knew Miss Quinn, poor dear. Such a lovely girl but no prospects, I can tell you. Waiting so long for Terrance Quinn would have ruined her—and he coming back missing a limb. Lucky for her that Mr. Braxton came along."

"You told Lady Breckenridge that Braxton was a banker's clerk?"

"Indeed, I did. A gentleman's son, but his family had no money, so he went into finance. Not a match I'd want for my own daughter, but better than Miss Quinn could hope for. He had ambition, did that lad. I'm certain he's become vulgarly rich by now."

"I heard from another that Mr. Braxton was a solicitor."

Lady Southwick looked surprised. "Not at all. He worked at a bank. He told me distinctly. I do not remember which, but I suppose one in Cambridge."

"You met him, then?"

"Well, I must have done, mustn't I? I introduced the pair of them. So exciting that they ran off together."

It was my turn to profess surprise. "You knew Mr. Braxton? And his family?"

"No, no, you misunderstand. I do not mean I *knew* him. I mean that I met him when he came to Blakeney. I liked him, I found out all about him, and I introduced him to Miss Quinn. I knew Helena Quinn well, you see. I quite liked her, such a pretty and unspoiled girl. A true lady, and you don't meet many of those these days. I know that Lady Breckenridge must have told you that I dislike ladies altogether, but I mean that I dislike *married* ladies. They are apt to be either too self-righteous for words or they try to steal one's husband. Widows are even worse." She leaned on my arm. "But young ladies, now, they are deferential, and it would never have entered into Miss Quinn's head to set her cap for any married gentleman."

"But she did for Mr. Braxton?"

"Well, *setting her cap* might be putting it a bit strongly, but they liked each other right off. Mr. Braxton was so very charming. All would have been well if Dr. Quinn and his wife hadn't cut up rough. They were adamant that Miss Quinn should fold her hands and wait for her cousin to return from the war. Lucky for her that she did not. Look at the poor lad. What is he good for now, I ask you?"

I thought of Terrance, angry, disappointed, broken by the loss of his arm and what he'd found upon his return home. I'd been miserable when I'd first come back to England, but I now thought it a lucky stroke that I'd chosen to live in London instead of trying to return to Norfolk. In London, I'd met Grenville and found an interest in pursing criminals. If I'd returned to Parson's Point, I'd even now be as sunk in melancholia as Terrance was.

"Mr. Quinn's injury is hardly his fault," I said, my voice going frosty.

Lady Southwick's eyes widened. "Of course it is not. He was most unfortunate, is all. But Miss Quinn is now married and gone, thanks to me."

"Did you help them elope?"

"I did, indeed, and good thing too. Helena came to me in tears, poor lamb. Her father and mother were about to send Mr. Braxton away, so I told her to leave it to me. I gave Mr. Braxton a bit of money and arranged that they should meet and go away together, without anyone being the wiser."

"Where did you have them meet? The Lacey house?"

"Good heavens, no. Your father was still alive then, and quite a curmudgeon. He took Dr. Quinn's side of the matter, thought Helena a disobedient child, and even wrote me, taking me to task for encouraging them. I beg your pardon, Captain, I know he was your father, but he was a tyrant and often got above himself. Lord Southwick could never stick him."

I did not argue with her. "Then where did you tell them to meet?"

"In the little copse north of your house, near that windmill. Easy for Miss Quinn to reach, and a spot her parents would not think her to go. And romantic."

A girl running away from home would think it romantic, in these days when we all had to read poetry, take long tramps through the countryside, and wax eloquent about skylarks.

"Have you heard from Miss Quinn since?"

"I did. One letter, when she first reached Cambridge. Telling me she was well, and that she had no wish to communicate with her parents. I did feel compelled to at least send her mother a note that she was alive and well, but I could not blame Helena for wanting to say nothing more to them. They treated her badly."

"Her father died soon after. She did not return to his funeral?"

"No. I did write her of the event, directing my letter to Mr. Braxton in Cambridge—Helena had given me no precise street or house—but I had no reply."

"Then you do not know if the letter ever reached her?"

"No, she never wrote again. Young Mr. Quinn went to Cambridge to find her, as you likely know, and he did find the house, but Mr. Braxton and Helena had gone north somewhere."

Lady Southwick made a *what-can-we-do?* gesture with her ring-clasped fingers, and my anger stirred. She'd been happy to help the girl thwart her parents and disappear into the mists but had felt no need to worry about Helena's well-being after that.

"Thank you," I managed to say.

Lady Southwick smiled again, sliding her hand up my arm. "Not at all, Captain. I am sorry we did not come to know each other better, but I understand you wished to be discreet while you were under Lady Breckenridge's eye." Her smile widened. "Lady Breckenridge, however, has departed."

"You flatter me, my lady, but I truly have much business to attend."

"What a liar you are." She gave my hand a little slap. "I will assure Donata that you were not tempted in the slightest. I release you, Captain, but in a few years' time, when you grow weary of marriage, remember that my home is but five miles distant from yours."

*** *** ***

Reaves looked pleased to see me depart. He shook my hand when I said good-bye, but I saw the relief in his eyes. I rode away from Southwick Hall, deciding to return to my house and the copse Lady Southwick had mentioned and have another look around.

Without the rain, I traversed the five miles fairly quickly, reaching the windmill that could be seen from the windows of my mother's sitting room. Its arms cranked steadily, a familiar *clack, clack* that brought back more memories than I cared it to.

This windmill not only pumped water but ground grain, and its gears had fascinated the small boy I'd been. The keeper who'd used to carry me home when I became too much of a nuisance was gone, replaced by a younger man. The windows in the windmill glowed with light, but I did not stop to pass the time.

To the west of the windmill was the copse, and beyond that sat the Lacey house, bleak under the gray skies. In the middle of the copse was a clearing, in which someone in my grandfather's time had fixed a stone bench. The perfect place for a rendezvous.

I dismounted and walked over the area, leaving large footprints in the mud. I examined the bench, a fancy thing of carved stone from the last century. I got down on the ground and looked under it, my bad knee protesting, though what I hoped to find after ten years I did not know. Nothing was there.

I climbed to my feet and sat down, wrapping myself in my greatcoat and bracing my hands on my walking stick. I was beset with questions: If Helena had met Mr. Braxton here, why was her dress in my mother's sitting room? Who had taken the church silver, and why had they stashed the things in the kitchen? The villagers had assumed Helena had stolen it, but its return made her look innocent.

Perhaps none of the incidents were connected, and perhaps I was chasing shadows. I'd find Helena and her husband alive and well in some northern county, the dress discarded by a maid who'd stolen Helena's things after she went, the church silver taken by a thief who'd never had opportunity to return for his prize.

I realized after a bit, sitting in the wind, that I was pondering these questions to avoid those that had swooped upon me all night: Who was the man my mother had loved? Why had she decided to run away with him? And why hadn't she, in the end?

Because of me? Had she not been able to bear the thought of never seeing her son again, or had she simply not wanted to leave me with my father? By law, a mother could not be guardian of her own child unless legally appointed. A boy belonged to his father, and that was all.

She had left me alone with him, in any case, by dying. But if she'd gone off with her lover, would she be alive today? And would I have forgiven her for going?

I needed to find out. But who to ask? Was my mother's love affair a secret between herself and whoever the man happened to be? Or was it common knowledge, one of those things known but not spoken of? And which man could I approach with the question? Had her lover been a stranger or someone local?

I pondered for a while longer, growing colder by the minute, until I fixed upon a person who knew all the gossip of the nearby villages and was kind at the same time. I led my horse to the bench, got stiffly onto the stone seat, and mounted up.

The rain started again as I rode the short way north. Not long later, I stood, streaming, at the kitchen door of the vicarage. Mrs. Landon's son led my horse to the warm, dry stables, and a maid let me into the equally warm and dry kitchen.

Mrs. Landon, her keys clinking on her belt like a medieval jailor's, welcomed me, bade me give the maid my wet things, and sat me down at the table.

"Mrs. Landon," I said, deciding to broach the topic as quickly as I could. "I want you to tell me everything you know about my mother. Her last year, especially."

Mrs. Landon pushed a steaming cup at me, looking in no way surprised at my command. "You've found out about that, have you, dear?"

I clasped my hands around the coffee, my heart beating faster. "I discovered a journal she kept. Who was he, Mrs. Landon?"

She gave me a sad look from her watery blue eyes. "Well, dear, I suppose it's right that you know. It was Mr. Buckley, the publican. Young Mr. Buckley, that is. The one who's publican now."

Chapter Sixteen

"Buckley?"

I stood, my chair sliding back on the flagstones. Thomas Buckley, the youthful-faced publican who'd welcomed me home as the "young master," remembered what I liked to drink, and offered me cheerful advice about Terrance Quinn—had been my mother's lover?

"You must be mistaken," I said. "Buckley would only have been in his twenties at the time."

"I am not mistaken, dear. I remember it well. You never knew, then?"

I scrubbed one hand through my hair as I paced. "Of course I did not know. What mother tells her child that she is going to run off with the publican's son?" I stopped. "Did my father know?" A horrible thought entered my head. Had he found out? Had he killed my mother in a jealous rage and then claimed she'd died of illness?

Mrs. Landon was shaking her head. "I do not believe your father ever tumbled to it. Your lady mother was most discreet, as was young Mr. Buckley. I know only because I came upon them by chance one day, but I promised my silence. The poor dear didn't have much joy in her life. Who was I to destroy that, even if she committed a mortal sin? When you have lived most of your life in a vicarage, you realize that there is sin, and there is sin."

I sat down, my legs suddenly weak. "But she did not go with Mr. Buckley in the end. He is still here, and my mother is dead."

"I know." Her voice was gentle. "I nursed your mother to the last. Such a sweet woman. You say that Mr. Buckley was in his twenties, and he was, but you must remember that she was not much older than he. Five or six years at most. And country boys grow up quicker, as much fancy schooling as the gentry have."

I balled my hands. "What made her decide not to leave? She wrote in her journal that she was prepared to go, but nothing after that."

"I cannot say. She never told me. But one day, when she was bringing flowers for the Easter service, your ma took me aside and said that the matter with Mr. Buckley was at an end. She apologized to me for having to bear the secret. She apologized to *me*, poor lamb."

"But she never said why."

"No, dear. And I did not ask her."

I rubbed a shaking hand over my face The idea that my mother and *Buckley* . . .

Was I outraged because he was a lowborn publican's son, or because she'd fallen so hard in

love with him that she'd contemplated leaving me
with my father? Or was I angry that Buckley *hadn't*
taken her off, out of my father's reach, where she
might have been happy?

I did not know. I knew only that I had to put my
hands on him.

I rose. "Thank you, Mrs. Landon."

She saw what was in my face and got to her feet.
"You leave him be, Captain. It was a long time ago.
Water under the bridge. He's got a good wife and a
fine son and grandson."

"I'm sorry," I said.

It was all that would come out of my mouth. I
shook off her well-meaning hand and strode out of
the house.

I was so angry that I walked all the way. Terrance
looked up from his tankard as I entered the public
house. "Lacey . . ."

I ignored him and made for Buckley, who'd come
out from behind his hatch to talk to a handful of
fishermen. The smell of frying fish came out of the
back, where Buckley's wife was preparing whatever
the fishermen had brought her.

"Captain." Buckley turned his publican's smile on
me. "Your usual?"

"I want a word," I said. "Now."

Buckley lost the smile, but he looked puzzled
rather than worried. He nodded to the fishermen and
Terrance, who also eyed me curiously, then Buckley
followed me out the front door.

The trouble with villages is that one cannot have a
chat in a corner without half the place overhearing.
The pub sat at the end of a row of flint cottages, each
built slap against the other. The space between the

row of houses and the one behind it was tiny, dark, and full of slops. Anything said there would echo up and down and through the back windows.

I walked out of the high street until I was well away from houses, on the path that ran up to the marshes. Buckley caught up with me, puffing. "What is it? What's happened? Is it Robert?"

When I determined we could speak privately, I turned to him, my walking stick firmly in my hands. "Why did she decide not to go with you?"

Buckley stared at me, perplexed, then the skin about his eyes pinched. He did not pretend not to understand what I meant.

"Because of you," he said.

"I was only a child." I clenched my walking stick so hard I feared the casing would break. "I was away at school. What could it have mattered?"

"It mattered to her. She did not want you to always be known for her transgressions. She did not want you to grow up in shame."

"And so she told you to leave her alone?"

"That's about the brunt of it. Yes."

I stood there, unsure what to do. My first instinct was to hit him, the small boy in me wanting to pummel the man who'd tried to take away his mother. My second instinct was to hit him for not persuading her harder.

"You should have made her go with you," I said. "She was miserable. Bugger what I thought."

Buckley stood with his arms loose at his sides, a stance of surrender. "I understood once I had a boy of my own. The sins of the parents, and all that."

"My father was a demon," I said. "He made her life hell, and mine. She died here, in that hell. If you'd taken her away, she might still be alive, and happy."

Buckley was shaking his head before I finished. "She would have died anyway." His voice was full of sadness. "She was belly-full. She lost the child, and that made her take sick."

I stood still while shock spilled over me. "Your child?"

"Aye."

He said it without shame. Only vast sadness for what might have been.

I remembered the words of my mother's diary: *I wish, I so wish, I could have another, a daughter such as she! But perhaps I will not have to wait so long. My limbs tremble as I think on it.*

I'd suspected she'd meant she was carrying a child, and now Buckley confirmed it. She'd hoped that the child would be a girl, a daughter. But she'd decided to stay here, to pretend the child was my father's, to raise her as a Lacey. My sister. Then the child had died, killing my mother as well. Buckley's child had killed her.

"Dear God," I said.

"She broke my heart, young master. That she did."

To resist the impulse to pull the sword from my walking stick and strike him down, I clamped my arm across my stomach and turned away. Not, alas, because I thought he did not deserve to be struck down, but because I knew everyone in the village would see me if I killed him.

"Tell me," I said. "I want to know. Everything. How long were you her lover?"

I heard Buckley move uneasily behind me. "Two years. I know she was older than me, and a lady, but she were a beautiful, beautiful woman. And so kind. Not condescending at all. Talked to me like I was the same as her. She always did."

I turned back as he paused. "What began it? Or did she one day decide to come to the pub and ask you to take her to bed?"

He reddened. "Nothing like that. I was helping with repairs to the church. We all throw in for that, one way or another, or the thing would fall down on us of a Sunday morning. Your mum was always there, assisting Mrs. Landon. She and I were alone in the back of the church, and Mrs. Lacey was holding a bit of wood for me while I nailed it over a hole. We were talking and making jests, as we often did. And then . . ." He shrugged. "I do not know how it happened, I will tell you honest, Captain. All the sudden, I was kissing her. And it was like angels started to sing."

"Mrs. Landon caught you," I said.

"That she did. Not then. She caught us months later, kissing in the sacristy. Adultery in a church. Can you credit it?"

He spoke wistfully, an older man recalling the follies of youth. I turned away again, wanting to rail at him, and at the same time, hungering for this new view of my mother.

I'd barely known her, I realized. My father hadn't known her either, seeing her as a vessel for his seed, a woman to run his home and nothing more. Buckley had known *her*.

"Why did you not tell me?" I asked. "Why did you never *tell me*?"

"Well, it'd not be easy, would it? To explain to a young man something like that? And then you were off to war and foreign lands and then London, never to return, we all thought. It was the past. I married and I had children of my own."

I stood still, uncertain what to do. The desire to hit him and keep hitting had not left me. Though the reasonable part of me agreed that it had been long ago, that it scarcely mattered any longer, the rest of me was quivering from this new and painful wound.

I walked away from him. It was the best thing, under the circumstances. I strode up the path toward the marshes, my walking stick pressing into the mud. Buckley did not follow me. The wise man went back to his pub and left me alone with my thoughts.

*** *** ***

I was never certain how long I wandered. The rain poured down, and my knee started to ache.

At least, I came across nothing gruesome—no severed hands, no bodies, no blood. Only me, the grasses, the rain, and sheep.

I found the shepherd under shelter of the bank that separated the salt marshes from the wet sands. He hunkered under a canvas tarp, taking nips from a flask while he kept one eye on his charges.

I sank to my heels, my game leg protesting, and he greeted me with a nod. "Now then, Captain."

I did not know the man, but I could not be surprised he knew who I was. Everyone in the area was aware of my return by now.

He offered me the flask but I declined, not because I did not want the gin or whatever was in it, but because the mouth of the flask was rust-stained and covered with sand.

"Are these Lord Southwick's sheep?" I asked. I did not much care, but I wanted to speak of anything to take my mind off my encounter with Buckley.

"Aye. And some from the villages. Parson's Point and Blakeney. We don't tell his lordship that we mix them together."

I watched the wet bundles of wool crop the marsh grasses, the aristocratic sheep unworried about being mixed with the common sheep. "How do you tell them apart?"

He shrugged. "Sheep are like people, Captain. They all have their little ways that make them different. I know which are which." He chuckled. "That and we mark them with a little dye."

His humor washed over me, unnoticed. "I suppose when you're out here all day long, you see more of the sheep than people."

"That I do." The shepherd grinned, showing broken teeth, and took another sip from his flask. "But I don't mind. Sheep know where they are and what's what, and they never mind it. It's people that fuss all the time."

"And hurt one another."

"Aye. Though the mamas can get protective of their babies."

"Do many people wander out here?" I asked. "Besides me, I mean."

"Not many. Saw you out here yesterday, with a horse."

"Yes." I rested my weight on my walking stick, my leg truly starting to hurt. "I'd lost it, and I found it grazing here. Did you happen to see it come out? Or a man with it?"

"Don't think so. But I move about, sometimes here, sometimes elsewhere. And this land looks flat, but it fools you. Little hills and ridges everywhere."

I'd noticed that. "He'd have been a large man, quite tall and broad. He might have had another man with him."

The shepherd rubbed his chin with the hand that held the flask. "Don't think so." He kept rubbing. "Did see a man, but not yesterday, and not with a horse. A few days ago. And he were alone. I think he were tall, though."

My moroseness fled. "Where?"

The shepherd pointed to his right, north along the ridgeline. "Up yonder. Walking away, heading westward. Not much out that way, but that's where he went. Didn't know who he were at this distance, and I never saw him again."

I stood up, my leg aching as I straightened it. I gazed down the ridge, shielding my eyes from the rain and the glare from the leaden sky.

"Thank you."

"If I see him again, should I tell him you're looking?"

I continued to study the direction he'd gone, the grasses bending under the wind. "No," I said. "No, do not mention it."

The shepherd touched his hand to his forehead in a mock salute. "Right you are, Captain. I'll keep your interest to meself. Can't speak for me sheep."

I looked down into his twinkling eyes and smiled with him. I was a native son; the man the shepherd had spotted, a stranger. He'd keep my secrets.

Now to find out whether the person he'd seen was Cooper, Cooper's killer, or someone else entirely.

Chapter Seventeen

I debated what to do. I walked along the ridge path a little way, but I soon found that the mud and pelting rain would defeat me.

I'd left my horse at the vicarage. I began my trudge back there, raising my hand to the shepherd as I passed. All I saw of him was the flash of lifted flask.

The rain became a gray curtain, obscuring the world. I bent my head to the wind, keeping my eyes on my feet. Pools of wet lined the path, which ran across a little rise of ground. If I stepped off the path, I would be knee-deep in boggy mud.

I knew that the path the shepherd had pointed to led to nothing. Or at least, twenty years ago, it had led to nothing. I had to remind myself I'd been away that long. Estate holders could have added outbuildings, and windmills continued to be erected. I hadn't walked that way in a long time.

And I would not today. I was thoroughly drenched by the time I reached the vicarage. Mrs. Landon, watching worriedly for me, wanted to fill me with hot coffee. I accepted a brief cup, but I needed to return to Easton's.

Before I departed, a carriage drew up and deposited Reaves at the front door. I recognized the carriage and the other man inside it. Grenville.

Reaves looked at me in surprise as the vicarage maid hurried forward to take his things. "Captain Lacey? What are you doing here?"

"I am equally surprised to see you," I said. "Has Lady Southwick ended her house party?"

"Pardon? No, some guests are remaining for a time. But it is Saturday, and when I enter the pulpit tomorrow, everyone will expect me to have something to say. I find this house quite conducive for composing sermons."

"Much quieter here," I agreed. And more restful. The vicarage was an old-fashioned cottage with flagstone passages and plain, polished wood that lined whitewashed walls. "What will be your theme, if I may ask?"

"I have not yet decided," he said. "I might work in the camel and the eye of the needle, in light of recent arrivals to our part of the world. Not meaning you, Captain."

No, I was hardly wealthy enough to worry about riches barring me from the kingdom of heaven. But if he meant Denis, I doubted Denis would care. Denis was not bothered by heaven and hell as far as I could discern. Nor would Denis likely attend the service. Easton's house was in a different parish anyway.

I could have pointed out the irony of a man who obviously loved the comforts of soft living lecturing on the sins of wealth, but I refrained. I wasn't certain Reaves would see my point.

I said good-bye to him and to Mrs. Landon and stepped back out into the rain.

Grenville's groom opened the carriage door for me, and Grenville called to me to get in. The groom would return my horse for me, he said.

I accepted. I'd had enough of the rain.

"You are exceedingly wet," Grenville said as my greatcoat spilled water onto the landau's floor.

The lanterns at our feet flickered as the groom shut the door. The welcome warmth of the coal boxes began to seep into my bones.

"I beg your pardon. I've been tramping about the marshes in the pouring rain. It is wet work."

Grenville drew his coat together under his chin. "Norfolk is lovelier than I thought it would be, but damp. Quite damp."

"Unlike London, which is only damp."

"You are in an interesting mood, Lacey."

"Exhaustion," I said, shutting my eyes. The carriage bumped hard over a hole in the road, and pain spiked in my cramped leg.

When I opened my eyes, Grenville was watching me. "Are you certain exhaustion explains everything? How goes the search?"

Grenville was canny. He'd learned the signs of my melancholia over the past year and a half, and he'd learned how to keep me from falling into it.

"Oddly," I said. I told him what the shepherd had said. "It is too foul to search today, but as soon as this lifts, I'll take a horse and go out there."

"With me," Grenville said. "Despite my performance as a soft-living dandy these past few days, I am a hardy sort."

"I know." I kept my tone light, still trying to banish the anguish of what Buckley had told me. "You've rowed on the Nile and across rivers in Canada, you've tramped across deserts and over the highest mountains."

Grenville shook his head. "Flippancy does not become you, Lacey."

"So Lady Breckenridge tells me." *Donata.* I'd sent her away, and I was happy I had, but at this moment, I longed for her warmth.

"Has something else happened?" Grenville asked me.

I debated what to tell him. I was still sifting through Buckley's confession and his revelation that my mother had carried his child, the miscarrying of which had led to her illness and death. Emotions chased through me—anger, shock, sadness, guilt. I could not fix upon one.

"Discovering things about one's own past is a jolt," I said.

Grenville nodded. "I know that well, my dear Lacey. I have told you of one or two of the shocks I've faced in my life, including discovering I had a grown daughter. You've found something out that has upset you. I understand. You may keep it private if you like."

"Thank you," I said.

"I have a healthy curiosity, but I will not pry into your darkest secrets." He held out a silver flask. "But you look like a man who needs sustenance."

His flask was free of rust and sand. I lifted it to my lips and gratefully downed the brandy inside.

I handed it back to him. "What troubles me has nothing to do with finding Cooper, or the paintings Easton hid, or Miss Quinn," I said.

"I did not think so. However, I *am* curious about what you've discovered regarding all three of those."

I was grateful to Grenville for bringing my mind back to the immediate problems. I told him what I'd learned since we'd spoken yesterday, and he listened without interrupting.

"So the hand was indeed Cooper's," Grenville said when I'd finished. "We must wonder — was it he the shepherd saw on the marsh? Or the murderer? And did the same man kill Mr. Ferguson?" He glanced out the window at the farmland we passed. "I must say, the idea of a nameless, faceless killer stalking about your marshes unnerves me."

"It unnerves me as well, and I know it unnerves Denis. I have been thinking that we are up against someone who wants Denis dead. One of his rivals. The woman who calls herself Lady Jane is cold enough and ruthless enough to send people after him."

"I would think that she'd send someone directly to the house to kill him," Grenville said. "Not pick off his servants in the wilderness one by one."

"But Denis guards himself carefully. He knows how many enemies he has. The way to reach him is to remove his guards, even one at a time. Thin the ranks. Or else, be hired on into the heart of his household. The killer might be residing with him even now."

"And you are taking me to sleep there. Thank you very much." Grenville took another pull from his flask. "I'd think that Denis would be careful enough to screen any who works for him. An assassin infiltrating his household takes a great risk. They'd not survive the mission."

"I wonder if Ferguson, the newest member, was sent to kill him," I mused. "Perhaps Cooper found out, fought him, and killed him."

"And then Cooper vanished. Perhaps. But why not rush back to Denis and proudly proclaim his deed? I have the feeling that the death of Ferguson and the disappearance of Cooper are unconnected."

I was not so certain. I'd learned to keep my mind open to possibilities, because in the past I'd gone wrong by fixing on a solution too soon. Ferguson, a big man and an experienced fighter, hadn't gone down easily.

I told Grenville about interviewing Denis's men and their thoughts about Ferguson and Cooper. We agreed that any of them might have killed Ferguson for their own reasons. We also agreed that Denis employed an interesting lot.

Grenville eyed Easton's square brick house uneasily as the carriage pulled to a halt in front of it. "Another adventure," he said. "I pray I do not regret it."

*** *** ***

Denis, of course, wanted me to report to him immediately, and I found myself in his study once more, relating the events of the day. He listened as attentively as Grenville had, but with less animation in his eyes.

When I put forth my idea that one of his rivals was trying to kill him, either by taking out his bodyguards one by one or infiltrating his household, Denis shrugged.

"That is always a possibility, one against which I take constant precaution. Ferguson was not an assassin. I investigate people thoroughly before they are allowed anywhere near me."

I leaned on my walking stick, neither of us having bothered to sit down. "Should I be flattered that you allow me near you?"

"Not at all. Notice that I have you watched at all times."

I did. Only recently had he begun speaking with me alone, and even then, I knew that one of his bodyguards had been within shouting distance.

"About this mysterious man walking about the marsh," Denis said. "I take it you will explore that?"

"Tomorrow, after chapel. Hopefully the rain will have lessened. I'll go on horseback and comb the area."

Denis's brows lifted. "After chapel?"

"I want to attend the morning service in Parson's Point. The Laceys have a pew there." For some reason, I was curious to hear what Reaves had to say. "Perhaps you would like to attend with me?"

Denis's eyes flickered. I'd surprised him. He studied me sharply, wondering what I meant by it, then he surprised me. "Of course," he said.

*** *** ***

In spite of Grenville's uneasiness, we spent an uneventful night. When I woke the next day, Sunday, the sound of bells drifted on the wind, filling the morning. The rain had stopped and the air was cold and crisp with autumn.

Denis provided his carriage for the ride to Parson's Point. Because he went nowhere without at least one bodyguard—today deciding to bring three, one riding inside—the carriage was crowded.

We reached the church at Parson's Point a few minutes before the service was to begin. Grenville studied the unadorned, twelfth-century church with an approving eye. "Quite a good example of Romanesque architecture," he said as we went in.

The church was rather full this morning, perhaps because the weather was good, or perhaps because of curiosity about whether I would attend. The church, large for the community, was mostly full.

Heads turned and people stared as, for the first time in many years, a Lacey opened the small wooden door of the pew at the front of the church and stepped inside. Grenville and Denis sat down with me, and Denis's bodyguards squeezed into the end of a pew behind us.

The service of morning prayer progressed, the familiar words read in Reaves' rather pompous voice. I found the murmured responses of the congregation somehow soothing. The church had no organ, and anything we sang was led by Mrs. Landon with a pitch pipe.

Denis read the responses with the rest of us, his voice rich and strong even through the confession of sins. *We have erred and strayed from thy ways like lost sheep; We have followed too much the devices and desires of our own hearts; We have offended against thy holy laws* . . . His bodyguards behind us said the same, and got through the Apostle's Creed and Lord's Prayer without stumbling.

Reaves mounted the stairs to the pulpit to read the lessons for the day then remained there for the sermon. He did indeed speak about the follies of wealth.

"And then Jesus said, *It is easier for a camel to go through the eye of a needle than for a rich man to enter the kingdom of God.*"

Grenville's lips twitched once. Denis remained smooth-faced. Most of the congregation did too, as they listened to Reaves, a man who loved the finer things in life, drone on about the evils of wealth.

People glanced at me as Reaves started to go on a bit, but they were not connecting me with the sermon. The Laceys had forsaken their wealth long ago, in any case. The villagers and farmers were simply curious about me, about why I'd returned and whether I intended to stay.

Buckley sat in a pew on the left side of the church and studiously did *not* look at me. Next to him was his plump wife and his son Robert, who had an equally plump wife and a sturdy-looking toddler. A respectable country family.

Robert was staring at the altar, his lips parted slightly. I looked in the direction of his gaze and saw that Reaves—or more likely, Mrs. Landon—had restored the silver candlesticks, well polished, to the front of the church.

The platen and cup were nowhere in sight, probably shut away in the sacristy. Parson's Point was decidedly low church, and communion was offered only at Christmas, Easter, and on a person's deathbed. Even then, most of the villagers refused it.

Reaves finished at last, and another village man passed around the offering plate. I put in my dutiful coins, and Grenville and Denis dropped in an extravagant five gold guineas each.

Mrs. Landon's eyes widened when she saw what they'd given. No doubt she'd be badgering me to make certain Mr. Denis and Mr. Grenville attended often.

After the service, we filed out and shook hands with Reaves, who waited at the door. I broke from Grenville, and stopped Robert Buckley, who was about to walk to the village for his Sunday dinner with his father and mother.

I shook Robert's hand and greeted his wife and child. Seeing I wanted to talk, he told his wife to take their son and go on with his parents.

"I'm afraid I've found nothing for you, Captain," Robert said. "No sign of the man."

I hadn't thought he would. "I want to speak to you of another matter," I said. "It's about my father."

Robert looked surprised. "Oh, aye?"

"I understand that you looked after him before he died."

Robert shrugged. "Not so much looked after as took him dinner that Dad sent."

"Even so, it was kind of you and your father to look out for him. I imagine he had no one else?"

"There was Mrs. Quinn, on occasion."

"*Mrs.* Quinn? The vicar's wife?"

"Aye. She went with me to see him sometimes. Plumped his pillows and the like. He'd talk to her."

The Mrs. Quinn I had known had been a bit of a valetudinarian, finding any excuse to stay home and not go about in bad weather. Mrs. Landon had taken over many of the duties of a vicar's wife, while Mrs. Quinn served tea in china as delicate as she was and smiled kindly on her husband's flock. As fragile as she appeared to be, she'd outlived her robust husband.

"Do you remember when Miss Quinn eloped?"

Robert's face creased with a smile. "That I do. I was potty in love with Miss Quinn. I was ten years old and thought she was an angel."

"But she ran away with someone else."

His grin became a chuckle. "And was I jealous? A bit, I suppose. I had dreams of her waiting for me to grow up, but at heart, I was a practical lad. She was a gentleman's daughter, I was a publican's son, and I knew she'd go off with the flash bloke. And she did."

"Did you help her go off with him?"

Robert lost his smile. "What are you getting around to, Captain?"

"I know she was to meet Mr. Braxton in the copse a little way from my house the night she went. I found a dress that was likely hers in my mother's sitting room. The house was little used, I understand, once my father shut himself up in his sickbed in the last years, the servants gone. You went up there most days, from what I hear. Did you help Miss Quinn meet her lover that night?"

Robert started to put a hand on my shoulder then seemed to recall that he was below me in social standing. "A bit of advice, Captain," he said. "The less you ask about Miss Quinn, the better. Her eloping is still a sore point around here. Mrs. Quinn hasn't gotten over the heartbreak of it, and young Mr. Quinn is still angry."

"I assure you, I have no wish to make the Quinns unhappy," I said. "But I want to know what happened in my house."

Robert glanced behind me, at the villagers still filing away, at Grenville and Denis now entering Denis's carriage. "They'll be waiting for you," he said.

"Tell me."

Robert heaved a resigned sigh. "All right—aye, they used me as a go-between. I'd have done anything for Miss Quinn, I told you. The night they were to have gone, Miss Quinn and I went to your house, as though she were helping me take dinner to your dad. I'd hidden a bundle of clothes for her there. She changed out in your mum's rooms, and then I walked with her to the copse. It was dark by then, and I didn't want her going alone. She meets Mr. Braxton, and that's the end of it."

"What about the candlesticks?"

Robert blinked. "The what?"

"The silver candlesticks and the chalice stolen from the church. The ones you were gaping at this morning. They were stolen at about the same time."

"She never stole them," Robert said hastily. "Everyone thinks Miss Quinn took them away with her, but there they are in the church—which proves she don't have them."

But *someone* had stuffed them up the chimney at the Lacey house. "You seemed quite surprised to see them this morning."

"Well, 'course I was. I didn't know they'd been found."

"A shock," I said in a mild voice.

He nodded, his grin trying to return. "Aye." He stuck out his hand. "They'll be holding my dinner, Captain, and mum gets right cross when anyone's late. My invitation to see my farm still stands, sir. We're a bit pressed just now, but come after dark and my wife will serve you a fine supper."

He looked proud of her, a woman he seemed fond of. The fantasy of the angelic Miss Quinn falling in love with him had been left in the past.

I shook Robert's hand, assured him I would visit, and let him rush after his family to the safety of the village pub. Closed today, as it was Sunday, but not to the Buckleys.

*** *** ***

Sunday dinner at Easton House meant Grenville and me sitting in the dining room, eating rather fine food served by Denis's hulking men. Denis never had female servants in his house.

Afterward, horses were saddled for me and Grenville, and we rode northward to the marshes to follow the path the shepherd had pointed out to me the day before.

Chapter Eighteen

Matthias and Bartholomew accompanied us, but on foot. Both had balked at riding horses — a gentleman's gentleman didn't ride with his master, Bartholomew argued. The brothers walked, but a five-mile hike across marshland to them was little more than an after-dinner stroll.

I found the spot where I'd met the shepherd. I saw sheep in the distance, but the shepherd had moved to another resting place.

From horseback, atop the ridge path, we had a fine view of the sea, which lay far out on the edge of the sands. The wind had pushed back the clouds, letting autumn blue sky arch overhead. The tall grasses bent, marshes stretching ahead and behind us. Lovely for a Sunday afternoon hack, but I was too impatient to enjoy it.

The path led into a hollow and the sea was lost to sight. Somewhere to the left of us was the coast road that went to Stifkey and on to Wells. Our way led straight through marshes that had yet to be drained, on a path that would be buried during high water. The tide was well out at the moment, but this path would be impassible at high tide.

"There," Grenville said.

He'd brought a small spyglass, which he'd been lifting to his eye from time to time. He stopped his horse now, pointed, and held the spyglass to me.

I peered through it, roving it around until I found what he'd seen. A windmill, standing alone on a headland. I nodded as I handed the glass back to him. It was worth investigating.

Grenville volunteered to ride back and tell Bartholomew and Matthias where we were going, while I went on. Generous of him, because I knew his curiosity was as whetted as mine.

Most windmills stood near villages, on streams that also served the village. This windmill stood by itself, probably at the end of a creek or fresh, with a house next to it. It was a large windmill, very modern, with glass windows, which meant the windmill keeper had probably set up lodgings inside it. Perhaps the house standing beside it belonged to a miller who used the windmill to grind grain.

As I drew closer, I saw, to my frustration that our path would not take us there. The windmill lay on the other side of a fairly wide river, and only by riding back to the coast road and finding a bridge could we cross, unless we had a boat. A scan along this side of the water showed me no handy rowboats, though I saw two tied up on the far bank.

I had no way of knowing how deep was the stream. It looked deep—the water was dark, and small eddies spoke of rocks a long way below the surface.

I put my hands around my mouth and called out to whoever might be in the house or windmill. The house looked abandoned, now that I was closer to it.

No one answered my call. Through Grenville's spyglass, I saw that the house had lost windows and shutters. Winters had been hard and harvests light of late—perhaps the miller had given up and moved on.

The windmill's windows, however, were whole and sound, the door and roof solid. The arms of the windmill cranked around, the pumps working.

I was still on the bank when Grenville returned on his horse, with Bartholomew and Matthias jogging behind him. I hadn't been able to get a rise out of the windmill keeper. Either he was hard of hearing, or he didn't like visitors.

"I could swim it," Matthias said, eyeing the water. "Grab one of the boats for you."

"You'd catch your death," Grenville said. "This wind is fierce, and the water will be cold. I don't have time to nurse you back to health."

Matthias shrugged, not ashamed of his idea.

"Nothing for it," I said. "We find a bridge. Keep an eye out, though, in case the keeper tries to leg it. A man who so guards his privacy will be worth speaking to."

*** *** ***

We had to ride west beyond Wells until we found a bridge across the stream and another path that led to the windmill. A helpful farmer pointed the way—

it was a fairly new windmill, he said, built about ten years ago. A miller tried to have a go grinding grain with it, but gave up and moved on. The windmill keeper, a man called Waller, was still up there. A taciturn man, but not a bad sort.

Grenville thanked him, sweetening the thanks with coin, and we rode on. The path petered out before we reached the windmill, but we were able to cut across a dry point in the marsh to the windmill's front door. The view from here was nothing but sky, grasses, and wet sands. When the tide was in, this place would be an island.

The windmill keeper wouldn't open his door, though I saw movement in an upper window. The miller's house next to it, two stories and made of brick and flint, had indeed been abandoned. I found a lone cow in the yard behind it, chewing hay and looking utterly uninterested in us.

I knocked again on the door, to no avail, so I asked Matthias and Bartholomew to break it open.

The keeper came barreling down the steps inside as the brothers slammed into the door. We heard locks scrape back, and then the door was flung open before the two could back away for another strike.

"Here," the keeper said in indignation. "What the devil be ye doing?"

His northern Norfolk dialect was decidedly pronounced, and Grenville and the town-bred brothers looked blank. I understood him but answered without bothering with the dialect.

"We're looking for a gentleman," I said. "He would have come here three, maybe four days ago. Possibly hurt."

"Don't have time of day for anyone." The man said, switching to common English, not to be polite, but so he could tell us we were bothering him. "Pumps don't keep themselves working."

"Then you won't mind if we have a look."

The windmill keeper growled. "I do mind. Who be you?"

"Captain Gabriel Lacey," I said, giving him a truncated version of a military bow. "From Parson's Point."

The man squinted up at me. "Lacey? Son of Mr. Roderick?"

No surprise that he had heard the name. "I have that distinction."

"You should have said right away. A fine man he was, old Mr. Lacey."

I hid my surprise. To me, the man had been a martinet and a bully. I'd been too young to notice what others had thought of him.

The keeper opened the door hospitably wide, and we squeezed into the foyer. A ladder-stair, much like the one in Easton's abandoned windmill, led upward, but this one was solid and fairly new. I introduced Grenville and the brothers, and the man told us he was Jonathan Waller. Born and bred in Stifkey, family going back generations.

"I'm looking for a man," I repeated, once we'd gotten the niceties out of the way. "He would have come this way in the last day or so."

"I'd have been here."

"And was he?"

Waller shook his head, pressing his lips together. "Do you see anybody here?"

"Perhaps I could . . ." I gestured to the ladder with my walking stick.

Mr. Waller, to my surprise, stepped out of the way. Bartholomew and Matthias seemed to make him nervous, so I told them to look through the miller's house next door while Grenville and I searched here.

The windmill was five stories high, the lower floors wider than the upper as the windmill tapered to its smooth roof. The huge paddles swung slowly past the windows, which looked out to the sea on one side, to green land and huddled villages on the other.

Grenville followed Mr. Waller into his living quarters, while I explored the mill rooms. I found a room in which gears would turn the huge wheels, but the millstones leaned against the walls, grain no longer being trundled here for grinding.

Back on the ground floor, I found a trapdoor. Pulling this open, I saw that it led down to a damp space beneath the windmill, and there I found the blood.

Not the huge quantity I'd seen on the marsh, but definite dribbles of it under the light of the lantern I'd borrowed from the keeper's kitchen. Enough blood to make me climb out and shout for Waller.

He came down, with Grenville, and I pointed at the blood, holding my lantern nearly on top of it. Waller at first looked blank then guilty.

"He begged me to keep quiet. Said someone was trying to find him, and to kill him." Waller shot me a frightened look. "Did he mean you?"

"No, I am a trying to help him." I flashed the light about, but the room was so dark, it seemed to drink in the lantern's flame. "You patched him up? Down here?"

Waller nodded. "He didn't want to risk being seen in a window. I told him we were a long way from God himself, but he insisted. Strong chap, to lose a hand like that and not be half dead."

"He rested here, how long?"

"A night and a day, then he was gone. He paid me good coin to say nothing, so nothing I said."

Waller's expression told me he expected more good coin from us for the information. Grenville, used to such things, already had a few crowns jingling in his hand.

"We agree that silence is best," he said, pressing them to Waller's palm. "We're the man's friends and are trying to help him. If you see him again, tell him to stay put. Send word to Lacey's house if you can."

Waller did not argue. "Are you going to be living there now?" he asked me. "Have a nephew who could help out with the grounds."

I was growing used to this refrain, but it stood to reason. The country people would consider it my duty to give them employment, and I agreed with them.

"Send him 'round," I said. "I am certain he will have plenty to do. To return to this man you patched up, where did he go after he left you?"

"Don't know, and that's the truth. He walked out into the storm and disappeared. He must have gone south, because he didn't take none of my boats. Never saw him again."

His words rang with sincerity. I imagined that Waller had been happy to see the alarming man vanish.

"You are certain he said that someone wanted to kill him?" I asked.

"He looked that frightened," Waller said. "Don't know who could make a big man like that so scared, but I don't want to meet such a one."

Grenville fed Waller another crown, and we took our leave. Bartholomew and Matthias joined us after coming out of the miller's house.

"Nothing there," Bartholomew said. "Plenty of birds' nests and animal tracks, but no Cooper, dead or alive."

"What now, Lacey?" Grenville asked as he let Matthias boost him onto his horse. "We search south? If Cooper worried about someone trying to kill him, would he not seek Denis's protection? Or at least get word to him?"

"I don't know," I said, not liking what I was thinking. "But I intend to ask Mr. Denis."

*** *** ***

We rode back to Wells, and from there turned south, asking everyone we saw along the way about Cooper. No one had seen any man they didn't know, injured or otherwise, in the last few days.

I rose in my stirrups as the day started to darken. To the north was a line of gray that marked the marshes, to the east, west, and south, green farmland, much of it enclosed now.

Many of the commons and heaths I remembered from boyhood had vanished. Enclosures beggared people as much as bad harvests did, because the poorer tenant farmers and villagers could no longer run their sheep on the commons or raise food on part of it. Large landholders were squeezing out the small, the way of the world.

I sank to my saddle in frustration. Cooper could be anywhere. He might have taken a mail coach to London or north to Lincolnshire or south to Suffolk. Or he could have paid a fisherman to take him to Amsterdam in Easton's wake. Combing the countryside was producing nothing.

"At least we have discovered that he was alive a few days ago," Grenville said, moving his horse beside mine. "If he could walk away after losing his entire hand, then he is indeed strong. He'll turn up somewhere. He's probably lying low, nursing himself back to health."

If he did not die of fever first. The wounds from amputations had to be burned, or the remainder of the limb—indeed, the rest of the body—could fester. Men died even when it seemed they'd recovered from the injury.

I recalled the remains of the campfire I'd seen near the blood. Cooper could have built that fire and plunged the stump of his arm into it once he'd cut off the badly injured hand. If so, Cooper had vast strength of will and the bravery of a lion.

But he might have done it. Denis had known, even as a child, that throwing in his lot with Cooper was the way to survival. Denis was no fool.

"We should return to Easton's," I said. What I would do there, I kept to myself.

Grenville adjusted his hat and pulled his greatcoat closer against the wind. "I'm afraid I'll be traveling back to London in the morning, Lacey. I've had a letter from Marianne."

His tone was so somber that I looked at him quickly. "Bad news?"

"No, nothing like that. She has reached London again and says she wishes to consult with me. I can only imagine what that means."

With Marianne Simmons, one never knew. Her urgent need might mean life or death or a shortage of the snuff she liked so much.

"I am certain Denis will be pleased to have me to himself," I said.

"Not if you come with me. Not that I wish harm to come to Mr. Cooper, but now that we know he's alive, surely Denis has better resources to send after him than you. Evidence of Cooper at the windmill should be enough to point him in the right direction. Let us go to London and be finished with Denis and his band of thieves."

I wanted to agree. I was ready to meet up with Lady Breckenridge and move on to planning what we'd do in our married life. How much more satisfying to discuss renovations to my old house from the comfort of her warm sitting room—even better, from the comfort of her bedchamber.

Or perhaps we should not return to Norfolk at all. I could try to find a way to break the entail and sell the house, if even for pittance. I would marry Donata and bury myself at the Breckenridge estate until her son grew up and tossed us into the dower house. Viscount Breckenridge's lands were in Hampshire, a beautiful place in a serene valley. Donata would always want her Season in London, but I could be the stodgy husband who remained in the country all year, seeing to the farms and fishing. I knew that Donata had no such life in mind for us, but it was a pleasant fantasy.

"I'm afraid I must stay a little longer," I said with reluctance. "There is more to Cooper's disappearance than meets the eye, and I have a few other things to resolve."

"The missing vicar's daughter?" Grenville asked. "I can be as suspicious as you at times, Lacey, but all evidence points to the fact that she eloped. And now the publican's son has confirmed he helped her run away."

"No, I do not mean Miss Quinn."

Grenville eyed me in curiosity, but I could not answer him. I had personal conflicts to resolve — between myself and Buckley, between myself and Terrance Quinn, between myself and my mother's revelations.

"Go to London," I said. "Give Marianne my best wishes."

Grenville shot me a dark look, but we spoke no more about it.

*** *** ***

Denis had shut himself away with other business, I was informed when I returned. I told the lackey who'd come out to meet me to report that I'd found trace of Cooper.

I washed and refreshed myself in my chamber, and Bartholomew brought me a glass of hock and a small, cold supper. After that, Denis sent for me.

Again he dismissed the man who stood guard and spoke with me alone in the study.

"The windmill keeper treated Cooper's injury," Denis said when I'd finished my tale. "And then Cooper vanished? You believed this?"

"I see no reason for Waller to lie about it. By all evidence he'd been happy to see the back of Cooper."

Denis's eyes went sharp. "I wager this Waller knows more than what he told you. Why did you not question him more closely?"

"I questioned him thoroughly, I assure you. Grenville's lavishness with coin loosened Waller's tongue."

"I disagree." Denis's voice was calm, but I heard rage behind it. "He told you what you wanted to hear. He would have told you nothing at all if you'd not seen the blood. Then you prompted him into the tale of patching up a man with a missing hand, and he agreed to it."

"If you believe him hiding Cooper, we searched. Cooper wasn't there."

"At first light, you will show me the way there, and *I* will search. And question the man. He will open up to me far quicker, no need for Grenville's coin."

"No," I said.

Denis's eyes widened, his anger no longer hidden. "What did you say?"

"I am finished with this search," I said. "Finished running about the countryside in all weather on your errands, while you lie to me. I have some private business to conclude, and then I will be returning to London."

"No, you will not."

"I say I will. Find Cooper on your own. Waller told me that Cooper was in fear for his life. I can imagine only one man Cooper would fear." I took a firmer grim on my walking stick. "That man is you. I refuse to hunt Cooper down and hand him over to you so that you can kill him."

Chapter Nineteen

The room went quiet, Denis facing me in the middle of it. I heard his men rumbling to each other as they shut down the house for the night, and the wind, cold and straight, rattling the windows and moaning under the eaves. Denis and I were nearly of a height, I half an inch taller. His dark blue eyes, staring straight into mine, held vast and cold fury.

"I told you why I needed to find Cooper," he said in a voice that could have chilled hell itself. "And what I would do if you did not assist me."

"And I grow weary of your threats. I will make one of my own. If you lay a finger on any of my friends or their families, I will kill you. I might have to wait a long time before I can find a way, but I will do it. I will come after you and never stop."

His eyes did not move, did not even flicker. "You have tried my patience many a time, Captain, and I have ever looked the other way. Do not imagine I have done so because I am kind. I've done it because I saw that your intelligence and your bloody stubbornness could be useful to me. I have aided you so that I would make sure you aided me in return. I have spent considerable time and resources on you. You owe me this favor, and you will do it."

"Not when you lie to me." I clenched my hand around my walking stick, feeling the sword loosen inside it. "If you want to speak of a man telling me what I wish to hear . . . Your tale of Cooper rescuing you from the streets was calculated to invoke my sympathy. It was very touching."

"I told you no lies. Cooper did rescue me, I am grateful to him, and we did form a bond of friendship. Enough that I am willing to risk being alone in a room with you in order to persuade you to help me find him."

"If Cooper believed that someone was trying to kill him, he would seek you, knowing that you could protect him better than anyone else," I said. "Therefore, I must ask myself why would he run in the opposite direction, unless you were the person who wanted to kill him."

"I do not *know!*"

Denis's voice rose into a roar, his façade cracked at last.

The door swung open, and the man who'd been standing guard looked in worriedly. "Do you need me, sir?"

Denis didn't bother to look at him. "No."

The man nodded but shot me a warning look as he withdrew.

After the door closed, I watched as, moment by moment, Denis reigned in his rage.

"I have not lied about Cooper," he said, when he'd regained control. "I admit that, in the past, I have not always told you the whole of a matter, but in this instance, I have given you everything. Cooper has protected me since I was a lad. If he met someone he thought would be a danger to me, he would lead the man on a merry chase through the marshes and pay the windmill keeper to stay quiet."

"Even while he's badly injured? Knowing that any moment could bring fever and death?"

Denis nodded. "He has defended me in similar fashion before, leading away danger and not returning until said danger was dispatched. I wish to find him before he dies because of it."

"You mean that he is being self-sacrificing rather than acting from fear?" I was not certain I believed that either.

"Cooper does not know the meaning of fear. He fears nothing, and that sometimes leads him into trouble." Denis stopped, the near-smile he sometimes employed twitching his lips. "He is much like you in that regard."

For some reason, I could not feel amused. And I had seen Cooper fearful before—when he anticipated the wrath of Denis.

"I will take you to the windmill," I said. "But you will not bludgeon the keeper into telling you what you want to know."

"Sometimes pain, or fear of it, loosens the tongue," Denis said.

"In such case, your victim will tell you anything to make you stop."

He gave me a nod. "I agree that there are better ways to bargain than with torture."

The argument hovered there, waiting for one of us to end it. "First light," I said. "If that's when we leave, I'll to bed."

"You do that, Captain," Denis said, forever needing to have the last word. As usual, he did not say good night.

*** *** ***

At first light the next morning, I rode out with Denis and one of his tame pugilists — three horsemen in the dawn.

The day was mostly clear, with a few thin, high clouds overhead. Last night's wind had died off, making for a pleasant Monday morning's ride.

Grenville had been up when we left, preparing for his journey back to London. He'd advised me to take care when we said good-bye. I agreed with him.

None of us spoke as we made our way north, taking the road that skirted Blakeney, on through Parson's Point and to Stifkey and Wells. We turned north after that, following the path that went nowhere but the windmill.

The windmill stuck up out of the salt grasses like a lone tree in the middle of a plain. Our horses headed for it steadily, Denis neither pushing too fast nor lingering. I'd never seen Denis use any transport but his lavish carriage, but he was proving to be a competent horseman. He'd not grown up in the saddle, as I had, but somewhere he'd learned good horsemanship.

The tide had turned in the night, and now the sea crept for the marshes slowly but steadily. We needed to finish our business quickly, or the water would cut us off.

We left our horses in the yard with the cow and mounted the few steps to the windmill's door. Denis tilted back his head to look up at the windmill, studying it, assessing it.

I wondered if his power came from his ability to learn—to look over something and decide right away whether he could use it, and then discover everything he could about it. People or windmills or horsemanship would be all the same to him.

The pugilist thumped on the door but Waller did not answer. When five minutes had passed, Denis signaled his man to break open the door.

The pugilist—Morgan by name—did nothing so dramatic as crash it down. He brought out a small iron bar and hammer, wedged the bar against the door handle, and brought the hammer down on the bar. The door handle broke away, and Morgan widened the hole it left until he could get his hand inside and unbolt the door. A housebreaking technique, one that did not make much noise.

We went inside through the small foyer and to Waller's living quarters. Food sat on the table, half eaten, the chair pushed back in haste. Waller had seen us coming.

Denis signaled to Morgan, who silently left the room and ascended the ladder to check above. I showed Denis the trapdoor which led to the small room beneath where I'd found the blood, and he insisted that we both descend to it.

I flashed my lantern around the low-ceilinged room, and Denis looked into every damp corner. He even thumped the floor in places, looking for more trapdoors. But the stone floor was solid. Anything dug below this would hit water.

We went back up the ladder and all the way to the top of the windmill in Morgan's wake. We passed the gear room, where the great wheel turned the gears that ran the pumps.

The keeper's bedchamber had three large windows, through which I scanned the surrounding land. The villages were small in the distance, nothing else out here but bending marsh grass and the wide gray sea, which was drawing ever closer.

Nowhere did I see a man, running or otherwise — not Waller, not Cooper.

"Check the house," Denis said to Morgan, pointing out the window at the ruined miller's cottage.

"The tide's almost here," I said. "We'll be cut off if we linger."

"Then we'll be cut off." Denis's voice was hard. "The keeper has plenty of provisions, and he obviously keeps his cow fed. We wait."

We went back to the kitchen while Denis's pugilist left the windmill and made his way to the miller's house. I found a pot of coffee, still warm, and poured liquid into a cracked mug. I took a sip and made a face. Still, I continued to drink, as it was better than no coffee at all.

Denis showed no interest in coffee. He moved to the window and watched Morgan disappear through the yard with the cow and into the miller's house.

I sat down at the table to ease my leg. "I know you long to say *I told you so*. If the keeper had nothing to hide, he wouldn't have fled when he saw us. I admit I should have been harder on him."

Denis didn't answer and didn't look at me.

The keeper had an old clock on the dresser where I'd found the mug, and the minutes ticked by. I heard the rush of the tide as it crept toward the house. Denis might not mind being cut off from the world, but I did not much fancy being alone out here with James Denis and a man who killed for him.

I put down the coffee and got to my feet. "Stay if you like, but I do not wish to wait the rest of the day for the tide to recede."

Denis looked at me at last, his expression unreadable. "Go, then."

I made myself walk out of the windmill without looking back. I knew in my heart that if I left the windmill keeper there with them, I might well be handing Waller a death sentence. Denis would not stop until he wrung from the man all he knew.

On the other hand, I did not believe Waller was still here. He knew the ways of the marshes better than we did and how to flee without being seen. He more than likely had run when he'd seen us coming.

I walked to the yard and to my horse. The cow moved aside for me, not really caring who came and went as long as her hay bin was full. We hadn't unsaddled the horses, though Denis's man had fitted them with halters so they could feed without restriction.

I pulled the bridle onto my horse and started to lead him from the yard. I knew that if I looked back up at the window of the windmill, I'd see Denis's slender and upright form framed in it. But I did not look back.

I'd have to search for a mounting block, but the ruined bits strewn about the place would let me find a good one. As I looked for the best candidate, I heard a soft noise.

The sound had come from the miller's house — not the cry of the keeper, caught, but a sort of low grunt. The cow continued to eat, but the horses lifted heads and turned ears, alert for danger.

I looped my horse's reins around a post and moved quietly out of the yard. The doorway to the miller's house stood open, an entrance into darkness. I heard nothing more from within, but I hefted my walking stick and quietly went inside.

I stepped immediately to the right of the doorway, to keep from being silhouetted against the bright light. I waited, making myself count to thirty, until my eyes adjusted to the gloom.

The miller's house was a two-story cottage, with two rooms opening off a center hall, one on either side. From what I could see, another room ran across the entire back of the house, its doorway dimly lit by windows beyond. The staircase was still intact, but the railing was broken, and spindles of carved wood littered the floor.

The place had been stripped of furniture, even of its doors. This house was much older than the windmill, probably having stood here for half a century. Why someone had built a cottage on this empty headland, I could not know. Obviously the windmill, when it had come, had brought no revenue as a grain mill, and so the house had been abandoned. The keeper lived cozily enough inside the windmill — likely there was no need to pay for the upkeep of the larger house.

I waited for a long time in the dark hall, but the noise did not repeat itself. I wondered whether Denis would rush down here to investigate why I'd gone inside, walking stick ready, but I doubted it. He was very good at letting others take care of problems for him.

I heard another sound, but this was a muted clatter, as though someone had tripped over a loose board. I moved quietly down the hall, the wind coming through the open windows and doors stirring dust.

I stepped into the room at the back of the house, again moving sideways as soon as I'd cleared the entrance.

I surprised the man in the middle of the room. He turned suddenly, holding a cudgel—one of the staircase spindles, thick and heavy. He balanced that menacingly in one hand, while his other arm ended in nothing but a blank stub.

"Cooper," I said in relief. "Damn it, man, we've been searching high and low for you. Are you all right?"

Cooper lowered his cudgel. "Captain. Is James with you? I thought I saw him ride up."

James. I started to answer then decided better of it. Where was Denis's other man, Morgan? And Waller, the keeper?

I heard a step behind me. Something was very wrong here, but I did not have time to stop and decide what.

I swung around, bringing up my walking stick, to find the terrified Waller standing in the doorway, blood all over his face. At the same time, I felt air move behind me.

I stepped sideways as I turned, letting fighting instinct take over. I brought up my walking stick and met the wood of Cooper's cudgel.

Before I could register surprise that Cooper was attacking me, I had to fight for my life. He brought the makeshift cudgel down with precision, gouging my shoulder as I swerved out of the way. The weapon whooshed past my ear, and I came up under Cooper's reach.

Fighting this close made my walking stick useless. I dropped it to drive a fist to Cooper's jaw.

His head snapped back with the blow, and I followed that with a jab to the throat. I'd learned the rules of boxing in Gentleman Jackson's rooms in Bond Street, but I'd learned survival on the battlefield. This fight was for survival.

Cooper had learned *his* fighting on the streets of London. He kicked at my bad leg, following that with a blow to my head as my knee buckled. I blocked the strike and at the same time I punched him in the gut. Cooper doubled over, but he was up again faster than I'd thought he could recover, and he kicked my leg again.

I grabbed for my walking stick as I went down, rolling on the board floor and trying to ignore the pain. I yanked the sword out of the stick and got onto my back, the point upward.

Cooper was coming at me, still hefting the cudgel. He tried to bash the sword with the wood, but I swung the blade out of its way. That meant that the wood came down on my arm, but I also managed to jab the sword's point into Cooper's thigh.

He grunted and jerked back. Blood oozed onto his dun-colored breeches, but not much of it. I hadn't cut deeply.

We kept fighting in the dim light, him swinging his cudgel and kicking at me, me thrusting the sword up at him and scrambling out of his reach. I got to my knees, but I'd need something to help me to my feet. We were in the middle of the room and the walls were too far away.

"Waller!" I yelled. "Get help!"

I heard no answer and no running feet. Waller could be dead or halfway down the path to the village. I did hear the rush of rising water. The tide.

Cooper kicked at my bad knee again, and this time I managed to catch his boot and shove him backward. He lost his balance but didn't fall, but the time it took him to recover allowed me the chance to push against the floor and get my feet under me.

My gloves had ripped, and sweat and grime dripped into my eyes. My breath came fast as I went at Cooper again. He and I were about the same age, but he was a few stone heavier, and he was strong, despite his missing hand.

He'd been holed up here, recovering, I realized. When we'd arrived yesterday to search, he'd hidden from Matthias and Bartholomew, somehow eluding them. Cooper would have been wise enough to hide signs of habitation, and I'd made plenty of noise shouting for the keeper from the other side of the river. He'd have been warned and had time.

His missing hand off-balanced him, but Cooper compensated well. Any time I tried to hit the stub of his arm, to give him a taste of what he was giving me, he manage to evade the blow. He was good.

"I didn't come here to kill you," I yelled at him. "If you think Denis did, I won't let him."

Cooper did not reply and kept trying to hit me. I did not know if he meant to kill me or simply beat me to a pulp, but either way I intended not to let him.

I went down again, facedown this time, while Cooper agilely came after me. My hand landed on a loose floorboard, and I dug my fingers under it, planning to yank it up and beat him with it.

I remained on my stomach, stunned, because what I saw under the floorboard was canvas. Painter's canvas, old and soft, with gloriously bright colors from two hundred years ago peeking around one edge.

Chapter Twenty

The roll of canvas was thick, paintings around paintings. Under the roll lay small, perfectly painted pictures, gleaming with gold leaf, from even longer ago.

As I stared at them in shock, Cooper grabbed me around the neck with his large hand. I didn't have time to shout accusations at him before he had me up and thrown against the wall.

As the breath went out of me, I saw now what the shadows had not allowed me to see, Denis's bodyguard, Morgan, facedown in a corner, blood all over his head. Dead or alive, I could not tell.

Cooper's fist caught me full in the face. My head rocked back against the stone wall. Cooper put his boot heel into my bad knee, and I fell again. I put my hands over my head, but Cooper beat me thoroughly with the stout wood.

He'd have beaten me to death if the roar of a pistol hadn't filled the air. Cooper jerked to the side at the last instant and the bullet clinked to the wall. But the shot caught him on the fleshy part of his bad arm, and Cooper yelled as his blood rained over me in a warm shower.

Cooper turned in fury to face James Denis, who held a black pistol in his hand. The acrid bite of smoke filled the air.

Waves crashed on the breakwater around the house and windmill. If we weren't cut off by now, we soon would be.

I tried to get to my feet and gave up. Instead, I crawled to the paintings.

Cooper stepped on my knee. He brought up his cudgel, still ready to fight. "You should have stayed in the windmill," he said to Denis.

"You've been with me for twenty years," Denis said, voice calm, as though we stood in his pristine study in his Curzon Street house. "You have seen what I do to those who betray me."

"Twenty fucking years." Spittle flew with Cooper's words. "Twenty years watching you take the best bits for yourself and giving me the leavings. Even when you were a lad. You had to have *everything*."

It might have been the light, or lack thereof, but I swore I saw pain flicker through Denis's eyes. Denis trusted so very few, and now the man he'd admitted to caring for was throwing that caring back in his face.

"If you go now," Denis said to Cooper. "I will let you live."

"Your pistol is spent, and your men are down. I might let *you* live. I haven't decided."

"You are badly injured."

"I can still best you, you little runt. I always could."

I sat with my back to the wall, my bad leg out in front of me. I longed to be able to leap to my feet and bash Cooper over the head, but I could barely move. "Why kill Ferguson?" I asked him.

Cooper did not take his eyes from Denis. "Ferguson is dead? He were alive and well when I left him."

"You did fight him, though. With a cudgel, your favorite method."

"Aye. But I left him still breathing. He's a strong fighter, is Ferguson."

"Was," I corrected. "He is certainly dead, sent back home to his mother for burial. I believe I know why you fought him. He found the paintings, did he not? Brigadier Easton hid them in the windmill. Ferguson found them, you found Ferguson, you beat him, took the paintings, and lit out. Did he cut off your hand?"

"He's wicked with a knife, is Ferguson. Thought I could save it, but when I knew it was done for, I built a fire and sawed it the rest of the way."

I imagined him, knife in hand, sweat pouring down his face, knowing what he must do. I could not stop myself thinking of him making the final blow with the knife, the agony of thrusting the end of his arm into the flames. He'd stumble away in horrific pain, too distracted to care about leaving behind the horse and his own hand.

He must have found the isolated windmill and threatened Waller to keep his presence secret. He'd not been too distracted, however, to leave behind the paintings.

"You're a smart man, Captain," Cooper said. "But you don't know any of this for certain."

"I am certain," I said. "But it doesn't matter, because Ferguson will never tell his tale."

Denis and Cooper were watching each other. Two animals, ready to battle. I started to climb to my feet, not because I thought I could help, but because I wanted to divert Cooper's attention.

He never looked at me. A glance out the window confirmed what I'd thought—the water had risen, filling the low ground around the windmill and house. We were now on an island.

Cooper went for Denis. Then the two men fought in silence—close, ugly, hard fighting. Thinner and younger, Denis was wiry and fast to Cooper's strength and bulk.

Cooper had taught Denis to fight. Now Denis was trying to kill him, fighting as dirty as Cooper ever had.

I got my hand around my walking stick. The sheath had rolled away somewhere, but the blade was still whole. I would have to kill Cooper, but so be it.

As I raised the sword to deliver the death blow through his back, Cooper managed to break Denis's hold and shove him away. Before Denis could duck out of the way, Cooper slammed his cudgel across Denis's head. Denis tried to roll from the blow, but blood streamed down his face and his eyes lost focus.

Cooper raised his stick, ready to end Denis's life, but I lunged my sword at Cooper. In my hurry, I missed his back but caught him on the healing stump of his wrist. He howled.

He swung around to me, cudgel swinging. I fought him back with my sword, but his cudgel landed on my wrist and the sword fell from my nerveless fingers. He crowded me into a corner, and then he beat me, swiftly and thoroughly, until I slid to the floor.

Denis had not moved, and I could not see whether he still breathed. I could barely move myself. Cooper ripped up more of the floorboards, never turning his back to me while I lay in a crumpled heap, pathetic and in pain. He pulled up a ring of a trapdoor, similar to the one in the windmill. There wouldn't be much room down there but enough in which a man could hide. Cooper must have gone to ground there when Matthias and Bartholomew came searching.

Copper dragged Denis by the feet to the hole and dropped him in. Then Cooper came for me. I was still awake, still ready to fight, but Cooper stepped his entire weight on my bad knee. Horrific pain spread through my body.

"Get down there, Captain," he said. "Keep him company."

He assisted me with his boot. I slithered face-first through the hole, and landed seven feet down, on the inert body of James Denis. The trapdoor slammed shut above me, and all was darkness.

*** *** ***

I did not have the good fortune to lose consciousness. I rolled off Denis's body, lay on my side, and hurt.

I could not see in the dark, but when I touched Denis again, he remained unnaturally still. My heart beat swiftly in worry as I turned him over.

He was alive. His skin was warm, and I felt his breath on my fingers.

I exhaled in relief. Ironic for me to be thankful that the man I'd so often wanted to kill had survived.

I had the opportunity to kill him now. He was unconscious, vulnerable, helpless. I could close my hands around his throat and squeeze until he died.

But, no. I had a modicum of honor left, and killing him in such a manner would be less than satisfying, in any case.

I retrieved a flask from my pocket, slid my arm under Denis's head, parted his lips with the head of the flask, and poured a bit of brandy into his mouth.

The brandy spilled, but Denis coughed and then swallowed. I fed him more. He swallowed that and pushed the flask away with a shaking hand.

"Is that you, Lacey?" His voice was little more than a croak. "Where are we?"

"In a cellar underneath the miller's house. You'll ask me next where Cooper is, but I do not know. He's hurt, but he survived."

"If Morgan is dead, Cooper will pay." His tone held finality. Cooper would not escape.

"Only if we can get out of this cellar," I said.

"It will not matter. He will pay. Even if I do not survive, Morgan's brother is not the forgiving sort." Denis groped for the flask in my hand, took it from me, and had another sip. "What interests me more is why Cooper did not kill us."

"Maybe he has. If Morgan and the windmill keeper are both dead, we might be stuck here. The tide has cut us off. It might be a week or more before anyone realizes that Waller has not come to the village for his provisions."

"I do not intend to wait a week. Tell me about this cellar."

In the pitch dark, I could do no more than recall what I'd seen before the trapdoor slammed shut. "About ten feet by ten feet, seven feet to the ceiling. Nothing down here but earth."

"Seven feet should not be difficult to overcome," Denis said.

"And I intend to make the attempt once I can stand up without falling over," I answered.

I heard Denis push himself to a sitting position. His voice, when it came, was close to my ear. "I haven't had to fight anyone in truth for a few years now. I am going soft."

"I suppose attending Gentleman Jackson's is not something you can do."

He made a quiet sound, like a laugh. "Gentleman Jackson would turn away the likes of me. I do have a go with my bodyguards to keep my hand in, but the trouble is, they hold back."

"They are afraid of the consequences if they hurt you," I said.

"I know. I will have to correct this oversight."

"You can always spar with me," I suggested. "I am a good fighter, in spite of it all, and I would not hold back."

"No, I imagine you would not." Denis made another sound, this one of pain, as he shifted. "Which begs the question, why did *you* not kill me while I lay here?"

I shrugged, though I knew he could not see me in the dark. "Maybe I had no wish to be trapped down here with your dead body."

I knew he did not believe that, but he said nothing. We sat in silence for a time, each of us gathering our strength.

The fight had taken much out of me, and my leg hurt like fire. Denis was younger and stronger—he'd recover faster. Then I might have to face the possibility that he, who had far less honor than I pretended to have, would kill me here, ridding himself of the captain who so irritated him.

But then, he'd shot Cooper, when the man would have beaten me into certain death.

"I am sorry about Cooper," I said.

He did not answer right away. I imagined he was glad of the dark, where he could fight his demons without me being able to see.

"Cooper was a mistake," Denis said. "I'd thought. . ."

He'd thought Cooper had come to care for him as he had for Cooper—*like father and son,* one of Denis's men had said. Cooper had taught Denis to fight, had brought him safely through the rough life on the streets. If Denis had not become wealthy, had not provided Cooper a soft billet and much money, would Cooper have turned on him long ago?

Denis must be wondering the same thing. I might have taken satisfaction that he was getting a taste of what it felt like to be used, but at the moment, I pitied him.

"You shot at him," I said. "But you only grazed him. On purpose?"

"Not at all," Denis said, voice as cold as ever. "I shot to kill. He heard me and moved in time. Believe me, my aim is true."

I could not stand. I had to half crawl, half drag myself to the nearest wall, brace myself on it, and climb to my feet. I did not bother stifling my sounds of pain. I leaned against the wall and struggled to catch my breath.

"Perhaps you should pay your lackeys more," I said. "Easton tried to take all those paintings from you. Ferguson found them in the windmill. I wonder whether Ferguson would have tried to make off with them, if Cooper hadn't come across him."

"I pay them more than they would get trading their talents to anyone else," Denis said. "Easton made more out of me than from his farm or the half-pay he receives from the army."

"Even so, those paintings could bring them much more."

I heard Denis trying to leverage himself to his feet. His words came breathily. "What you are seeing is the natural greed of man, Lacey. If a man catches a whiff of untold wealth, he will do anything to get it. Even a small amount of money can release the greed." One more puff of breath, and his voice returned to normal. "I've seen men kill each other over a few coins."

I had too, so I could not argue. "*You* now have untold wealth," I said. "At least, you seem to."

"Yes, and I did everything I could to get it. I vowed, when I was a lad, that I'd never sleep in a dung cart again. Granted, the cart was warm."

"I am sorry about that."

"You are, aren't you? Captain Gabriel Lacey, friend to the downtrodden. You grew up in a manor house, protected by many, while I grew up alone, fending off those who would prey on me. Now, you eke out a living while I live in luxury. And yet, you are highly respected, while I will ever be the boy who slept in the dung cart." He did not sound resentful. He stated a fact.

"I am sorry about that as well," I said.

He actually laughed, but it was a controlled laugh. "You may keep your respectability, Captain. I will take the disapprobation of the many, while I lie in clean sheets and gaze at beauty created by men who also had to grub for their living. So many artists never received the money promised them for their paintings. They died in poverty while their patrons ate from silver spoons and hung the stolen artwork on their walls. At least what was in the painters' hearts lives on for us to enjoy today."

"Very poetic," I said.

"I am apt to wax poetic in dire circumstances. Can you walk over here? I believe I have found the trapdoor."

I limped toward his voice. My walking stick was in the room above us; at least, it was if Cooper hadn't absconded with it. He'd been badly hurt, and the tide must still be rising. Had he made it to dry ground or would he be waiting for us to emerge?

One obstacle at a time.

I reached Denis. I lifted my arms to feel what he felt, but I had to lean against him to do it. He remained firmly in place, letting me rest my weight on him.

"Here," he said.

I felt wood set in stone, boards about a foot above our heads. Without a word, we both pushed.

The boards would not budge. Cooper must have wedged the trapdoor or dragged something heavy over it.

"Hmm," Denis said, as though we faced nothing more dire than a bad hand of cards. "How are you at digging?"

"With my bare hands, through the walls?" I thought of the cool, damp stone that lined the room. "It could be done, I suppose, but I imagine we'd hit water right away. We might drown instead of starving to death."

"How about digging upward? We find floorboards instead of whatever Cooper has used to wedge the trapdoor."

"Worth a try, I suppose."

In the next hours, I realized what a resourceful man Denis was. He had both of us turning out our pockets for whatever useful tools we might have, and allowed neither of us time to speculate what would happen if we did not escape.

My pockets produced, in addition to my flask, a small knife, a gold card case—a gift from Lady Breckenridge—a few coins, and a handkerchief. Denis had a knife—larger and sturdier than mine—a handkerchief, a short piece of rope, and balls and powder for his pistol. Denis also had a watch fob, but it was unadorned, unlike Rafe Godwin's, which had been hung with all sorts of junk. Like Grenville, Denis dressed expensively but austerely.

"Rope," I said, touching the small coil.

"Useful for tying things," Denis said. "The black powder interests me the most. We might use it to shatter stones above us."

"Or bring the ceiling down on us. And there is the question of lighting it."

"It takes only a spark, and fortunately, inhabitants of Norfolk use much flint in the building of their cottages. A challenge, yes. Impossible, no."

"May we try that as a last resort?" I removed my knife from its leather sheath and carefully poked at the stone surrounding a beam.

It was painful work, balancing on my good leg while I worked my already sore arms. Painful, yes, but I had no wish to remain in this cellar forever.

"Over here," Denis said. "The earth is a little softer, and this beam is rotting."

I hobbled over to join him. "Cooper might be up there, with your pistol. And my sword."

"If he is, then we will face him."

Nothing more to be said.

We worked in silence, chipping away at stone that rained in our faces. I understood what Denis was trying to do. Even if we brought down the beam and part of the ceiling, if we could shield ourselves from the falling debris, then we could climb out.

I continued our earlier conversation. "I suppose that, to you, I grew up privileged and protected. The truth is we were quite poor but not allowed to let on. I was protected from everyone but the one supposed to be protecting me."

"Yes, your father," Denis said. "I have heard the tales." No doubt he had.

"A boy's public school can be as mean as the London streets, believe me," I said. "A lad is at the mercy of bullies until he learns to be a bully himself. There is little tolerance for the weak."

"I imagine you held your own," Denis said. "And I know that you are fishing for more information about my childhood, Captain."

I grunted as I worked. "I profess to curiosity."

"Let me see—when I was seven, I lived in Lancashire with a lady who loved gin and young boys, in that order. The least said about that, the better. One night, she drank a few gallons of gin and never woke up. I stole everything I could carry and left on my own, making my way to London. From there my life took the turns I've already mentioned."

"Why on earth did you stay with the woman?" I took a step back as dirt rained into my face. "I did not think you were the sort to put up with much."

"Fortunately, she spent most of her nights stone drunk and asleep. But she fed me and taught me to pick locks. She was friends with a housebreaker who sent me down chimneys to open doors because I was so thin. I grew tired of chewing on soot, so I asked the woman to teach me about the locks. I knew she could pick them, because whenever she took a job as a maid or charwoman in a respectable home—bringing me with her to help her—she came away with bits of their valuables that had been locked away in cabinets."

"And if the discovery that they were missing was connected with her stint, she blamed you," I finished.

"Naturally. The boy from who-knew-where was a more likely suspect than the respectable-looking maid. Beat the boy, cry and return the things, and all was well."

Denis spoke coolly, with his curious detachment, as though these things had happened to someone else. But his tales explained some of his coldness. Every person in his life had used and betrayed him. He'd learned to remain distant, to watch and learn people's weaknesses. He soaked up whatever knowledge he needed from them and walked away.

"Is your curiosity satisfied, Captain?" he asked.

"For now. Except—is James Denis your true name?"

"It suffices for the moment."

I was not certain whether to believe him, or whether I pitied him. The world threw at us what it did, and we chose what to make of it. Denis could have become an enraged and violent man, or drunk himself into nothing. Instead, he'd made himself into this emotionless being who did what he pleased and dispatched those who got in his way.

I'd noticed that he avoided the excesses of other men—never drank much, nor indulged in enormous meals or cheroots or beautiful women. He could have all that now, and yet, he chose an almost Spartan existence, excepting his comfortable house and brilliant artwork. He was no hedonist.

Denis had chosen control. His early life had given him none, and so he'd learned to wrest control from those who'd tried to rule him.

"Few know my sad tale, Captain," Denis said. "I will not threaten you to keep you from telling it, but I will ask you, as a courtesy, to refrain."

"I never repeat confidences," I said. "I will treat this as one."

"Of course you will. Your honor. And you cannot be certain that what I have told you is the truth."

No, I could not. With Denis, nothing was certain.

His tale did explain to me why he had never married, or I thought it did. Falling in love, pledging oneself to another, unto death, was the ultimate giving over of control. I was rushing headlong into it for the second time, and I did not mind at all.

The thought of Donata, dressed in her finery, complete with the odd, feathered headdresses she favored, cigarillo in her gloved hand, made my heart twinge. I would leave this place, travel to her home in Oxfordshire, pluck the cigarillo from her fingers, and show her how much I reveled in the chaos of marriage.

"I find it ironic," I said, "that one of the few people who hasn't betrayed you, is me."

"Yet." We both stepped back as another rain of dirt showered to the floor. "Everyone betrays, in the end. I should have remembered that before I grew sentimental about Cooper."

"I also find it ironic that you shot at him to keep him from killing me."

"Because I still need you, and he was, after all, trying to run off with my paintings. This beam is giving, I think."

Chapter Twenty-One

The beam did more than give. It tumbled down, worn through with salt and damp. Stone, flint, and dirt fell with it. I grabbed Denis and hauled him out of the way, landing with him against the wall as half the floor poured down.

I shielded him, feeling rock batter my back, while I pressed my forehead to the wall so my face would not be cut. Dust filled the air, and we coughed.

With the dust came light, not much, but enough for me to see the pile of rubble that had fallen. I also saw, when he raised his head, the pale smudge of Denis's face, splotched black with blood.

He pushed me away, his arm over his mouth, and shuffled back to the fallen ceiling. The debris made a scattered pile, and the hole above was small. Denis reached up with his knife and broke the stone and floorboards that hemmed it in.

"I'll boost you out first," he said. "You're not steady enough to hold me, but you're big enough to pull me out."

"Are you not worried I'll run and leave you here?" I asked. Not that I'd run far on my weak and aching leg.

"No," he said without inflection. "I've come to know you well, Captain."

He had, damn him. "Better make the hole larger, then," I said. "Or I'll stick like a cork in a bottle."

Denis did not smile. I supposed he reserved his laughter for the pitch dark when no one could see him.

Together we widened the hole, pulling down rock until our fingers bled. Denis put his hands around my right boot and heaved me upward.

I landed facedown, scrabbling on the floor to get purchase. Denis shoved some more, and I crawled out.

The light came from the cottage's back windows, the afternoon bright outside. The wind blew, bringing chill sea air through the broken panes. I heard the water on all sides of the house and knew we were cut off.

But alive. The windmill keeper had food and water, and we could rest inside and either wait for the tide to turn, or take one of his rowboats and make for shore.

I turned around on my stomach and reached down for Denis. He lifted his arms to me, clasping mine, and I started hauling him upward. I'd gotten him halfway through the hole when I heard a step.

I looked up—and let go of Denis. Denis fell back into the cellar, but he didn't ask why I'd dropped him, didn't say a word.

Cooper stood above me, blood caking his face and body. He had Denis's pistol, cocked and pointed at me. Where he'd gotten more powder and a bullet, I did not know, but I had no doubt the thing was loaded.

"You did not make it away before the tide," I said, stating the obvious, so Denis would hear and understand.

"I was coming back for ye," Cooper said. "You didn't have to work so hard. You are going to row me out of here, Captain, and he will die."

"Leave the paintings," I said. "And him. I'll take you somewhere safe. I know all the hidden places on this coast. You can go and never see him again."

Below me I saw Denis stop short of rolling his eyes.

"And what would that get me?" Cooper asked.

"Your life."

"You will row me anyway, Captain. *With* the paintings, after I shoot him."

"And then you'll kill me," I said. "I'll not do it."

"You will. This pistol is loaded and primed for him, but I have a long knife to take care of you if you give me trouble. Or I could do it the other way around. I haven't decided. Bring him out of there. Or I'll shoot you first."

In the cellar, Denis nodded. I reached down for him. He let me pull him out by the arms again, but he used only one hand to assist me. The other was tucked against his chest.

As soon as he got himself onto solid floor, Denis rolled hard away from me and flung a large handful of gunpowder up into Cooper's face. Cooper jerked back, but the powder clung to his face and chest, sticking in the blood all over the right side of his body.

Cooper swung the gun around, but I shouted. "The spark could ignite you, man. Stop!"

As Cooper hesitated in rage and confusion, Denis launched himself up like a cat. He grabbed the pistol from Cooper and slammed the butt of it into Cooper's forehead. Cooper, spent from bleeding and pain, went down.

Cooper groaned, and Denis hit him again. This time Cooper's big body went limp. Denis lifted the man's head, opened his eye, and let the head fall again.

I got myself to Denis and took the pistol from him. I unlocked the hammer and gently closed it before it could spark. "You have gunpowder all over you too," I said.

Denis ignored me. "What the devil did he do with my paintings?"

I had thought Denis would take out his knife and stab Cooper to death then and there, but he left the man on the floor while he went outside into the wind.

I limped across the wrecked floor and found the sword and sheath of my walking stick on opposite sides of room. I retrieved the pieces and slid the blade into the cane, happy that the thing had survived intact. I breathed a sigh of relief as I leaned my weight on it.

Cooper was alive, I knew from his loud breathing. Morgan, on the other hand, was dead.

I walked out of the miller's house to see Denis pull a canvas bag from one of the saddles and take a quick look inside it. The windmill keeper was nowhere about, but I saw that one of the rowboats had gone. Had Waller rushed to the nearest village to bring back a constable? Or fled entirely?

"Morgan is dead," I said.

Denis did not look up. "I know." He closed the bag. "Are you a good oarsman, Lacey?"

"I have not used an ocean craft in years," I said. "Though I rowed on a pond in Oxfordshire this summer and seemed to remember a bit."

Denis did not look in the mood to be amused. "You told Cooper you know all the secret ways around this coast. Were you lying?"

"No."

"Good. You row and tell me where to steer."

He handed me the bag of priceless paintings and went back into the miller's house. He came out with Cooper's body balanced over his shoulders, his slim build in no way bent by Cooper's weight.

Denis walked past me and dumped Cooper into the rowboat. He got into the rocking craft, holding it steady by the line tying it to a lone wooden post sticking out of the water.

I stood for a moment on the bank. I still held the pistol, and I had the paintings. I could shoot Denis there and then, row myself to shore, take the paintings to a magistrate I knew, and return home a virtuous man.

I got into the boat.

Denis took the bag from me, wrapped it well, and stowed it on the bottom. If we foundered, thousands upon thousands of guineas worth of valuable and historic paintings would go down with us.

"I assume you know the difference between port and starboard," I said, unlashing the oars.

"I do."

I cast off, thumped down onto the seat, and started to row. "Hard aport," I said, and we moved.

*** *** ***

I rowed west and north, around headlands, past drained marshes, and to an area where little creeks ran everywhere, water and land blending into one. Here, the villages were far inland, and no fishing boats were in sight.

Denis did not want me to pull up in the marshes. He had me row out into deeper water, right into the sea.

I did so with some trepidation. This craft was meant for floating through creeks and rivers or along the shore, not for tossing about on waves. If we went too far, we'd not get back.

When the land was a only wide line on the horizon, Denis had me stop. I shipped the oars, and the boat bobbed heavily on the waves. The sun was sinking far to the west, over the green smudge of Lincolnshire in the distance.

Denis grabbed the unmoving form of Cooper and hauled him to the gunwale. The boat tilted alarmingly. Cooper groaned, and his eyelids fluttered.

"He's alive," I said.

"I know." Denis hooked his hand around the seat of Cooper's pants. "You might want to look to shore, Captain."

I did not think Denis meant to dunk Cooper's head in the water to revive him. I had hoped we'd brought him out here for a good talking to, but Denis's lectures tended to be final. Cooper started to struggle, regaining consciousness but still weak.

"You cannot dump a man overboard and leave him to drown," I said. "That is too cruel, even for you."

"Do you hear, Cooper?" Denis asked. "The captain has compassion."

He took up the pistol I'd left on the bench, heaved Cooper up so that his head was over the water, and stuck the pistol's barrel into the back of Cooper's neck. Cooper dragged his head around to look at me.

What I saw in Cooper's eyes was not terror but rage. He fixed me with a glare of hatred stronger than any I'd ever seen. He was still glaring at me when Denis pulled the trigger.

The gun's boom was deafening. The life abruptly died from Cooper's eyes as half his face vanished into blood.

Denis had arranged the execution so deftly that almost all Cooper's blood sprayed into the water, very little touching the boat. Denis laid down the pistol, caught Cooper's waistband again, and heaved the man into the water. Cooper sank, blood and bubbles in his wake.

Denis took a long breath and stripped off his ruined gloves. I thought he meant to say something to me, but he turned away, bowed his head, and pressed his hands over his face.

*** *** ***

Denis sat for a long time—saying nothing, doing nothing. He remained motionless, in silence, while the waves pushed at the boat.

We started to drift too far north. I took up the oars and quietly turned us around, picking a path back to shore.

Eventually, Denis raised his head and caught the tiller. His eyes were as cool as ever, no tears, no redness to betray grief. But the sun was full in my face, doubled by its reflection on the water, and perhaps I could not see.

Denis said nothing at all as we traveled. He steered competently, and we avoided breakers to move smoothly back toward the windmill. I offered to row him closer to Blakeney or Cley, which would give him a short walk over fields to Easton's, but he declined.

"He will wash ashore sooner or later," I said after another long silence.

Denis did not ask me who I meant. "I know." His mouth was a thin line. "If you worry that any accusation will fall on you, do not. Your name will not be involved."

I had not thought that far ahead—I'd barely thought past landing the boat. I said nothing, and Denis went on.

"When there are questions, I will answer them for you. You are under my protection." He looked to shore at the windmill drawing closer, its arms turning with slow patience. "Morgan will have a proper burial and a grand funeral service."

Whereas Cooper, the man he'd trusted for twenty years, would be food for the fishes.

We landed and tied up the boat. Waller hadn't returned, and I decided he must have run off for good.

Denis entered the windmill with the paintings, then came out with a blanket and went into the ruined miller's house. I unsaddled and unbridled the horses to let them again share the cow's manger, which I replenished with hay from stacks on the leeward side of the house.

When I looked into the miller's house, Denis had turned Morgan over and laid him out, hands on his chest. Denis covered Morgan with a blanket and came out of the house without a word.

The day was darkening, and we sought shelter from the night in the windmill. I lit lamps and stoked the fire against the cold.

Denis's finely tailored suit was shredded and blood-spattered, his face smeared with blood and gunpowder. I imagined I did not look much better, which was confirmed when I bent over the washbasin in the bedroom upstairs. I caught a glimpse of my parchment-white face in the mirror, my dark eyes burning with a strange, feverish light.

I found bread, cheese, and ale downstairs in the kitchen, and I fell hungrily to my repast. Denis declined my offer to share the meal with him. He sat on a straight-backed chair, his hands on his lap, staring out the window through which he could see nothing.

"Grieving for him is only natural," I said around bites of thick bread. "He was a part of your life."

Denis turned his head to look at me. "Please do not speak of it."

"The man who gave me the life I needed betrayed me too."

"You mean Colonel Brandon, punishing you for loving his wife." When I did not answer, Denis looked back at the window. "You do not like to speak of that either."

"No," I said. "But Brandon and what he did to me made me realize that men are who they are. We try to make them into something they are not, and then are astonished when they turn out not to be what we wanted. We betray ourselves."

Denis got up from the chair. "Pardon me, Lacey, but I have had enough of your philosophy for one day." He walked steadily across the kitchen and opened the door. "You have fulfilled this commission for me. Pack your bags when we reach Easton's and go."

He went out into the night, closing the door behind him—not slamming it. I resumed my supper and my own troubled thoughts.

*** *** ***

The tide turned, and the road south was dry in the morning. Waller did return, with a constable from the nearest village and the magistrate for the area: a well-fed squire on a well-fed horse.

Waller had witnessed Cooper attack us and kill Morgan, plus Cooper had held Waller hostage. The constable and magistrate were satisfied with the tale that Cooper locked Denis and me into the cellar and then ran off, fascinated by my explanation of how we'd managed to climb out through the floor. Denis said nothing, only stood looking out to sea, his back to us.

I had cleaned the boat before I'd fallen into heavy sleep the night before and had checked this morning to make sure I'd missed no smear of blood. I hadn't, but no one even looked at the boat. The magistrate went off home and the constable sent for a carter to deliver Morgan's body back to the Easton estate. They considered Cooper to be a fugitive, and the magistrate said he'd put out the hue and cry.

I knew they'd find nothing for a very long time. Denis had known exactly where to drop the body. When Cooper did eventually wash to shore, he would be too disintegrated for any but an expert to tell how he died, and then they might believe he'd fallen in with ruffians or was attacked by them. Cooper was a killer—no one would care very much how he met his end.

Denis and I spoke not at all as we rode back. Bartholomew, who'd spent an uneasy night waiting for me, had plenty of questions when I reached Easton's, especially when he saw my blood-spattered clothes. I put him off with short answers and bade him draw me a bath.

As I soaked in the hot water, I told Bartholomew to pack my things. We'd be moving into the pub at Blakeney. I did not want to go to the Parson's Point pub, because Buckley would be there, and I still did not have the fortitude to face him.

Denis summoned me before I could leave, and I went to the study.

Everything was as before—Denis sitting behind the desk, one of his lackeys at the window, looking on. The desk was bare.

Before Denis could speak, I said, "One final thing puzzles me. Cooper says he did not kill Ferguson. If he did not, then who did?"

"Cooper lied," Denis said.

"He seemed genuinely surprised that Ferguson was dead. Your surgeon told you that Ferguson had been well beaten, but before his death. The wounds on his face were made by Cooper, who was good with a cudgel. But the death blow could have been made afterward."

Denis shrugged. "Cooper delivered the final blow, Ferguson died slowly of the wound, and Cooper did not realize."

I was not so satisfied. "A second person might have come upon Ferguson later, when he was too weak to fight."

Denis rose, not caring. As far as he was concerned, the matter was at an end.

"Come with me," he said, and walked out of the room without waiting to see whether I followed.

Chapter Twenty-Two

Denis led me downstairs to the dining room. The chandelier above the long table had been lit, and under its glowing light, Denis unrolled the canvases I'd found under the floorboards in the miller's house.

It was as though paradise had opened itself into this small, quiet room. I saw Venus and Adonis in a misty green garden; a beautifully dressed Dutch man and woman standing together in a tender moment; the haughty face of a princess with a ruff around her neck; glorious blue skies over classical ruins in a world that did not exist.

Beauty always struck me mute. I could only walk around the table, stunned, looking at glory.

"I thought you would like to view that for which you nearly died," Denis said.

"What will happen to them?" I felt as though I asked about orphaned children.

"They will go to the gentlemen who paid me to obtain them. Those buyers are growing rather impatient. Brigadier Easton angered me not only because he stole from me but because he was ruining my business."

"But you stole these in the first place," I said. "Or had others steal them for you."

"I remember telling you—rather poetically, you remarked—that the rich patrons who commissioned the works in the first place usually came up with every excuse why they could not pay the artists once the work was done. Consider that I am taking only that which has already been stolen."

I met his gaze. "Do you spin this tale to make yourself feel better?"

Denis looked well rested and almost as normal, his well-made suit perfectly pressed, his linen pure white, his bruises and abrasions already fading. But even so, I saw in his eyes an emptiness that had not been there before. "I spin it to make *you* feel better," he said. "With your sense of honor, I thought you would enjoy the justice."

Denis pushed a tiny painting at me, a miniature done in exquisite detail. The picture depicted a young woman in a dark dress, a white cap over her fair hair, a rather elaborate silver necklace around her throat. She kept her gaze serenely downward, but she was so real that I expected her at any moment to look up and speak to me.

"By Holbein the Younger," Denis said. "Give it to your lady."

I touched it, sorely tempted. "What about whoever asked you to find this?"

"No one did. I pick up pieces here and there for my own enjoyment. You have done me several good turns. Take it as a token of my gratitude."

"Or as a payment for not telling a magistrate all that has happened?"

"You are a highly suspicious man, Captain. Make of it what you will. I still believe that Lady Breckenridge will enjoy the picture."

If I took it, I condoned his thievery and Cooper's execution. The picture would forever haunt me. He knew that, devil take him.

I also knew that someone had tried to kill him yesterday, and instead of assisting the killer in ridding the world of James Denis, I'd saved Denis's life. I'd then helped cover up a murder and was about to look the other way at Denis stealing a fortune's worth of paintings.

True, after the confusion of the recent war on the Continent and the constant looting of each nation by the others, it was difficult to know who owned what. And Denis was not wrong about the artists. Wealthy patrons could be the most canny criminals of all.

I put out my hand, picked up the miniature portrait, dropped it into my pocket, and walked away without a word.

*** *** ***

The bed in the small room above the pub was not as comfortable as the one I'd had at Easton's house, or indeed, at Lady Southwick's, but I slept heavily, nevertheless.

I had horrible dreams. Again and again, I saw Cooper's eyes going blank when Denis shot him, his body falling into the waves, and felt my arms aching as I pulled for shore. I dreamed of the paintings

Denis had spread across the table, the astonishing colors that suddenly became stained red-brown with blood.

When I woke, my arms did indeed hurt, both from fighting and the hard rowing through ocean waves. The rest of my body did not feel much better.

Before I could get myself out of bed, Bartholomew came in bearing a tray heaped with a well-needed repast. The brown bread, warm cheese, bacon, and coffee tasted of ambrosia.

"Are we going back to London, sir?" Bartholomew asked as he dressed me.

"Not yet. One or two things I need to clear up."

I'd thought Bartholomew would look disappointed, but he smiled. "Good for you, sir. You always finish the job. How can I help?"

*** *** ***

We returned to the Lacey house. The pile of debris in the back was now cool ash, and I asked Bartholomew to start raking it up.

The local men began drifting in, asking for work. I had them begin testing and shoring up beams, while I sorted through whatever papers and things had been left in the house. I had to promise to pay the men later, but they took me at my word.

Terrance Quinn also came. "I'm not much use," he said. "But there must be something I can do. At least pretend there is, Lacey."

"You can be of enormous help," I answered. "I need a caretaker, a steward. I return to London soon, and my wife-to-be informs me that we'll live here only in the summers. She is a determined lady, is my wife-to-be."

Terrance unbent enough to smile. "You are up against it."

Not that I minded one whit. "If you moved in here to direct the repair work, and then stayed on and looked after the place in general, I would be extremely grateful. So would her ladyship."

So would her ladyship meant a salary, a decent one. Terrance regarded me in surprise. "You would want me?"

"Why not? You know the local men, and they respect you, you know who can be trusted. Why stay home and carry pots for your mother's cook?"

"Why indeed?"

We shook hands, Terrance offering his left. I now had someone to look after the old place, and Terrance had a purpose.

I turned to other matters. Despite Denis's conviction that Cooper had killed Ferguson, even accidentally, I was not so certain. I wanted again to go over the exact sequence of events leading up to Ferguson's death.

Before I could begin, however, a lavish coach and four pulled up the drive that was now being cleared of weeds. A horseman followed the carriage, and I saw, when he dismounted, that the horseman was Grenville.

I came out of the house to greet him. "I thought you were in London."

Grenville handed his reins to his groom, who'd descended from the back of the coach. "I did start for there." He neared me, saw my battered face, and stopped in shock. "Good God, Lacey, what happened to you?"

"Many things. Suffice it to say that the paintings and Mr. Cooper were found, and I am released from my duty to Mr. Denis. You did not answer my question."

Grenville's brows rose. "I will certainly bribe you to tell me all about it, later. But for my part . . ." He closed his mouth, put his hand on my shoulder and led me into the house, out of earshot of the other men. "I decided to travel to London via Cambridge. While in Cambridge, I stopped and asked a few questions—I know quite a few people there. I believe, Lacey, that I have found your Miss Quinn."

I raised my brows. "In Cambridge?"

"Indeed, no. The information you received about her was correct. She is in Lincolnshire. In a place called Market Sutton, to be precise. I thought to jaunt there and speak to her. Are you free to come?"

The coach and four, I realized, was for me. Grenville had been riding instead of sitting inside the carriage, because of his motion sickness, but he knew I'd never make a day and a half journey on horseback. He was good at anticipating the needs of others, one of the reasons he was well liked.

He was also afire with curiosity. I was alight with the same curiosity, but I was still battered and slow from my ordeal.

"Denis sent someone to Cambridge to inquire on my behalf," I said. "You did not have to go."

"I know, but I could not help myself. I met Denis's man, and he was happy to turn the problem over to me. If you are up to traveling, please join us. If not, I will go alone, at your service."

"Us?"

Grenville's smile deserted him. "Marianne is in the coach. When I sent her word I'd be pausing in Cambridge, she came down to meet me."

"And she is willing to continue to Lincolnshire on the moment?"

"She professes to be. We will find a comfortable inn in which to spend the night on the way." He peered at me. "You do not seem frightfully keen, Lacey. Which means you must have been badly hurt. I do apologize, my dear fellow, for bouncing in here with my news."

"I will recover," I said. I was not ready to talk about the adventure, not yet. "By all means, take me to Lincolnshire. I need to be quit of this place for a time."

*** *** ***

I could not rush off in an instant, but it was within the hour. Marianne descended to look over my house while I gave instructions to Terrance and had Bartholomew run back to the inn in Blakeney for my things.

Marianne looked around at the stripped walls of the main hall and the rust on the solid wrought iron of the stair rail. "I cannot decide which looks worse, Lacey, you or your house."

Ever tactful, was Marianne. Grenville had gone outside to speak to his coachman and Matthias, so Marianne and I stood relatively alone in the hall.

"I hope that both will mend," I said to her.

Marianne craned her head and looked up the open staircase. "It is interesting to see where you came from, though. Quite posh, it must have been. I imagine Lady Breckenridge rubbing her expensively gloved hands and planning supper balls and summer fetes."

"Possibly," I said.

"Definitely," Marianne answered.

"Why on earth are you agreeing to ride all the way to Lincolnshire?" I asked. "Surely Grenville would hire a chaise to take you back to London."

She gave me a dark look. "Because obtaining time to speak to his worship is difficult. He does rather avoid conversation, as you can surmise by the fact that he rode horseback almost the entire way here from Cambridge."

"He grows ill in carriages. Perhaps he does not like you to see that."

"Perhaps he does not like to actually speak with me. But he will with you, and so I will listen and pretend I am part of it."

"He said that you wanted to 'consult' with him. You meant by that, what?"

She put her head on one side. "Not really your business. Perhaps I simply want to converse with him."

"I cannot blame him for avoiding you, if you are this maddening. Conversation with you, Marianne, can put a gentleman off."

"Rot. I know exactly what sorts of things to say to a gentleman. The trouble is, he won't sit still long enough for me to say them."

I made a noise of exasperation. "Because he is not looking for conversation with a courtesan who knows how to flatter and tease. He wants a real conversation—with the real Marianne."

Marianne looked at me a moment, then her voice went soft. "That is what I fear."

"I speak the truth. Grenville is not a stupid man. He has no use for Spanish coin and flummery. He wants to know *you*."

"And then I will watch him run from me as fast as his legs can carry him. Maybe to a lady who has a cultured tongue and can converse about art and music with her nose in the air."

"Ask him to teach you about them. And you have a more cultured tongue than you know. I've often observed that you speak far better than your colleagues at the theatre. You were never gutter born. Stand amazed at my discretion in never asking you."

"Yes, I had noticed that," she said. "Thank you, Lacey."

Out the open door, we saw Bartholomew come dashing back, toss my bag up to his brother, who was now on top of the coach, and climb up to join him.

Grenville said nothing to us as I escorted Marianne out of the house and handed her into the carriage. Grenville got in beside Marianne, leaving the empty backward-facing seat for me. In any other circumstance, this would be a discourtesy, but I'd grown used to riding backward in Grenville's coaches. Grenville became even more violently ill if he did not face forward.

"Are you certain you will be well?" I asked him.

"Not at all," he said. "But I can hold out long enough to tell you my tale. Besides, my backside is a bit sore from all the hours in the saddle."

He spoke glibly, but as soon as the carriage jerked forward, Grenville looked as though he regretted giving up the steadiness of a horse. He opened the window and breathed deeply.

"Tell me what you discovered," I said. "It will take your mind from things."

Grenville dabbed his pale lips with a handkerchief. "I discovered Denis's man," he said. "He'd spoken to the people Terrance Quinn told you *he'd* spoken to, but found nothing new. However, when Denis's man broadened his inquiries a bit, he found a woman who'd looked after Helena when she first arrived in Cambridge. She was the person who persuaded Helena to move on to Lincolnshire and found her a place there."

I frowned at the heaths and farmland of inland Norfolk moving by us. "I am confused. I thought Miss Quinn and her husband settled in Cambridge and then moved north. That is what Terrance reported Braxton's neighbors as saying."

"Yes, but I have not told you the crux of the matter. Miss Quinn is not married. She is living as a lady's companion to an elderly woman by name of Edgerton, in Lincolnshire."

"A lady's companion?" I stared at him. "Did she jilt Braxton, then? All those years ago?"

"Ah, now I come to the crux of the crux." Grenville's smile became triumphant. "There is no such person as Edward Braxton, who came to woo Miss Helena Quinn. The man does not exist."

Chapter Twenty-Three

After the violence of the day before and with the continuing pain in my body, I was in no mood for riddles.

"Of course he exists," I said. "Mrs. Landon and Lady Southwick met him. Robert Buckley met him, as did Miss Quinn's mother and father. Please do not tell me that people in three parishes, including Lady Southwick, conspired to invent him."

"No, indeed. There *was* a man who came from Cambridge to Norfolk and seduced away Miss Helena Quinn. He told everyone his name was Edward Braxton, but it was not. There is a true Edward Braxton, neighbors of the people Terrance Quinn spoke to, but upon further investigation, this Mr. Braxton is seventy, and he and his wife, a woman of his same age, went to live near their daughter and grandchildren in York some years ago.

He was certainly not the young and handsome gentleman who swept into rural Norfolk to woo a naïve vicar's daughter."

"Then who on earth was Helena's Mr. Braxton?"

"No one seems to know," Grenville said. "A ghost."

"A smooth-tongued devil, that's who," Marianne broke in. "A confidence trickster. Do not look so amazed, gentlemen; I have seen this sort of thing time and again. A man takes whatever name he pleases, invents whatever background he pleases, and seduces a woman—usually for her money—and then disappears, leaving her ruined, humiliated, and destitute. No doubt the true Edward Braxton is a respectable solicitor or banker's clerk, so that if people do inquire, they'll find a man of impeccable reputation behind the name. Better still if he's recently moved elsewhere, so no one can say he hasn't traveled to Norfolk for a holiday. If inquiries turn up that the man of the same name is of venerable years, those asking will assume he is the father or grandfather of said trickster, which will lend still more credence to his story. A respectable name, passed down through generations, is always esteemed."

Grenville listened with interest. "But why would a confidence trickster travel to a remote corner of Norfolk and entice away young Miss Quinn? What could he hope to gain? Miss Quinn did not come from a wealthy family."

Marianne shrugged. "These men will take anything they can find. A man such as the false Mr. Braxton might persuade a woman to marry him, perhaps with a sham ceremony and sham special license, only to take the family silver and leave the poor lady high and dry. Or he might have come to convince local men to invest money in some scheme—a new invention that's sure to make them all rich, or some such. In that case, the respectable vicar's daughter putting in a good word for him does not hurt."

I did not hear half of what she said, because one word had caught my attention. "Silver," I said.

Grenville's brows rose. "You mean the candlesticks from the church? He stole them? Or persuaded Miss Quinn to?"

"You can be certain that he persuaded the girl to nick them for him," Marianne said. "A man like that never gets caught with his hand in the pot. He likely convinced her that they needed the money the silver would fetch to make their escape."

"But she'd be stealing from her own father's church," Grenville said.

Marianne gave him a pitying look. "Vicars' daughters are not necessarily the pious beings you imagine. They mostly do not give a toss about Sunday services, and she might have reasoned that a country church did not need extravagant candlesticks. Mr. Braxton likely convinced her, if she worried about hurting dear papa, that Protestant modesty would be assisted by the loss of glittering silver on the altar. These gentlemen think of everything, believe me."

Grenville eyed her in curiosity, his motion sickness momentarily forgotten. "Have you had wide experience of this?"

"I have watched others have wide experience of it," Marianne said. "You'd think girls in a theatre company would have more wisdom, but no. They cling to the belief that a fine gentleman will sweep them off to riches and comfort."

As Grenville had done with Marianne. I deliberately did not look at him. "Innocent country girls would be even more susceptible," I said.

"Precisely," Marianne said.

"How do we find this man?" I asked. "I'd like a word with him."

Marianne shook her head. "You do not. They take what they came for, and they vanish, turning up elsewhere with a new name to fleece a new flock of sheep. The best ones are never found."

"Well, this Edward Braxton could not have been terribly good at being a trickster," I said. "He told Mrs. Landon and Lady Southwick slightly different versions of his story, which was why Mrs. Landon swore he was a solicitor, and Lady Southwick swore he was a banker's clerk. He left the silver plate in my chimney, and Miss Quinn never married him."

"Yes," Grenville said. "Odd that. And so, a visit to Miss Quinn is in order." He took out his handkerchief again and patted his damp forehead. "I beg your pardons, my friends, but I am afraid I must . . ."

Both Marianne and I knew what he needed. She vacated the seat, and the two of us helped him pull it out into the special bed he'd had made. Grenville collapsed onto it and closed his eyes. Marianne sat down next to me and pulled out a newspaper, not seeming to think a thing of it. I leaned my head against the wall and let my fatigue overcome me.

*** *** ***

We traveled the rest of that day, put up in a coaching inn for the night, and resumed the journey the next day. Grenville's money ensured that we had a private parlor and bedrooms, and Marianne assumed the role of Grenville's respectable wife so that the innkeeper did not questioned her presence.

She played the part astonishingly well, never overdoing it or behaving awkwardly. Grenville raised his brows at me once or twice but did not remark upon it. Theatre companies had done poorly to keep Marianne buried in the chorus.

By noon on the second day, we rolled into Market Sutton, a fairly large town a few miles from the coast, and found another inn. Marianne was surprisingly understanding about staying behind, while Grenville and I made our way to the house of Mrs. Edgerton.

Mrs. Edgerton proved to be a lady of large girth, who had to be pushed about in a Bath chair. She met us alone in her parlor, bade us to sit, and then looked us over, seeming in no hurry to summon Miss Quinn. Grenville explained that he'd written ahead, and Mrs. Edgerton acknowledged this, but I had to assure the lady that I was a friend of Miss Quinn's family.

"She does not wish to return to her family," Mrs. Edgerton said. "And if she does not wish it, she will not go. I have charge of her now."

"Then she will not go," Grenville said smoothly. "We wish only to speak to her. Her family is worried about her well-being."

"You cannot accept my word that she is well?"

"Please," I said, sitting forward. "They would want to hear that I actually saw her. I promise you, if it turns out that Miss Quinn does not want me to tell her family where she is, I will not."

Mrs. Edgerton ran a hard gaze up and down me and let it linger on my walking stick. The fact that I was lame seemed to reassure her for some reason. She summoned her maid who was instructed to fetch Miss Quinn, and we all waited.

When Helena entered the room, I was struck by how little she'd changed. I'd left Norfolk at age twenty, when Helena had been twelve. She'd been tall for her age, and robust—not an ethereal beauty but a sturdy and pretty girl.

She was twenty-two when she'd disappeared from home, and now she was in her thirties. Though still robust and still pretty, Helena wore a resigned look. This was her lot in life, the look said, her dreams of marriage and a family of her own now dust.

I rose, as did Grenville. When Helena saw me, she halted, the color draining from her face. I stepped forward, thinking her faint, but she waved me off.

"I beg your pardon," she said. "I did not mean to . . . It is just that you look so like your father."

I supposed it inevitable. "My father passed away a few years after you left."

"My condolences," she said, quickly and politely. She did not mean them.

I introduced Grenville and told Helena the briefest bit of my changed circumstances since she'd last seen me.

"Your cousin Terrance is worried about you," I finished. "He returned from Waterloo to find you gone. He tried hunting for you in Cambridge."

Miss Quinn flushed. "Yes, well, I was long gone by then. I came to stay with Mrs. Edgerton, who has been so kind to me."

Kind Mrs. Edgerton intended to sit there, I saw, her cane planted on the carpet, keeping me from asking the questions I needed to ask. Miss Quinn also understood this, because she turned to Mrs. Edgerton. "May Captain Lacey take a turn with me in the garden? I wish to ask him about my family."

Mrs. Edgerton did not like the idea, but she gave a conceding nod. She lifted her cane and pointed the end of it at Grenville. "*You* will remain."

Grenville bowed with his practiced aplomb. "As you wish, my lady."

"I do wish it," Mrs. Edgerton said. "That is why I said so."

"She really is quite generous," Miss Quinn told me as we walked through the small garden. Mrs. Edgerton's house was square and brick, large but not ostentatious. Everything about it shouted extreme respectability, money spent wisely, a vivid contrast to Lady Southwick's monstrosity.

"She must be very generous," I said. "To take you in — alone, away from your family, running from . . . from Mr. Braxton?"

Helena's flush deepened. "As you no doubt have discovered, given that you have found me, I was once a great fool."

"You were young," I said. "And I have it from a good source that gentlemen like Braxton can be very persuasive."

"I was twenty-two." Helena spoke with a severity directed at her younger self. "Old enough to be wiser than I was. I was on the shelf but still wearing debutante's clothing. Still hoping."

"As is natural."

"You are kind, but I know you also think me a fool. Miss Austen's novels were a great favorite of mine, and I should have paid better attention to the lessons in them. The dashing gentleman usually turns out to be the scoundrel, while the friend one has known all one's life proves to be steadfast and true." She sighed. "Poor Terrance."

"He is still concerned about you," I said.

"And I am ashamed of what I did to him. But I am pleased he returned from the fighting, safe and sound."

I stopped. We'd reached a fountain in the middle of the garden, the fountain not running. Mrs. Edgerton did not strike me as a woman who would condone wasting water on something as frivolous as a fountain on a brisk September day.

"Terrance returned safe, but not sound," I said. "He lost an arm, Helena, and his spirits are low. I quite understand—when I learned that the surgeon would not have to cut off my leg, I wept for joy. Terrance did not have that happy news."

Her face had gone ashen. "Lost his arm? Dear Lord."

"There is more to your fear of returning home than shame at your foolishness," I said, my voice taking an edge. "Your family would have forgiven you if you'd turned back that night, regardless of whether Mr. Braxton had touched you. Terrance would have forgiven you. Your family is good at heart. Things would have been difficult for you, but not impossible. Yet, you carried on with your plan to ran away. Why?"

Helena pressed her hands together and shook her head. She did not want to tell me.

"I found the church plate," I said. "Did Mr. Braxton coerce you to steal it for him?"

She looked up at me in anguish. "Robert did it. Little Robert Buckley, the publican's son. He did it, because I asked him to. Gabriel, I am so ashamed."

Robert, who'd told me he'd been potty about Helena Quinn. "He stole the silver and brought it to you. Then what happened? It was stuffed in the chimney of my house, so Mr. Braxton obviously did not abscond with it."

Helena bowed her head, and her voice was almost inaudible. "I have taught myself not to think on it. But it happened . . . such a horrible thing happened."

I realized the last piece of it, an idea that had been swimming in my mind, just out of reach. "Edward Braxton is dead," I said. "Or at least the man calling himself Edward Braxton. Was it an accident?"

Helena looked up at me again, her hazel eyes clear and intelligent. "It might have been. Robert killed him. He struck Mr. Braxton with one of the candlesticks, and Mr. Braxton fell stone dead. Poor Robert killed him. For me."

Chapter Twenty-Four

Her words fell into silence, the violence she spoke of incongruous in this tidy garden. Clouds were filling the sky, the afternoon turning cold.

When I spoke, I did so slowly, my thoughts arranging themselves as they emerged. "Lady Southwick suggested to Mr. Braxton that you met him in the copse near my father's house, and from there you would run away together. That evening, you went to the Lacey house. My father was ill in his bed, and he'd not have known that you'd crept into my mother's sitting room, always shut, and changed from your gown into traveling clothes." I paused. "Why leave the dress there?"

Helena shook her head. "I am not certain. I remember laying my dress across the chaise. The gown was so pristine and white—a symbol of the girlhood I was leaving behind. I was to be married, to have my own husband and my own house, and I did not need such a dress anymore."

"Robert helped get you into and out of my house," I continued. "He'd brought the church silver to the meeting place. What happened there? Did Braxton show his true colors?"

Helena shuddered. "Dear heavens, yes. He laughed at us, told us we were good trained dogs to do what he said. He was going to take the silver and go, and let it be a lesson to us. I could not believe my ears. I'd fallen in love with him . . . No, truth to tell, I was infatuated and flattered by him. No one else had said the things to me that he did. To realize that I'd fallen for his pack of lies, that he'd used me to get the silver from my own father's church, that he thought of me as nothing more than a stupid, childish, frump of a girl . . ." Her eyes filled with tears. "It hurt. It hurt so much."

Braxton had probably used those very words—*stupid, childish, frump of a girl.* I wished Braxton weren't dead, so I could get my hands on his throat and teach him some manners. I imagined Robert Buckley growing enraged, as I was doing now, except with the fury of a boy watching his angel being beaten down. It must have seemed right to raise the heavy candlestick and go at Braxton. I could imagine the pattern of the carved silver against my hand, sense the candlestick's satisfying weight, could feel the triumph of swinging the thing and smacking Braxton's gloating face.

I drew a breath, trying to banish the picture and my angry glee.

"Foolish of him to linger to boast of his misdeeds," I said. "That was the end of him."

She looked surprised at my matter-of-fact statement. "Robert—he grew so angry. I was crying. Robert snatched up a candlestick and struck . . ." She shivered. "I thought he'd only stunned Mr. Braxton, that we could run to the constable's house and tell him that we'd caught Mr. Braxton running off with the silver. We would look like wise creatures to have found him out, instead of fools duped by him."

"But he was dead."

"He lay so still. I felt for his heartbeat, but he had none, and no breath. Robert could not believe what he'd done. But he never lost his head, as young as he was. He went through Braxton's pockets, found all his money—fifty pounds it turned out to be—and gave it to me. He told me to go, said he'd take care of the rest. He would put it about that I eloped with Mr. Braxton, and that would be that. I cried, but I went."

Fifty pounds. Lady Southwick had said she'd given Braxton "a bit of money" to help the pair elope. Braxton had duped and flattered her as much as he had Helena.

"Why did you run?" I asked. "Why not go to a magistrate and explain the accident? Braxton was trying to rob the church, after all."

"We were young, and we were so frightened. We could not be sure, could we, that we wouldn't simply be dragged away for the murder and the robbery— Robert had done the actual theft, not Mr. Braxton. And I was a coward. I did not want to face the world and confess what Braxton had done to me."

True that their fate would depend on the kindness of the magistrate. If the magistrate had been an unreasonable and suspicious man, Robert could have been tried for murder and stealing from the church, perhaps Helena as well, as his accomplice. A conviction, even for a child and a young woman, would be hanging or transportation.

The magistrate at the time had been fifty yards away—Mr. Roderick Lacey. If he'd been too ill to give a judgment, Brigadier Easton might have stepped in, a man equally as adamant about the letter of the law. Robert and Helena had been wise not to chance that either one of them would be lenient.

"What happened to Braxton's body?" I asked. "How did Robert hide what he'd done?"

"I never knew. Robert found me a horse, and I fled. I rode across country until I came to a posting inn, in a town in Cambridgeshire where no one knew me. From there I took a mail coach into Cambridge. I met a woman on the coach who felt sorry for me and decided to look after me. She thought me escaping an unhappy home. She let me stay with her a time, then she heard that her acquaintance, Mrs. Edgerton, was looking for a gentlewoman to be her companion, and she sent me to her."

"You never heard from Robert Buckley again?"

"Never. Not until this day have I heard a thing from Parson's Point. Robert must be quite grown now."

"Robert is twenty and married. He has a boy of his own."

Helena gave me a look of apprehension. "What will you do? I have told you this because you were once my friend, and I know you were a friend to Terrance. Everything about Mr. Braxton can hardly matter now, can it?"

I privately agreed with her. Braxton had been a thief and a trickster and had duped two youths for his own gain. Cooper had been a thief and a bone-breaker and had tried to kill me and Denis, a man who'd graced him with his trust. Both Braxton and Cooper had died by the hands of the people they'd betrayed. Rough justice.

Robert should not have covered up the crime. But he'd been ten years old, afraid and uncertain. He'd done what he'd done.

The murder in the past was understandable, and perhaps not really murder. A frightened and angry child had struck out and killed without meaning to. But that did not change the fact that Robert had murdered again in the present.

I did not say this to Miss Quinn. She'd had enough guilt and regret in her life, and I would not pile on more.

I took her hands in mine. "I will say nothing."

Her eyes widened. "You would keep silent? Why?"

"Because Braxton was the villain, not you. And because you are right. It was so very long ago, and it hardly matters now."

She frowned in puzzlement. "You said that he was not really called Edward Braxton?"

"He stole the name, just as he stole the silver and planned to steal your virtue and reputation."

"Then you do not know who he truly was?"

"No. And I suppose we never will."

Helena squeezed my hands the slightest bit. "Thank you, Gabriel."

"I will tell no one of your whereabouts if you do not wish me to. But please, write to Terrance and tell him that you are well. I will carry the letter back with me."

She flinched. "I am not certain I want to see him again. To return to that life. My life is here now."

"I will leave you to decide whether you face him or not. But Terrance is a broken man. Hearing that you are alive and happy with Mrs. Edgerton will do much to ease him."

Helena still had no wish to draw back the curtain from this enclosure she'd made for herself, but I saw her realize that Braxton's actions had hurt more than herself and Robert. "Very well. I will write."

There was nothing more to say. We returned to the house, Helena to her rooms. Grenville and I took tea with Mrs. Edgerton, Helena came down with the letter, and we departed.

*** *** ***

In the inn that night, I told a truncated version of the tale to Grenville and a curious Marianne and bade them to keep silent about everything until I decided what to do. They agreed. Marianne voiced the opinion that Mr. Braxton had brought his death on himself, and good riddance. I could see that Grenville agreed with her.

We traveled back to Norfolk in easy stages, Grenville again spending most of it on the bed in his coach or riding his horse when he felt better.

Terrance greeted me more cheerfully upon my return. He'd spent every day at the Lacey house, directing the work and enjoying it.

His exuberant mood changed when I handed him the letter, penned in Helena's hand.

"You found her," he said, staring at the folded paper. "Where is she?"

"I promised her that she could tell you, if she chose."

"Dear God, Lacey. This is the woman I was to have married. Tell me where the devil she is."

I shook my head. "I am sorry. Read the letter."

Terrance gave me a dark look, but turned away, deftly breaking the seal and unfolding the letter with his one hand.

He went out through the back of the house to read in private, and I made my way on horseback, alone, to Robert Buckley's farm, south and east of the Lacey estate, the setting sun at my back.

Robert's farm was not large, but the fields were enclosed by neat green hedgerows, and he'd hired laborers to work it with him. His wife gave me a pot of homemade ale while I sat in her warm kitchen and waited for Robert to come in from the fields. She baked as I sipped, the homey, yeasty smells reminding me of the bake shop below my rooms in Covent Garden. I realized, sitting here, that I missed the place.

Robert trudged in as the sun was going down. He greeted me with a grin and a work-worn hand, and took the ale his wife handed him.

The two of us went outside, walking around the thatched cottage to look at the view. Green fields rippled away from us down a slight slope, the wide Norfolk sky streaked crimson and gold.

"Lovely," I said.

"I am a lucky man, Captain."

I took another sip of the meaty, dark ale. "I came to tell you that I have been to Lincolnshire. I spoke to Helena Quinn there."

Robert froze with his ale halfway to his mouth. His good-natured look deserted him. "Miss Quinn."

"Indeed." I kept my voice down so his wife and the workers in the barn would not hear us. "She told me that you killed Edward Braxton—or whoever he truly was. And I believe you killed the man called Bill Ferguson, a week ago, in Brigadier Easton's windmill."

Robert stared at me, his dark eyes fixed. "You cannot know that."

"You are correct—I am only guessing. What I believe is that you heard that Brigadier Easton had fled to the Continent, and that Mr. Denis's men had moved in and were tearing up the place. You had no idea what they were looking for, but it scarcely mattered. If they confined their search to the house, you had no need to worry, but if they started looking through the abandoned windmill . . . It was a good hiding place. Easton used it to hide things that did not belong to him. You used it to hide something else. Braxton's body?"

Robert nodded, his movements wooden. "In the cellar. I chopped him up with an axe I found in your house, I carted him there, and I buried him under the cellar. No one used that windmill anymore."

"And the windmill was far enough from Parson's Point and the places Braxton used to meet Miss Quinn that he would likely not be looked for there. No one bothered to search for him at all, as it turned out, but you could not anticipate that. Once he was hidden, it was easy enough for you to make it look as though he had absconded with the silver and the vicar's daughter, never to be heard from again. Family too ashamed to pursue it, matter closed. You shoved the silver up the chimney in my house—why did you not simply take it back to the church?"

"Couldn't," Robert said. "By the time I was . . . finished, Mrs. Landon had discovered that the silver had gone missing, and everyone was up in arms. I thought it best that it stayed hidden for a while. And then, as time passed, it did not seem worth the fuss. If it turned up, there would only be questions."

"I think I understand. The Lacey house was a good hiding place for it—I commend you. My father kept no servants by that time, I was away at war, and the house was falling to ruin. I made no announcement that I was returning, and you had no idea that Denis's men would be hunting there as well. Still, even if someone found the silver, most people would believe that an incompetent thief had hidden it long ago and never returned for it. Which they did. Did Ferguson find Braxton's body? Or did you only fear he would?"

Robert looked miserable. "I don't remember what I was thinking. By the time I reached the windmill, someone had done him over already. His face was all bloody, but he was on his feet, and so angry. When he saw me, he ran at me like a madman, murder in his eyes. I saw a thick stick on the floor. I caught it up and struck out. He went down, just like Braxton."

Tears stood in his eyes, and fear. I could imagine the scene as vividly as I'd imagined the boy Robert killing Braxton—only this time, he'd struck out in terror. Ferguson had been a large and violent man.

Whether Robert had given Ferguson the killing blow accidentally, or whether he'd known exactly what he was doing, I could not know. I'd never know. Robert had killed to defend his own life and his past secrets.

"What about Lady Southwick?" I asked. I thought about the pistol ball going past Lady Southwick's nose, Donata's idea that two people had shot at the same time, Grenville's report of Rafe Godwin's utter bewilderment. "Did you shoot at her? Perhaps because she helped Braxton in his scheme with Helena? Unwittingly on Lady Southwick's part, of course. But she might begin guessing what had happened after I came poking around, asking questions about Miss Quinn and Mr. Braxton."

Robert looked blank. "Someone shot at her ladyship?"

"With a pistol. She'd set up a shooting match, and she was nearly clipped."

"I don't have a pistol," Robert said. "And I haven't been near Southwick in years."

His puzzlement was genuine, and I believed him. Perhaps we had been seeing sinister things where none existed. Rafe Godwin was simply incompetent with a pistol.

Robert turned away from me. He looked at his beloved farm, made golden by the setting sun. We heard the sounds of the men in the barn, the cows as they were fed, Robert's wife humming in the kitchen, the high-pitched squeal of his little boy as he tried to talk to his mother. An idyllic place.

I asked, "Where did you put Braxton's bones after you took them from the windmill?"

"Binham Priory," Robert said. "Under the rubble of the ruins. It is still consecrated ground."

The villagers now used part of the ancient nave, the only thing spared by King Henry's men, as their parish church. I remembered the tranquility of the rest of the ruins, standing tall on the green, the sadness of a life stripped away and gone long ago.

"Mr. Denis believes that Ferguson was killed by one of his own men," I said. "And that man is also now dead."

Robert said nothing. He only watched me, certain I'd come to strip away *his* life, this son of the man who'd fallen in love with my mother.

"I am content to let Mr. Denis continue to believe this," I said.

Robert watched me in continued apprehension. "What about Mr. Braxton?"

"We'll never know his real name." I gave Robert a tight bow. "May he rest in peace."

I handed him the jar of ale, turned my back, and walked away.

Chapter Twenty-Five

I returned to London the next day. I rode with Grenville and Marianne, Grenville again spending most of the journey on his back. Marianne seemed to take this in stride, reading a newspaper and inhaling snuff while he slept.

I asked to be left at my rooms in Covent Garden, though Grenville extended me an invitation to stay at his house. Marianne rolled her eyes at me, amazed I'd not prefer a more comfortable bed, but at the moment, I wanted to be alone.

I greeted Mrs. Beltan, who'd not yet left for the evening. She gave me some fat buns with butter and coffee without asking for payment. She also gave me my post.

My rooms were stuffy, and I opened the windows to admit the cool September air. Summer in London, with its heat and stink, was almost unbearable, but fall could be soft and pleasant.

I ate because I was hungry, drank coffee because I drank any coffee put in front of me. I sat back in my wingchair, feeling the bite of coming winter in the air.

My post sat untouched. I closed my eyes and thought about all that had happened since I'd hired a coach to take me to the Lacey family estate in Norfolk.

Home. Or was it?

I'd thought that there, I'd discover things about my father, about the brute he was, to justify my hatred of him. Instead, I'd found that most people looked the other way at his brutality. I'd found that my mother had taken a lover, had feared to go away with said lover, and had died because she'd fallen ill miscarrying his child.

I'd learned much about my adversary, James Denis, and I'd helped him kill a man. I'd unraveled a mystery involving the disappearance of a young woman, and murder, past and present, and agreed to let things lie.

Three years ago, when I'd left the army and moved to London, I'd had a rigid sense of right and wrong. Since then, the people I'd met and the things I'd seen and done had changed that. Now I'd participated in and covered up murders.

Life had a strange way of tearing apart one's convictions.

Three years ago, I had been alone, those I loved out of reach. Now I was to be married — to an aristocratic woman I'd disliked at first sight.

As though the Fates enjoyed toying with me, I heard my unlocked door open and caught a soft whiff of perfume in the night. My beloved stepped into the room, and spoke.

"Lacey, why the devil are you sitting alone in the dark?"

I did not open my eyes. "Why are you not in Oxfordshire with your son?"

"Because I knew in my bones you'd return to London before you journeyed there. I told Mrs. Beltan to send me word when you did."

She shut the door. Moments later, I felt the weight of her warm body on my lap, her arms around my neck.

She ran her fingers over the healing cuts on my face. "I take it you had adventures," she said.

I finally opened my eyes. "Terrible things, Donata. I did terrible things."

I knew she'd ask me to tell her all. She was not the sort of woman to distance herself from a man's affairs.

But she did not ask just then. I felt her cool lips touch mine then brush my cheek. "It is warmer at the Audley Street House," she said.

I was exhausted. "That is so far away."

"True."

My bedchamber was much closer. I rose, took her hand, and led her there.

End

Author's Note

Many of the locations in *A Death in Norfolk* are real—Blakeney, Binham Priory, and several other villages on the northern Norfolk coast—but are, of course, used fictitiously. I invented the village of Parson's Point, placing it between Morston and Stifkey, just west of Blakeney. Likewise, I invented the locations of the windmills where some of the action takes place.

Norfolk windmills are very real, however. The windmills, or wind pumps, were constructed throughout the eighteenth and nineteenth centuries, on into the twentieth century, to drain lands for farming, some also grinding grain. The use of windmills was discontinued in the early twentieth century in favor of electric pumps. However, many windmills are still standing throughout Norfolk, and can be visited.

Please turn the page
for a preview
of Captain Lacey's next adventure

A
Disappearance
in
Drury Lane

Captain Lacey
Regency Mysteries
Book 8

Chapter One

London, 1817

Marianne Simmons came to me on a cold December day when I was packing away my old life in order to begin my new.

Tomorrow, I would journey through sparkling frosts and possible snow to Oxfordshire. I would go via warm, private coach, but no amount of luxury could keep away the winter winds that were decidedly blowing now.

Marianne walked into my rooms and looked about with critical interest. She was resplendent in an ensemble created for winter afternoons — a gray skirt topped with a black and silver, long-sleeved bodice, a silver-gray spencer, gray leather gloves, a bonnet trimmed with feathers and ruched black ribbon, and a large fur muff. A far cry from the rather desperate, tawdrily dressed young woman who used to come down the stairs from her rooms above mine and filch my candles, my coal, my snuff, and anything else she could carry.

Marianne was now the mistress of Lucius Grenville, one of England's wealthiest men, and he believed in turning his ladies out well. The dressmaker he employed was the most sought after in London.

"I need your help, Lacey," Marianne said without preliminary.

"On the moment? I am rushing off to be married, as you can see."

"I thought you did not leave until tomorrow."

"I do not, but Bartholomew and I must clear everything from these rooms and have my baggage ready for Lady Breckenridge's coach tomorrow. Her coachman is not the most patient of beings."

"Good. Then you have this evening."

I looked up from where I was packing the contents of the drawers of my chest-on-frame into a wooden box. When I'd moved in three and more years ago, I'd had little in the way of possessions, but things tend to accumulate, especially in drawers.

"I have this evening to pack," I said. "You would not wish me to be late to the happiest day of my life, would you?"

Marianne plunked herself into my wing chair and slapped her muff to her lap. "Well, if it will be the happiest day of your life, then all the others can only be worse, can't they? Perhaps you ought to miss it altogether."

"I fear that my good lady would not see it in that light. Besides, her mother is going to much trouble with this wedding."

"To which I am not invited."

I ended up simply dumping the entire contents of the drawer into the box. "No one is invited but members of the immediate family. Donata's immediate family, that is. Pembrokes, all. The only Breckenridge attending is Donata's son, Peter, and he with his nanny."

"Grenville will be there."

We came to the heart of her sour mood. "Grenville will be there because he is standing up with me. I assure you, the rest of the party will be elderly matrons and gentlemen related to Lady Breckenridge's mother and father. My family will be represented by my daughter."

And my heart sang.

I had not seen Gabriella since the summer, when she'd come for a too-brief visit to the country house of Lady Aline Carrington, where I also had been staying. Gabriella had arrived at Dover a few days ago, chaperoned by her French aunt and uncle. Earl Pembroke had dispatched his personal carriage to take them straight to Hampshire.

Marrying Donata Breckenridge was one reason I hurried away from dank London, but seeing my daughter again put wings on my feet.

"The matter is a simple one," Marianne said. "I am sure you could clear it up in a trice. You always do."

Not quite. The last problem I'd cleared up had taken nearly two weeks, and I'd ridden miles and been battered and beaten for my pains. I'd also done things, and looked the other way at things done by others, that still made me uncomfortable at night.

"What matter?" I asked. I knew that trying to put Marianne off would never work. She could be persistent to the point of madness.

"A friend has gone missing," Marianne said. She stroked the fur of her muff as she frowned, the short, jerky movements telling me she was more worried than she wanted to let on. "One I knew when I was in the company at Drury Lane. I thought you might look into it for me, since you excel at finding the missing."

About the Author

Award-winning Ashley Gardner is a pseudonym for *New York Times* bestselling author Jennifer Ashley. Under both names—and a third, Allyson James—Ashley has written more than 35 published novels and novellas in mystery and romance. Her books have won several *RT BookReviews* Reviewers Choice awards (including Best Historical Mystery for *The Sudbury School Murders*), and Romance Writers of America's RITA (given for the best romance novels and novellas of the year). Ashley's books have been translated into a dozen different languages and have earned starred reviews in *Booklist*.

More about the Captain Lacey series can be found at www.gardnermysteries.com. Or email Ashley Gardner at gardnermysteries@cox.net

Books in the Captain Lacey Regency Mysteries series

The Hanover Square Affair
A Regimental Murder
The Glass House
The Sudbury School Murders
The Necklace Affair (e-novella; collected in print with the stories in *The Gentleman's Walking Stick*)
A Body in Berkeley Square
A Covent Garden Mystery
The Gentleman's Walking Stick
  (short-story collection)
A Death in Norfolk
A Disappearance in Drury Lane
And more to come!

6153859R00173

Printed in Great Britain
by Amazon.co.uk, Ltd.,
Marston Gate.